LOVING HER HIGHLAND THIEF

Time to Love a Highlander Series
Book One

by Maeve Greyson

ARE YOU SIGNED UP FOR DRAGONBLADE'S BLOG?

You'll get the latest news and information on exclusive giveaways, exclusive excerpts, coming releases, sales, free books, cover reveals and more.

Check out our complete list of authors, too!

No spam, no junk. That's a promise!

Sign Up Here

www.dragonbladepublishing.com

Dearest Reader;

Thank you for your support of a small press. At Dragonblade Publishing, we strive to bring you the highest quality Historical Romance from some of the best authors in the business. Without your support, there is no 'us', so we sincerely hope you adore these stories and find some new favorite authors along the way.

Happy Reading!

CEO, Dragonblade Publishing

**Additional Dragonblade books by
Author Maeve Greyson**

Time to Love a Highlander Series
Loving Her Highland Thief
Taming Her Highland Legend

Highland Heroes Series
The Guardian
The Warrior
The Judge
The Dreamer
The Bard
The Ghost

Chapter One

Highlands of Scotland
An unknown cave near Loch Lochy
Late April 2019

"Ramsay! Back here, ye devil!" Kenzie MacMartin leveraged her way past a jagged boulder, clambering over it with the aid of her shepherd's crook. "Brodie, hie to the right. Back to me now."

Brodie, her devoted black and white border collie and best friend in all the world, skittered around, over, and through the stony obstacles of the ravine in hot pursuit of the most stubborn ram Kenzie had ever known. And the most expensive, too. The prize blackface had cost her so much she'd be eating nothing but neeps and tatties for a while. The wicked animal was also an escape artist. She had yet to find a fence or barn that could hold him when he decided to break free and go exploring.

The fugitive in question paused several yards ahead, looked back, and *baa'd* long and loud, like a bratty child chanting *neener neener.*

"If ye hadna cost me so much, ye'd be mutton stew this Sunday!" She scrambled over a downed tree uprooted by sizable chunks of stone that pushed up through its root system like the ruins of an ancient cathedral. She hopped downward and sank ankle deep in the sandy muck left behind by spring rains. Thank goodness for thick socks and her bright red wellies.

"Brodie! Hie to me! Quick now!" If the dog could head the ram off and turn him, it would be so much better. The farther the woolly escapee forged, the more cave-like the area became. Up ahead, it looked as though earth and rock met and closed over the ravine, making the recovery of the pedigreed stud promised to sire more livestock next to impossible. If she returned to the farm for a lantern, who knew where the creature would get to by the time she got back?

An angry *baa* and a loud thunk told her the ram wasn't in the mood to cooperate. The herd dog parried with the stubborn beast, all the while doing his best to turn him. The sheep ran at the canine, then came to an abrupt halt, lifted his head as though harkening to a call, and spun about and bolted deeper into the maze of stone. Brodie paused and looked back at her, waiting for the signal to either give chase or relinquish the animal to the cavern gods.

Kenzie waved him on. She couldn't afford to give up now. When the sandy mud ebbed away to solid ground, she appreciated the end of slogging through mire, but didn't care for the sight up ahead. The washed-out ravine had become the worrisome trial she had feared. Grand spires of squared off stone, crude black obelisks streaked with veins of sparkling quartz, connected at the top like hands folded in prayer. Narrow beams of sunlight filtered down through the cracks, lighting a cave-like enclosure she had never realized was there. The earth displaced by the great rocks clung over them, nurturing a lush layer of moss, ferns, and small trees that concealed the place from the glen above.

Both dog and ram had gone out of sight, but their sounds echoed back to her. She had to retrieve that stupid animal or Da and her brothers would never let her live it down. Staff in hand, she stomped the gloppy mud off her galoshes, then forged onward. She would get that infernal sheep returned to his pen if she had to herd him across all of Scotland.

Even though walking became easier, she tapped out the path with the crook to make certain she didn't fall through any fissures hidden by the shadows. She prayed no clouds blew in and blocked the shafts of sunshine lighting the way, or she'd be trapped in darkness until light returned.

"Brodie!"

His answering yip eased her mind a bit. But sounds seemed distorted now. The tap of her staff. The clop of her steps. She worked her jaws and swallowed, trying to pop her ears. An odd buzzing filled the air. She couldn't tell if it came from somewhere in the cave or from up above, in the overgrowth covering the strange place. A glance back at the opening caused her head to spin.

She blinked hard to clear her sight, then frowned. The sun-dappled ravine rippled and shimmered with what looked like heat waves rising from blistering hot pavement. That made no sense. While it was a fine spring day, by no means was it warm enough for that. She had even worn her thermals and sturdy farm jacket because of a lingering nip in the wind.

After rubbing her eyes, she pressed her temples and tried to pop her ears again. At this rate, she'd soon be losing her lunch. The sudden nausea reminded her of the time she had gotten airsick. The queasiness felt the same.

"Brodie! Back to me! Come, lad!" They would wait in the ravine for the fool ram to decide he was ready to come home. They had to get out of this cave. The place must have a buildup of some sort of gases. Whatever it was, she didn't like it.

Uneasiness overrode the nausea when no response answered her call. That never happened. "Brodie!" she shouted louder. Moving faster, she squinted through the murky darkness as she edged between and under overhangs of stone. The way opened up, making breathing easier, but the uncomfortable pressure building inside her head was worse.

Another series of hard swallows didn't ease the sensation, nor did coughing or sticking her fingers in her ears. Violent shivering took over, and she broke out in a cold sweat. A telltale throbbing right under the hinge of her jaws warned her. The bread and jam she'd had for lunch came out with such force; it left her sagging against a stone. She wiped her mouth with the back of her hand, then fumbled through the multiple pockets of her canvas coat, searching for a tissue.

"Jings alive, we have to get out of here. Fast." She held her head, gasping to catch her breath. Cave gases. Had to be. Sheep or no sheep, she and the dog had to leave. "Brodie, come to me! Now, lad. Come."

A noise she didn't expect answered her call. Not her precious dog's bark, but what sounded like—

"Nah, it canna be. I've gone barmy with the foul air." She pushed off the rock, steadying herself with her shepherd's crook. "Brodie, come," she repeated, but it came out so weak, she doubted the sweet lad heard her. That doubt brought a smile. Nay. He heard. Many a time, when training him as a wee pup, he had responded to the softest whisper. Her precious dog was pure dead brilliant.

The noise that could only be described as sounding like the reenactment battle she had watched at Bannockburn festival came to her again. Clash of steel. Loud bangs of shield hitting shield. Roared curses and shouts. While she massaged her throbbing temples, outrage took hold and grew. This was her land. Her family's land. Da hadn't leased it to any re-enactors. "We'll see about this." She pushed through the nausea and headache and charged forward.

The cave split off into three potential routes. She listened at each of the tunnels, straining to pick up on any clues. "Brodie!" A curt bark turned her to the passage farthest to the right. Less and less light filtered through from… wherever. It wasn't coming from above anymore, but for some odd reason, she could still see well enough to continue on. The battle sounds grew louder, heating her blood. Those fools better have proof of who had given them permission to come onto her land. If not, she would have their arses thrown in jail and their vehicles impounded especially if they'd buggered up her meadow.

A joyous bark greeted her as she wormed her way free of the tight tunnel. Brodie bounded to her, his tongue hanging out the side of his smiling mouth. She bent and gathered him into a hug. "Good, lad. At least ye're all right. That's all that matters."

An indignant, grumbling *baa* disagreed. The ram stomped his front feet as though throwing a tantrum for attention.

"So, ye decided to stop playing chase, did ye?"

The animal marched over and nosed her jacket pocket, tossed his head, then bumped her again.

"No, sir. Ye've earned no treats." She stamped her cane, then tapped it against his rump to get him moving. "Ye'll have yer feed and water this evening and be thankful for it." Pointing to what looked like an opening of wondrous daylight up ahead, she waved Brodie forward. "Away wi' him, my fine lad. We'll take the long way home as soon as we settle our business with these trespassers."

The dog nipped at the ram's heels, herding him into a fast trot toward the sunshine.

From the sound of it, the battling had increased to a raging frenzy. Kenzie halted just outside the mouth of the cave, surveying the area. Her anger shot to a bloody fury.

Clots of her precious land filled the air, kicked up by charging horses that looked to be Shires or Clydesdales. Whatever they were, the monstrosities were huge. And cattle! Where had those Highland cows come from? At least a dozen or more of the hairy beasts milling about as the men played their game of swords. How had they brought in all these animals?

"I bet they've rutted the place with their trucks and trailers. It's too wet to be driving in these fields!" The nearest road was over a kilometer away. She shuddered to think of the damage they had done.

A nearby roar made her step farther out of the cave in time to see one man slash another across the chest. The wounded actor fell from his horse with a red streak staining the front of his dingy yellow tunic. It looked realistic enough. She'd give them that.

Whipping out her cell phone, she powered it on and tapped her father's speed dial. Da had several constable friends. They'd take care of this blatant vandalism. For that's what this was—pure disregard and destruction of her land.

"No Service" flashed across its screen.

"Still?" She held it higher and turned in a circle as if that might somehow help. "Bloody hell," she muttered, tapping on the contraption.

Brodie interrupted, transforming into a snarling, protective beast. Ramsay joined in, rumbling with the furious sound he only made when protecting his ewes.

Kenzie shoved her phone back into her pocket and whirled to face whatever had triggered their reactions.

A wild-eyed man, sword raised and costumed as if he belonged somewhere in Scotland's long-ago history, slunk toward her.

"Who gave ye permission to play yer games on my land?" She resettled her stance and readied her staff. If this idiot thought to scare her, the trespasser would be disappointed. If he wanted a battle, she'd gladly oblige him. With five rough-housing brothers, she knew how to fight to win.

"Games?" the man snarled. "MacPhersons dinna play games when it comes to thievery." He loomed closer, sword still ready. The wind picked up, whipping his long brown hair to one side and carrying his stench to her.

"Shew! Ye go all out in yer reenactments, dinna ye? Did ye roll in pig shite to smell like that?" Surely, he hadn't dyed that tunic yellow with urine to be *that* historically accurate. But the powerful stink of piss added another level to his disgusting body odor.

The man glared at her. Then he charged. "Ye'll be coming

with me," he shouted and lifted his weapon higher. "The Stronachs can pay for this insult with one of their women!"

"Are ye on feckin' drugs?" She parried, avoiding the slash of his heavy sword and countering with an effective hit of her staff, cracking it across the back of his neck. Her animals jumped into the fray. Brodie sank his teeth into the man's thigh, while Ramsay took out the trespasser's other leg at the knee.

The enraged actor rolled as he fell, beating at her precious beasts with his sword.

"If ye hurt my babies, I'll kill ye!" Kenzie bore down on him, whacking the fool with the seasoned hardwood crook Granddad had given her. It worked for many things besides herding sheep. "Drop yer weapon! Now!"

"She's thrashing yer arse for ye, Ellar," shouted someone from behind.

Kenzie didn't let up in her fight. A glance over her shoulder assured that the trio of grinning men weren't an immediate threat. She'd deal with them later. First, this idiot trying to hurt her pets needed some sense and manners beat into him. She leapt and attacked from the rear, scoring a well-placed hit that caught him dead in the bollocks.

He roared in pain, and the sword fell from his hand.

"I'd say yer done, Ellar," observed one of the men in her audience.

"Aye, and yer guard's deserted ye," called out another. "Already gathered yer wounded and rode off. Dinna ye think ye'd best give up and be on yer way as well?"

On hands and knees, Ellar bared his yellowed teeth and gave Kenzie a murderous glare. "This isna over," he hissed, spitting blood with every word.

"Ye're right. It isna over," she agreed. "Brodie, hie to me."

The dog unlatched his jaws from the man and goaded the ram to stand behind her. One foot planted on Ellar's sword, she took out her cell and pointed it at him. "As soon as I get a signal, the constable will take care of yer drugged-out, trespassing arse."

She frowned down at the phone. Still no bars. She'd thought sure she had gotten a decent signal at this end of the glen before.

"This yer witch?" Ellar growled to the three observers as he held his crotch and tried to stand.

"Aye, we'll be claiming her," said the largest of the trio.

That one had long dark hair, too, but it looked a great deal cleaner and had been pulled back from his face and tied. The historical look suited him and made Kenzie wish he wasn't a bloody trespasser. She wouldn't mind sharing a dram or two and getting to know this one if he hadn't already proven himself to be such a disrespectful arse.

The actor strode forward, smiling as he lifted both hands to show he bore no weapons. Amusement gleamed in the light coloring of his eyes. Gray or maybe blue. She couldn't decide.

"Mathias Stronach at yer service, m'lady."

Her confidence wavered the slightest bit. He looked like a bodybuilder. On steroids. Taller than most men she knew and bigger than any she had trained with in her self-defense classes. Chest so broad, the linen of his tunic stretched taut across it. She could almost hear the threads screaming with the strain. Narrow waist. Leather belt riding low, sporting not one but two swords, one long and one shorter. His massive legs bulged with muscle, their sculpted cording visible through his snug leggings. This actor was definitely a feast for the eyes.

With a slow rotation of her shepherd's crook, she squared her shoulders. He might be big as a mountain and a beauty to behold, but she had speed and determination on her side. "I'm Kenzie MacMartin, and this is my land. By what right do ye play yer games here and tear up my meadow?"

His dark brows drew together, matching the confused tilt to his head. "*Yer* land?"

"Aye, MacMartin land. It's still in my Da's name, but his solicitor's got the papers showing where this part comes to me when he passes." She stopped working the staff but kept it clutched in front of her. Why was she explaining herself? She wasn't the trespasser. "Answer me. Who gave ye permission to be here?" She pointed the crook at the bedraggled field, now peaceful and empty except for the herd of cows and other men who had ridden closer to eavesdrop. "Look at the mess ye've made of my glen. And cows? Cows where my sheep are to graze? This isna the dark ages anymore. Ye canna be using someone's farmland without their leave."

"She's tetched as old Annag," remarked a man not quite as large but still bigger than most.

Mathias shot him a silencing look, then returned to studying her. He scrubbed his fingers through the stubble of reddish-brown beard shadowing his jaw. "Ye speak strange, lass." He looked her up and down, head tilting the other way now. He frowned when his gaze hit her bright red rubber boots. "Ye dress even stranger."

"I dress strange?" She tugged on her jacket, then pointed at his garb. "When ye're not playing yer games, do ye wear that everywhere?" The swords at his side caught her attention. "Have much trouble going into the shops with those?"

"Throw her on yer horse and be done with it," said the third of the original trio, the one closest in stature and build to Mathias. He strode forward, a sour look on his face. With a jab of his finger at Ellar, he growled, "Hie yer arse back to yer chief. We've reclaimed what is ours."

"As I said," Ellar threatened. "This isna over." His attention shifted to his sword still under Kenzie's boot.

"Dinna even think about it." She leaned toward him with a warning swish of her cane.

Ellar backed away until the length of several long strides stretched between them, then turned and took off with a fast-limping hop.

"Ye said his name was Ellar?" She tapped on the notes app on her phone. "Ellar what? I'll need his full name for the constable."

"Ellar MacPherson," Mathias replied, sounding as though he'd found a puzzle he couldn't solve. He nodded toward the phone. "What is that in yer hand?"

He had to be joking. Trying to throw her off guard so she wouldn't set the constable on them. Even though the man was a pleasure to look at, he'd soon find out she wasn't a pushover for some handsome, silver-tongued devil.

"Ye can drop the act." She typed both his name and Ellar's into her phone, then turned to the others. "Names?" She'd turn every one of them in and see that they paid for any damages.

The two looked at Mathias. He shrugged. "Give her yer names."

The sour-faced jerk who had suggested she be thrown over a horse gave a defiant tip of his chin. "Bhaltair MacSorley."

"Eumann MacVail," said the heavyset man next to him. His crooked nose and lopsided smile possessed a charm all their own and more than made up for his tubby appearance.

"And the rest of ye?" she said to the horsemen who had moved closer to observe from their mounts.

"Moray Cleireach," called out the rider farthest to the right.

"Lyle," said the next one, then added an air kiss and a wink. "Lyle Stronach."

Apparently, the Stronach family thought flirting would get them off scot-free. She typed the name and placed an asterisk by it. She looked up. "And yerself?"

"Ruari Stronach, m'darling. Best of the lot of them." This one resembled Mathias. She wondered if he was a brother or something. He waved her forward, then grabbed his crotch. "Ride with me, lass. I'll keep ye safe and warm. Ye have m'word."

Kenzie ignored the rude offer and eyed the next man. "Name?"

"Hew MacVail." The gravelly-voiced rider cleared his throat and spit. His mount pranced from side to side as he shifted in the saddle. "We're wasting daylight and risking the MacPherson's return with more men. Their chief willna bear the thrashing Ellar just took at the hands of a mere woman. We need to move, aye?"

Mere woman? Kenzie placed an asterisk beside MacVail's

name, too. He'd pay double for that remark. She fixed her scowl on the last trespasser. "Name?"

"Ye'll nay have *my* name," the twitchy little man retorted. He jerked a nod at the phone. "I dinna ken what that there thing is, but ye'll nay be stirring my likeness into it to help ye with yer spell casting."

"May I present Daw MacSorley," Bhaltair said with a taunting flip of one hand. "My only brother and, as ye can tell, the bravest in all of Clan Stronach." He blew out a long, bored huff, then turned to Mathias. "I'm all for a bit of levity to lighten our days, but Hew's right. We need to be moving. Throw her on yer horse and be done with it, aye?"

"Throw me on a horse?" Kenzie powered off her phone to conserve its battery and shoved it in her pocket. She hefted her shepherd's crook in both hands and pointed it at the men. "I advise ye to get yer arses and yer livestock the hell off my land. Now."

"Or what?" Bhaltair growled as he stormed forward.

Mathias blocked him. "Enough." His jaw tightened as he made a curt tip of his head toward the horses. "Hie to yer mounts and leave her to me, aye?" He eyed the dog and ram. "Her and her animals. The rest of ye tend the cows. The Stronach will be pleased when he sees we've recovered so many."

"I'm sure the lass would rather ride with me," Ruari crooned in a tone that made Kenzie remember which pocket held her pen knife. It might be small, but it'd do well enough at splitting that arrogant fool's bawbag.

"I said," Mathias repeated in a voice rumbling deep as thunder. Somehow, it made him seem even larger. "Tend the stock. I will handle her." He stared down the men with a fearsome scowl that left no doubt who was in charge.

Each of them gave an obedient nod. Their defiance checked, they mounted and went to the herd, urging the hairy, ruddy-coated beasts into a southwesterly walk.

"Hie to me, Brodie," Kenzie whispered, easing backward into

the mouth of the cave. She wasn't confident to the point of being foolish. While she believed it might cause significant damage, she doubted she could best Mathias one-on-one. He seemed more intelligent and a great deal more agile than Ellar MacPherson. But if she could reach the tunnels, she would have it made. The cave's tight twists and turns would be hard for a man his size to manage with any ease or speed.

"Heel, lad," she breathed out softly. The collie stepped to her left, and surprisingly enough, the ram followed suit.

Mathias turned to her, his ferocity fading into a pained frown. He held out a hand. "I dinna wish to hurt ye, lass. Come."

"The only place I'm going is home." She took another step backward. "Leave me be, aye? Or the trespassing charge will be the least of yer worries once my Da and brothers get hold of ye." He appeared to have a kind, sensible vibe about him. Surely, now that his cohorts were busy with the cows, he'd see the reasonable thing to do was leave her alone and join them.

He took another step toward her. "Word will be sent to yer kin, so they know ye are at Stronach Keep. They can collect ye there."

Her devoted dog rumbled a warning growl that clicked low and ominous. Hackles raised and head lowered, he stood ready to lunge. The ram grumbled, stomping from side to side behind her.

Mathias eyed her defenders, his jaw flexing as though this chore had turned out to be a lot more difficult than it should. "I shall see that ye're…that yerself and yer animals are kept safe." He waved her forward. "Come, lass. Ye can either join me willingly and ride in comfort or travel like a sack of grain tossed over my horse. The choice is yers."

She spun and ran, determined to make the tunnel. A glance back stopped her. Brodie and the ram stood fast, blocking the man's way, the canine with its teeth bared and the sheep with its great curved horns lowered.

"'Tis admirable yer beasts will die for ye," Mathias observed in a chilling tone. Slow and steady, he drew a *sgian dhu* from each boot. He flipped the daggers and held them by their blade tips. He lifted both hands and stared down at the dog and sheep. "Will ye sacrifice them, then, and continue with yer escape?"

She knew what Da would say. And each of her four brothers. *They're just animals, Kenzie. Dinna be a tenderhearted fool.* She couldn't help it. It was who she was. A tenderhearted fool. And Mathias, damn him straight to hell, had spotted that weakness and used it.

"Dinna hurt them." She meant to sound strong, but her voice cracked, and the words came out like a plea. "Please," she added, forcing the word through clenched teeth.

"Then come with me." He held steady, daggers ready, steely glare locked with hers.

"First, tell me where we're going." If these over-achieving re-enactors were stupid enough to leave her with her phone, she'd call for help as soon as she reached somewhere with a bloody signal.

His hardened air softened. "I told ye. Stronach Keep." He bent and shoved the daggers back in his boots without taking his gaze off her. With a worried squint, he straightened and motioned her forward. "Are ye unwell, lass?"

"There is no such place as Stronach Keep," she countered. And there wasn't. Unless *Stronach Keep* was the name of their acting team's building. Her hopes rose. If they passed an inn or one of the tourists stops in Gairlochy or Stronaba, she could make a call through Wi-Fi. Da would have a fit about this. So would her brothers. Her riding off with this oversized ox and his gang was lunacy itself. But she had no choice, and a gut-feeling told her he was safe enough. Instinct had never failed her before. She prayed it wasn't wrong now. "Where are we going, really? Fort William? Kinlochleven, maybe?"

"Stronach Keep," he said again, repeating the words slowly. "Glen Loy." He glanced down at the animals. "The journey will take us a few days, what with the coos and yer beasties there." The sentiment in his forced smile didn't reach his eyes, making her second guess everything. "But no harm will come to ye. Ye have my word."

No harm would come to her? Why had he added that again? Were some of his men dangerous? She bet that Ruari one was. And Bhaltair. Both looked like trouble. "A few days?" she repeated.

"Aye." He glanced at his horse, then back at her. "Come."

A few days. That meant they'd stop at one of the hunting lodges. Many of those promised Wi-Fi as a selling point to prospective travelers. She lifted her chin, pulled in a deep breath, and blew it out. "Fine, then." With a single tap of her shepherd's crook, she strode forward, giving the collie the hand signal that let him know to stand down. "Well done, Brodie lad. Close now, boy."

The dog shifted from fierce protector to all business, spurring the ram into a quick trot beside Kenzie.

"Braw animal ye have there," Mathias said with another placating smile that tempted her to smack him right between the eyes. In fact, if she hit him hard enough with the hardwood crook, she and the beasties could make the tunnels before he recovered.

"Dinna try it, lass," he warned, snatching the staff away before she could put the thought into action.

"Give that back! It was my Granddad's!" She flew at him, not caring that she sounded like a spoiled child fighting for a toy. "Give it to me now!"

Her best spinning kick thumped hard against his muscular gut, bending him forward slightly but otherwise causing minor damage. Quick as a cat, he caught hold of her ankle and flipped her to the ground. She leapt to her feet, ready for more.

The dog joined in, aiming for the man's leg. Mathias booted the dog while beating off the ram with the cane. "Dammit, woman! Ye can have yer wee stick when ye've enough sense not to use it as a weapon." He kicked harder. Brodie yelped and tumbled across the ground but jumped up and came back for more. "Call them off, or it's my sword for them next." To add weight to his words, he unsheathed the lethal blade that looked more deadly than any reenactment prop. He pointed it at her. "And then I'll be taking the flat of it to yer arse!"

"Brodie! Ramsay! Come to me." Dammit, she didn't mean to cry. She hated that. It always happened when she was madder than hell. "Hie to me now," she ordered, tears coming so fast she wanted to scream.

The dog corralled the sheep, and both animals returned to her side.

"Dinna weep, lass," Mathias said with a hurried sheathing of his sword. Her captor looked more pained than when she had kicked him. "Forgive me, but ye…ye left me no choice." He shuffled in place, obviously uncomfortable but not enough to stir any sense of forgiveness in her. With a glance down at the shepherd's crook, he gave her another infuriating smile. "Ye can have it once we reach the keep. I promise."

"I hate ye." She spit at his feet. "I'll make ye pay if it's the last thing I do."

"I am certain ye will," he agreed with a resigned sigh. Pointing at his monstrosity of a horse, he held her staff behind his back. "To my horse now with ye."

Stomping past him, Kenzie plotted all the ways she would get her revenge. She'd have him thrown in jail. Sue him. Go online and expose him for the disrespectful, animal abusing, kidnapping swine he was. He'd never work in Scotland again. Or England. Or Ireland. She didn't have a clue how to ruin a person in such a way, but by jings, she would figure it out.

He sheathed his sword, threaded her crook under the ropes securing a rolled bundle to the back of his saddle, then hoisted her up and seated himself behind her. His muscular arms caged her in as he took hold of the reins and set the animal in motion with the slightest shifting of his legs. "We'll be joining the others to help with the cattle. Highland coos dinna move that fast. Leastwise, long as we dinna startle them. Yer wee dog and sheep should have no trouble with the pace."

She ignored him, aiming a sad smile down at her beloved collie, who kept the ram moving along beside them. "Good lad, Brodie," she encouraged. *We'll get out of this,* she added silently. *And I'll feed ye this one's bollocks for supper.*

CHAPTER TWO

THE LONGER THEY rode, the more Mathias pondered his wisdom in taking ownership of this strange woman who, in his opinion, was *more* tetched in the head than the clan seer. Perhaps they should have let the MacPhersons have her.

He consoled himself with another deep breath of her beguiling scent. The wind obliged and whipped her long dark hair into his face, offering a stronger sampling. She smelled better than the chief's garden when his daughter's flowers were in full bloom. That was one good thing about claiming her. And he'd have to be blind not to appreciate that, even though she was a tall woman, her fine shapeliness made her height easily forgettable. Odds were this lovely lass would give whoever managed to tame her a horde of sons built for battle.

Three cows slipped through the riders and split away from the main herd, pulling his attention from the tempting prisoner seated in front of him. "Ruari! Eumann!" He tipped his head toward the escaped beasts. His conniving cousin, Ruari, probably had his wicked mind on their lovely captive rather than the cattle, and knowing Eumann, that man was dreaming of food and drink.

The two spurred their mounts into full gallop, but the shaggy cows were wily. The animals veered off in three separate directions.

Mathias watched his men bungle the task. No wonder the MacPhersons had reclaimed their prized herd with such ease. 'Twas amazing enough that his guard had managed to lift them in the first place. And also, that the initial harmless thieving had triggered a clan feud, he still harbored some guilt about. His ailing chief couldn't handle the rigors of an all-out war. Not now. Such a thing would make the man's journey to the grave that much shorter.

One of the escaped cows disappeared through the trees. Another looked to be ambling toward a shallow ravine. The third had turned around, attempting to go back to MacPherson territory. "God's teeth, how hard can it be to herd a few coos?"

"Brodie!" the woman barked with such authority that Mathias jerked to attention as if he had been the one she summoned. "Gather!" The lass gave the order like a commander leading a battle charge.

The black and white dog shot away, fast as an arrow released from a newly strung bow. One by one, he recovered the strays, circling and nipping at their heels until they rejoined the main group. Satisfied, he fell back and trotted around the perimeter of the herd in case any others wandered.

"Fine wee mongrel ye have there." His admiration grew for the unusual woman and her animals. She had already proven herself canny enough in fighting, even though Ellar MacPherson had never been much of a challenge. Still, she had shown she feared nothing. Quite the accompaniment to her beauty. "Thank ye, lass. I fear my guard is better at lifting cattle rather than herding them across the Highlands."

She remained silent.

So, it was like that, was it? He understood but wished it wasn't so. "What did ye say yer name was again?" He didn't know why, but he truly wanted her to talk to him.

"Kenzie MacMartin."

"MacMartin," he repeated, trying to place the surname, but

failed. "Is it a sept? Which clan do ye owe fealty?"

She shifted with an irritated exhale, blowing out the air as though answering him was pure torture. "Cameron."

"Aye, good then. Stronach is counted among Clan Cameron, too."

"How lovely." Her icy tone betrayed her true feelings.

The more he attempted conversation, the more she bristled like an angry, wee hedgehog. She yanked her outer garment closed, securing it by rubbing her knuckles up the strange strip of cloth edged with tiny metal teeth. Once finished with her smoothing of the rough ribbon, she pressed on small brass circles on the flap covering the toothy material. Each one popped, and when she was done, the front of her surcoat stayed shut as she shoved her hands into her pockets. What a grand piece of clothing.

The poor thing must be cold. Clouds had rolled in, casting a chill across the balmy spring day. He tugged free a fold of his plaid and wrapped the length of it around her. "Here, lass. My brat will keep ye warm."

She stiffened but didn't speak.

He expected her to shrug it away, but her good sense won out over her stubbornness. She pulled it closer and snuggled down into the wooly folds.

"Thank ye," she said with a little less hostility.

Mathias's spirits lifted. He liked this lass. Odd though she might be, he wished to know her better. "Ye mentioned a father and brothers. Is there no man who will worry after ye as well?"

"I farm alone." With a yank, she pulled the fold of his plaid closer around her neck, then swept loose strands of hair out of her face.

That didn't tell him what he really wanted to know, but it was obvious he had rubbed her fur the wrong way again. Best veer to something safer. "Yer surcoat. I dinna recall ever seeing one fashioned like that."

"My what?" She turned her head as though trying to hear him

better.

"Yer surcoat." He pulled back a fold of his plaid and tugged on her garment's hood. "This."

"I told ye before, drop the act." Loathing dripped from her words.

"What act?" Her ill humor bothered him. Aye, he held her prisoner, but there was no call for her snappishness. He had treated her with nothing but kindness and respect. Well…he had threatened her animals, but surely, she understood he'd had no choice. "My politeness is nay an act," he added.

"Politeness?" She barked out a bitter laugh. "Ye think kidnapping falls under the definition of politeness?" With a shake of her head, she muttered something under her breath that he didn't quite catch but felt sure it wasn't the words of a proper lady.

"What say ye?"

"Never mind."

God help him, he should have let the MacPhersons take her for certain. Mathias gave up on talking to her. He'd never been all that good at charming the lasses anyway and was ill-prepared to win over one who despised him. They ambled along for several hours before it occurred to him she might need to relieve herself or sate her thirst. Lyle carried their provisions. Perhaps she would like an oatcake or two. The River Spean lay straight ahead, close enough to water the livestock and give them all a chance to stretch their legs before they attempted the crossing. With all the rains of the past few days, the task would be a chore. They had best rest while they could.

He halted his mount and signaled the others to do the same. "We'll let the herd tarry here a bit before we maneuver the Spean," he called out.

"The Spean?" Kenzie twisted around, staring at him as though he had threatened to drag her behind his horse. She pointed at yon river glistening through the sprinkling of trees along its banks. "What are ye trying to pull? That canna be the Spean. We've not even crossed the motorway yet. The B8004."

Lips parted, her breathing hitched ever faster. She jerked back and forth, searching the landscape. What she sought, he had no idea.

"The fences. Where are the fences? The placards for Gairlochy Holiday Park? The telephone wires?"

Most of what she babbled made no sense. All he recognized was her fear. She needed water or perhaps something a mite stronger. Bhaltair always packed whisky. Said he brought it for healing in case someone had a wound in need of cleansing. They all knew that for the lie that it was. The lass probably yearned for a good piss in the privacy of the bushes as well. Aye, all those things would help her calm herself.

"Come." He dismounted and reached to lift her down. "We'll get ye a drink and one of Lyle's oatcakes. That'll settle ye."

Still glancing around, she clutched at the plaid as though he had tried to rip it away. "I dinna need a drink. I need to know where we are."

"Glen Spean. Ye see the river there beyond those trees." Her sudden pallor concerned him. She looked about to faint. "Come, lass. Before ye fall from the saddle."

Still shaking, she stared down at him. Silent. Eerie. Eyes wide and round as shields. She appeared overwrought and confused.

"What did ye do to her?" Eumann asked as he rode up and joined them.

"Nothing." Mathias watched her, ready to snatch her down if she threatened to topple off the other side.

With a labored grunt, Eumann dismounted and stood beside Mathias. "Then wha's wrong with her?"

"I am nay quite certain." Mathias snagged hold of her strange surcoat and tugged her down into his arms. For the briefest moment, she curled up against him like a frightened bairn. He rather liked the feel of her sweet-smelling warmth. Striding to a patch of sedge that was soft and newly sprouted, he eased her down. With a glance back at Eumann, he jerked his head toward Lyle. "Water for her. And an oatcake, aye?"

"Looks as if she needs *uisge beatha* more than water." Eumann turned and flagged down Bhaltair, then pointed at the lass. "Whisky! Make haste, aye?"

She balled up in the plaid, sitting upright but hugging her knees. Chin tucked, gaze locked on the ground in front of her, the poor thing seemed trapped inside her thoughts.

As he reached to pull the brat higher around her shoulders, a growl warned him to move his hand away. The dog shoved between them, teeth bared and hackles raised.

"I am nay going to hurt her, lad," Mathias quietly reassured. "I mean to help her best I can." He had already decided he liked this sweet lass. No harm would come to her under his watch.

"Where are we?" she whispered again without looking at him.

"Glen Spean," he gently reminded. "Remember? The River Spean is there ahead. Hear the water tumbling against its banks? It's swifter with the rains."

"It canna be," she mumbled, either trembling or shaking her head. He couldn't tell.

"What did ye do to her?" Bhaltair asked, striding up with a small leather flask in one hand. "Did she fall from yer horse? Did ye give her a good smack for disrespecting ye?"

"I willna grant such idiocy with an answer." Mathias snatched the drink away. He despised Bhaltair but tolerated the arrogant fool because of the man's warring skills. Pulling the stopper out with his teeth, he rolled back on his heels and studied the dog still ready to attack. He didn't wish to hurt the beast. The lad was merely protecting his mistress. "She needs this." He showed the animal the flask. "Let me close to her, aye?"

The mongrel flicked an ear and tilted his head, not moving from his station but at least no longer growling.

"Use yer sword," Bhaltair said. "It's good at herding, but we've nay time for this shite."

Kenzie snaked an arm around her dog and hugged him to her side. "If ye hurt my dog, I'll kill ye." The glare she fixed on

Bhaltair left no doubt she meant every word.

"Bah!" Bhaltair shooed away her reaction. "She's fine." He reached for the flask. "Gimme back my whisky."

With a vicious snapping, the canine lunged and sank its teeth into the man's hand.

"Damn ye, filthy cur!" He drew his dagger but came up short and stumbled a step back. Chin jutting upward, he flinched as the animal dangled from its hold on his hand.

Mathias nudged the tip of his sword harder against Bhaltair's throat. He pricked him enough to make the man wince again. "No harm to these beasts. Either of them. Understand?"

The ram, standing on Kenzie's other side, *baa'd* long and low, pawing at the ground.

To be certain Bhaltair understood, Mathias nudged the blade until a trickle of blood seeped downward. "Is my meaning clear, Bhaltair?"

"Aye." The man's eyes narrowed, and he bared his teeth. "Clear enough."

Satisfied that the short-tempered fool knew better than to challenge him, Mathias eased back down beside Kenzie and leaned close to get her full attention without touching her. "Call him off, lass. Make him know I mean to help ye. Bhaltair willna harm yer wee pup. Ye have my word."

She dragged her stare away from Bhaltair and locked it on him. What odd eyes she had. Greenish gray like the curly moss clinging to the bark on the trees. A coppery-brown shade circled her irises, matching the tawny flecks sprinkled through the field of pale green. She blinked. Her dark lashes were long and full. "Where are we? she repeated, forcing the words through clenched teeth.

That again. He wasn't sure how to make her understand. "Call off the dog and have a wee nip. We'll talk after that, aye?" He had dealt with such odd unreasonableness before. During battle. Right before his only brother had died in his arms. "All will be well. I promise ye."

"Brodie. Release."

The way she spoke gave Mathias chills. Poor lass sounded like she had resigned herself to her own execution.

The dog turned loose of Bhaltair's hand and returned to its mistress's side. She pulled him into her arms and rested her cheek against him. "I dinna ken what's happened," she said softly. The tickle of her breath made the animal flick its ear. "But they might can help us, aye?"

When nothing else happened, Mathias risked leaning forward and put the flask to her lips, thankful when the dog didn't attack.

Hands trembling, she took hold of the leather vessel, tilted it up with a quick flip, then brought it back down. She made a face and covered her mouth as she pushed it back at him. "I thought ye said that was whisky?"

He shrugged. "It is. Just not verra good whisky." With an encouraging nod, he pressed it back into her hands. "Another. 'Twill do ye good."

Eumann appeared with an oatcake and water. "Here. If she's unwell, should we make camp here?"

"Aye." Mathias glanced around. The place would do well enough. "Set up a shelter for her case it rains."

"'Twill be done." His friend paused and turned back. "And a hunt? Meat for supper wouldna go awry. A full stomach might make her feel better."

Mathias chuckled. One to always think of food, Eumann made a fair point this time. A hearty meal would do the lass good, and her dog would more than likely enjoy a bone or two. "Aye, man. A hunt, too." He turned back to the strangest woman he had ever met and held out his offerings. "An oatcake for ye, lass. And water to wash away the taste of it and the whisky."

With shaking fingers, she took it, staring at the rough brown disc as if she had never seen an oatcake before. "Thank ye." She rubbed her thumb back and forth across it. Her unblinking stare grew more worrisome by the minute.

"Where do ye hurt, lass?" He didn't have a clue what else to ask her. She had seemed fit enough moments ago.

"I am not hurt." She frowned at the food, then snapped it in two. "Something's verra wrong here, but I canna figure out exactly what it is."

He looked around, surveying the area. No one was here other than themselves, the cows, and her animals. It might rain soon, but elsewise, nothing seemed amiss. "Have ye been here before?"

His question brought a trembling smile to her pallor, a smile not meant for happiness. "Many times." She nibbled at the oatcake, then handed it to the dog. The other half, she handed to the sheep. "Throughout my life," she added.

"Was the glen not the same as it is now? What is different? What troubles ye about the place?" He couldn't fathom what could be wrong. He'd been through here all his life as well. The place hadn't changed a whit.

Her quivering smile faltered, then melted into a frown. She barely shook her head. "I doubt ye would understand." With a quick sniff, as though fighting the possibility of tears, she pinned him with a worried gaze. "The date?"

"The date?"

"Aye, the year and the day? What is today's date?"

"Twenty-eight April. Year of our Lord 1203."

She flinched as though he had struck her. "Twenty-eight April. 1203?" she repeated in a breathy whisper.

"Aye." He had never seen such a look. Shock. Fear. Panic. "Tell me, lass. What troubles ye? I'll help ye if I can."

She didn't answer, just closed her eyes and massaged her temples. Her face crumpled, and tears flowed, but her sobs remained silent.

God's teeth, he couldn't handle a woman's weeping. If it was the ache in her head making her cry, they could fix that. "I'll send Daw to find ye some willow bark. Soon as we get a fire going, we'll set some water to boil and steep it for ye, aye? 'Twill help with the pain in yer head."

She balled up tighter in the folds of the woolen brat, sagged over onto her side, and pulled her dog into a hug. The beast snugged into the curl of her body but kept its head propped on her hip, eyeing Mathias with distrust. The ram settled down against her back with a loud, grumbling *baa*. What bothered Mathias most was that she didn't close her eyes. Just stared straight ahead like someone trapped in madness.

"Kenzie?" he whispered, leaning as close as he dared without setting off the dog. "Tell me what I can do to make ye better, lass. I dinna understand what ails ye."

"Ye canna help me," she said. Her helpless tone wrapped chilling fingers around his heart and squeezed. Then her eyes flinched, and her gaze shot to him. "Take me back to the cave. Back where ye found me."

When she asked that, he felt taken in, gullible as a lad manipulated by an experienced lass. This had all been a ploy to regain her freedom. Nay. He'd oft been accused of soft-heartedness, but he wasn't a fool. He shook his head, not letting on that he had seen through her act of the distraught maiden. "That, I willna do. Ye must return to the keep. If the chieftain sees fit, yer kin can collect ye there."

"And if not?" she snapped, making him feel a great deal better since the fight had returned to her tone.

"If not?"

"If yer chief doesna see fit or my kin canna collect me, what will he do then? Have me hung from the skirting wall? Toss me in a dungeon? Throw me to his guard to abuse as they see fit?" She'd risen back to a sitting position, her fear and out-of-control imaginings renewing her strength.

"*Haud yer wheesht!*" It took all the control he possessed to keep from grabbing her up and shaking her. "Ailbeart Stronach is not only a good chief but a fair man. He would never treat ye harsh unless ye gave him reason to do so." Straightening, he gave her his sternest scowl, the one that made his men take a step back. "And I am the commander of his guard." He jerked a thumb at the men setting up camp. "All of them, not just these.

Have I once hinted at letting the men harm ye?"

"Not yet, but that doesna mean ye willna do so." She glared right back at him. "How do I know what ye'll do? I dinna know the lot of ye." A toss of her hand took in the men gathering around them to listen. "I've seen none of ye before. What do ye expect me to think when ye look like a horde of blood-thirsty warriors ready to rape and pillage?"

Moray, the prankster of the group, laughed and thumped old Hew, the one who never smiled. "She called us a horde! Us? A horde. We're naught but eight of us."

Hew didn't comment, just gave Moray an eye roll that said he'd rather be anywhere but here. "I'll be getting wood for a fire," he grumbled, then turned and stomped away.

Still chuckling, Moray nodded to Mathias. "Wait 'til she sees our full Stronach guard. She'll think *horde* then, aye?"

"Shut yer maw and tend to the cows," Mathias ordered through clenched teeth. "Now." He rose to his feet and faced the rest of them. "Must I assign each of ye duties one by one as if this be yer first day as guard?"

The men scattered—all except Bhaltair. A more conniving man would never be found. Mathias took a step toward him. Bhaltair had challenged him once before, and it hadn't gone in the man's favor. Perhaps it was time to revisit that thrashing. "Bhaltair?"

Eyes narrowing the slightest bit, the man slid a look down at their prisoner, then returned his attention to Mathias. Without a word, he turned and strode away.

Good. Now back to battling with the wee hen. Although a fight with Bhaltair would probably be easier. He squatted down and leveled his eyes with hers. "Stronach guards dinna rape nor pillage." With a wincing pause, he clasped his hands and tapped his thumbs together. "I misspoke. We dinna rape. Occasionally, we do pillage." With a shrug, he seated himself in front of her. He couldn't squat for the length of time this conversation might take. "But we've never taken from the weak or defenseless. It isna our way. Those are the ones we defend."

"Ye defend the weak and defenseless," she repeated with the look he had already learned meant she was up to something.

"Aye," he answered slowly, sensing a trap in the making.

"Then, why am I yer prisoner?"

A simple question. "I consider ye neither weak nor defenseless." He allowed himself a grin. "Ye thrashed Ellar MacPherson's arse for him. Did ye not?"

She shrugged off what he had meant as a compliment. "The eedjit fought like he was fair blootered."

"Like he was what?" This woman came out with the strangest words. Where did she hear such things?

"Drunk."

"Ah." A laughing snort escaped him. "Ye're right there. Ellar always fights like he's too deep in his cups." She seemed calmer now. Maybe she would talk. "Who are ye Kenzie MacMartin? And why is that cave so important to ye?"

Once again, her gaze dropped to the ground, and she seemed to draw up, closing herself off from the world. She took a long drink of water, then poured some in her hand for the pup and the sheep. After the animals had drunk their fill, she set it aside. All the while murmuring to them as if they were her children.

"I'm a sheep farmer," she finally said, her half-smile directed at the dog and ram as she scratched them behind their ears.

Mathias decided to try a different tactic. "Right after ye put Ellar down, ye demanded our names. Said ye needed Ellar's surname for the constable." He drew up his knees and propped his forearms atop them. "I know of no constable in this area. I met one once. In Argyll." He worked his arm, rubbing his shoulder at the memory of wrestling with the man. "Fierce warrior, he was. Commander of the Lord of Argyll's *Gallóglaigh*." When would the lass realize he knew she had lied? "So, which constable did ye mean?" He nodded toward one of the large pockets of her surcoat. "And what is that flat piece of onyx ye carry in yer pocket? The one ye kept tapping on back at the cave."

"A…charm," she said, speaking as though in a daze. "It's supposed to bring me luck." She closed her eyes and rubbed her forehead. Her head must be aching fiercer. "Apparently, the luck's gone from it."

"I wouldna say that," Mathias reassured her. The poor thing seemed so lost. Defeated. "Ye ended up with us rather than the MacPhersons."

She blew out a heavy sigh while still rubbing her eyes. "Aye. I suppose it could be worse."

That stung. "Have we been all that bad to ye?"

"Aye. Ye have." She fixed him with a pleading look. "I need to get back to that cave."

"Why?" The cave was on the very fringes of Stronach land. Entirely too close to the MacPhersons. Why would she risk it? A woman alone?

"It is my way home," she said with such emotion, he knew it for the truth.

"Ye live in the cave?"

"No." Staring down at her lap, she paused, frowning at her fisted hands. "The cave is a… tunnel," she said without looking up. "Through it, on the other side, is where I belong."

"Yer farm lies on the other side of the cave?" While that sounded believable, it failed to explain her garments, her odd speech, and that charm stone in her pocket. "Why are ye nay dressed proper?" He hoped she realized she would be asked all these questions again once they reached the keep. The Stronach might be ailing, but he would still demand answers. 'Twas best to sort those answers out now. Mathias hated surprises. He'd rather have a plan in hand when they walked through those gates.

Another heavy sigh escaped her. She chewed on her bottom lip for the span of a few heartbeats, all the while studying him. The lass was working up another lie. He could smell it. She brightened and sat taller. Her lie found. With an affectionate pat of the ram, she nodded. "I always wear this when Ramsay's escaped his pen and gone off wandering." With a tilt of her head toward her boots, she tapped on one of them. "I never know if there's going to be mud, rocks, or caves to be overcome."

While her answer seemed sound enough, Mathias recognized it as the crafted falsehood that it was. She was a canny lass. He'd give her that. She was doing her best to answer all his questions without telling him a single thing that might reveal who she was or why she had been at the mouth of that cave. He nodded as though he believed every word. This wasn't his first time questioning a prisoner. Even one as sly as her. He'd leave her be for now and let her think he had swallowed every word. He rose to his feet and nodded toward a tangled cluster of saplings leafed out enough to give her some privacy. "If ye need some time to yerself, make yer animals know to stay here with me. I'll stand guard to ensure ye're nay interrupted."

She stood and let his plaid fall to the ground. "In other words, ye'll be holding my lads hostage to make sure I return."

He grinned. "Ye are as canny as ye are beautiful."

With a glare that shouted she was ready to kill him, she flung a strange hand sign at him. A lone finger stuck up in the air. The middle one. Her expression paired with the way she thrust the gesture made it quite clear it wasn't meant as a compliment. Then she whirled about and stomped off into the bushes.

"Yer mistress isna happy with me," he told the animals in a soft voice so she wouldn't hear. Pity she felt so sour toward him. He liked her. More and more with each challenging conversation.

"Where's the lass?" Eumann asked, a pair of limp ptarmigans dangling from each fist.

"Bushes." Mathias reached down to pet the wee dog, then thought better of it when the animal bared its teeth. "Why?"

His friend lifted the birds. "Thought she could clean these while I see if Daw and Lyle's snared any hares or mayhap gotten a fish or two."

"Leave them. I'll see they're readied proper." With the woman's current mood, the last thing Mathias wanted was a knife in her hands.

"Remember ye're meant for the Lady Lilias," Eumann warned in a low tone. "A fine lady who's been hurt enough in this life, ye ken?" He stepped closer and lowered his voice even more. "Mind—none of us would blame ye if ye decided to…" He arched a brow at the bushes. "But ye dinna need to shame the Lady Lilias by…" His words trailed off again, but his meaning didn't.

"Leave the birds and go," Mathias ordered. What he did or didn't do was no one's affair but his own, and he'd not be the center of their band's wagers.

"I'm just sayin'—"

"I know exactly what ye're saying, and I'm telling ye that I'll nay have my men gossiping like a gaggle of washer women. Is that understood?" They all should know better than to question his authority by now. He'd fought hard for the role of commander and intended to keep it.

Kenzie emerged from the bushes, looking just as irritated as when she had entered them. "I'm taking them to the river for a drink." She turned and looked in the direction she'd just come from. "Shallows are just past there." With a flick of her wrist, the dog sprang into action and nudged the ram into motion. With a bold air, she held out her hand. "Give me back my crook."

Eumann stepped forward, holding out the game. Mathias blocked him. "I've changed my mind, Eumann. Clean the birds yerself. Daw and Lyle dinna need ye gawking to see if they've had any luck catching fish."

"But—" the man began, but a sharp look silenced him. With a disgusted huff, he stomped away, muttering under his breath while the carcasses swung at his sides.

Without another word, Mathias fetched her stick but didn't place it in her hand. "Yer word that ye willna use it as a weapon against me or any of my men. I dinna wish ye harmed."

"Ye're a pompous arse, aren't ye?"

Mathias wasn't positive what *pompous* meant, but he had a fair idea. He ignored the insult. "Yer word, m'lady?"

"Fine," she snapped with another step forward and her hand

still extended.

He handed over the staff and braced himself in case she had lied.

"When I give my word, I mean it." She snatched the staff away and stormed off with a wave for the dog and sheep to follow. "Come."

Even though he knew she meant the beasts and not himself, Mathias followed.

"I can do this myself," she called out without looking back at him.

"I have no doubt ye can." He lengthened his stride, easily catching up with her as they weaved through the bushes and trees along the river's edge. "But I think it best I come with ye." He could tell she wanted to say more by the way her jaw tightened. Instead, she just walked faster, stabbing the ground harder with her staff. Taking hold of her arm, he stopped her. "This doesna have to so unpleasant, lass."

"Oh, aye. It does." She glared at him. "Be warned, mighty Mathias, ye have no idea what ye're in for by holding me captive."

"Ye're wrong there, lass. I know full well what I've done, and I relish everything yet to come."

CHAPTER THREE

H ER SHELTER WAS saplings and branches woven into walls and a roof thick enough to block some of the rain. Kenzie yanked her hood lower over her eyes. Brodie and Ramsay lay curled on the plaid on either side of her. Their warmth radiated through the small space, helping to knock down the fierce chill of the damp night.

April in the Highlands might bring warmer days, but the nights still called for thick blankets and a crackling fire in her bright red wood stove back home. Visions of her dear little cottage that Da and her brothers had helped her renovate made her eyes sting with the urge to weep again, but she refused to give in to it. Tears brought nothing but a snotty nose, and the bedraggled tissue from her pocket couldn't bear much more. April 1203. How in the world had chasing a fool sheep through a cave sent her back in time?

As she stared into the darkness, she chewed on her bottom lip and pondered the impossibility. She had never enjoyed history classes, only taken them to get college credit. But the truth couldn't be denied. This was the thirteenth century. If she retraced her steps through the cave, would it send her home? Surely it would. For the health and wellbeing of her sanity, she couldn't allow herself to think otherwise.

Thinking over the day's journey and judging the landmarks she had spotted along the riverbank, she had a pretty good idea where they were. As soon as her captors slept, she'd nab one of their horses and ride off into the night.

The ram groaned and shifted in his sleep, nudging her as he rolled to his side. The bump of his overfed body reminded her that his short-legged trot would never keep up with a horse's gallop. Mathias and his men would overtake him, and who knew what they would do to her poor sheep just to spite her. She blew out a frustrated breath. Escape had to be achieved a different way.

On foot was the only option. She could travel along the tributary, hiding among trees, bushes, and washed-out embankments. The Spean would lead her to where it joined the River Lochy, then she would head north and follow that waterway until she found the cave beside the loch. This plan would ensure all three of them made it back to where they belonged. Even though it was the sheep's fault they were in this mess, she didn't have the heart to sacrifice it to the thirteenth century. Silly ram. He might be a pain in the arse, but she loved the woolly troublemaker.

She eased up to a sitting position, pushed away her hood, and strained to take note of everything in the camp. The sleeping men serenaded her with a chorus of snores and high-pitched wheezes punctuated with an occasional fart. Firelight silhouetted Eumann laying across the threshold of her shelter, his belly so large there was no way the ram could leap over him. *Climb? Yes. Jump over and not make contact? No.* They would have to escape through the rear wall. She prayed the tangle of limbs closing off the other end could be moved without alerting her captors.

With a firm hold on the sticks, she gave a gentle push, then hefted, testing the amount of give to the structure. Maybe she could raise it and slip under. Even though the men had used green boughs, it wasn't too heavy to manage. She glanced back at the animals and frowned. For the sheep to wriggle his way under, it would have to be lifted with enough of a tip to shower Eumann with loose leaves and debris. She didn't care. They were getting out of the thirteenth century, and that journey started now.

Patting the ram's side, she urged him to his feet even though he groaned the entire time. Brodie cooperated beautifully, alert and ready for any adventure. On her knees, she wiggled her fingers under the wall and lifted it enough for the dog to stick his nose underneath. The collie blew and snorted like a malfunctioning vacuum cleaner, snuffling the other side.

Kenzie cringed. "Nay, Brodie," she whispered. "Shh."

He drew back and cocked his head. She swore the animal frowned at her.

"We canna let them hear us," she mouthed. Pausing, she listened to see if they had been discovered. Nothing in the camp seemed to have changed. After resettling her knees and taking a deep breath, she lifted the wall higher until she could scoot under it and wedge a bent knee to keep it raised. She pulled the sheep to the opening, straining to push his head lower, so he'd take the hint and wriggle out. The beastie loved escaping. Now was his chance to shine.

The ram locked his legs and *baa'd,* glaring at her with obvious insult.

"Shh!" Kenzie grabbed hold of his muzzle, then tried to coerce him by scratching behind his ears. He shook her hand away and pawed at the ground.

"Do ye want to be roasted over their campfire?" she whispered. How the men hadn't caught on to them by now had to be a miracle from God Almighty. Giving the sign for the dog to herd the ram, she took hold of the sheep by the wooly fringe of his jowls and tried again. It took one more attempt for the hard-headed thing to get the idea and wiggle out underneath the wall.

Kenzie held her breath, hoping the animal kept quiet. Brodie slipped out next. Going over onto her side, she grabbed her shepherd's crook, then shimmied out sideways. She lay there for a long moment, listening. Snores. Wheezes. A mumbling groan, then Eumann must've rolled against the shelter because it shook and slid toward her.

She hopped to her feet and glanced around. All was still. Peaceful.

An enormous hand grabbed hold of her arm. Her self-defense training kicked in but did little against the mountain of muscle other than winning a huffing grunt or two during the scuffle. The overgrown thicket surrounding them hindered more than it helped. Her staff snagged in the branches, delaying her blows, and neither the dog nor the ram could position themselves to help her.

"Ye must stop this now!" Mathias caught hold of her wrist and twisted her arm behind her, forcing her to drop the crook. "I dinna wish to hurt ye."

"Then let me go!"

"I told ye nay before, and I havena changed my mind." He marched her around to the front of the shelter and booted Eumann in his arse. "This is how ye guard a prisoner?"

The man sat up with one eye squinted shut as he struggled to make sense of his surroundings. "She crawled over me?" With a jaw-popping yawn, he scratched his head. "Damn. I wish I hadna missed that."

Mathias kicked him again. "Get up and go round to the back. Prop yer sorry arse against the rear wall, ye ken?"

"Aye." The man huffed and groaned as he hauled himself up and did as ordered.

"In there. The lot of ye." With a gentle but forceful shove, Mathias bent her forward, then pushed her inside. Her animals followed, taking a seat on either side of her and staring out at their captor. He pointed at her, jabbing the air with every word. "Ye had best sleep now and give up any plans of escaping. We leave at dawn, and there'll be no time for rest until we make camp again."

"Give me back my crook." She didn't think he would do it, but it never hurt to ask.

"Ye shall nay have yer wee stick again until we reach the

keep. Not before, ye ken?"

"I hate ye." And she meant it. Before Mama died, she had always told her children it was wrong to hate anyone. Kenzie sincerely doubted Mama had ever found herself in a situation like this. "Did ye hear me?" She wanted to be sure the fool man knew how much she loathed him.

"Aye, I heard ye lass." He blew out a resigned sigh and stretched out in front of the entrance on his side, his back to her. "I wish ye didna feel so, but I reckon there's no helping it."

He wished she didn't hate him? *Why?*

"What difference does it make whether I like ye? Ye're just going to dump me at the keep and let the chips fall where they may."

"What chips?"

She clenched her teeth, grinding them together to keep from screaming. Heaven help her, she couldn't even communicate in this blasted century. "It's a saying. It means you'll get rid of me and go on yer merry way, not caring what happens to me."

"Of course, I care what happens to ye."

He actually sounded like he meant it. And also, as though her words had stung. Had she really hurt his feelings? She flopped down on the plaid, curling into a ball with her head toward the opening instead of the other end next to Eumann's timber-rattling snores. Defeat triggered a sudden weariness deep in her bones, one that made her throat ache with wanting to cry. Maybe when she woke up, she'd discover this all to be a bad dream. But she couldn't sleep.

"Why would ye care what happens to me?" she argued, pulling her jacket closer. "Ye dinna even know me."

"I would like to know ye," came his soft reply in the deep rumbling way she would have found so inviting under any other circumstance. "But it doesna appear ye will allow it."

"It's because I dinna belong here," she defended just as softly. "My home, my family, friends…" Her voice cracked, and a tear broke free, rolled down the side of her nose, and dripped off the end. She sniffed and batted at the wetness with an angry swipe of her hand. "They're all gone, and I dinna ken if I'll ever see them again." Speaking the fear aloud only made it worse. She closed her eyes tight and prayed for rescue.

"Was yer village raided? Were they taken prisoner?" Mathias moved. His rustling interrupted her panicked prayers and made her open her eyes. He now faced her. "Tell me, lass, mayhap I can help. There's more to the Stronach guard than these few men. Might we could recover yer kin and give them sanctuary at the keep."

"And why would yer chief allow ye to do that for a complete stranger?" While his offer to do the impossible was touching, even if it could be done, she doubted any chieftain would risk a clan's resources for nothing in return.

"He would do so because he values family. The man lost his wife during a Norse raid." Mathias paused, his expression unreadable with his back to the fire and his face hidden in the shadows. "They crippled him during that fight and…hurt…his young daughter. A wee lassie of some seven years. Poor thing spoke nary a word for quite a few years thereafter."

"Hurt?" Kenzie didn't want to imagine how the Vikings had *hurt* the child. The history books suddenly felt very watered down by detached professors more intent on droning on about names and dates than teaching what really happened to the people living in that time.

Mathias shifted as though ill at ease. "Aye, but the Lady Lilias is a fine young woman now. Ye will meet her once we reach the keep. Ye must try and sleep now. 'Twill make ye feel better, ye ken?"

Sleep? What a ridiculous notion. She had reached the point of exhaustion where even if she closed her eyes, sleep would never come. With a slow rake of her fingers through Brodie's thick fur, she tried to soothe herself by thinking of all that had gone right with the day rather than all that had gone wrong. Mama had taught her that habit long ago when she came running home from school one day with her feelings hurt by a bully. Another tear slid free. Mama had been so wise. She wondered what Mama would suggest she do in this situation.

"Close yer eyes, lass. Sleep, *mo nighean donn*," Mathias whispered.

Mo nighean donn. My brown-haired lass. Both Mama and Da had often used that pet name, but somehow, when Mathias said it, it had a unique ring to it. *Warm. Possessive. Lonely.* The memory of her hardworking Da's favorite phrase brought her a sad smile.

"I'll sleep when I'm dead," she replied soft and low.

Mathias shifted again, reached out, and clumsily stroked the top of her head as if to comfort her. An action she would have found touching under different circumstances.

"If that be the case, then dinna ever sleep because I dinna wish ye dead," he said.

Then a sudden realization dawned. Mathias was a decent man doing the best he could in the time in which he had been born. If he had belonged in her time, they might have been friends. A sad smile came to her. Maybe even more than friends. Who knows? It didn't matter. She would return to where she belonged as soon as she could get back to that blasted cave.

"Ye're a good man, Mathias," she said, relenting to at least offer him that much.

"So, ye dinna hate me like ye said before?"

With a heavy sigh, she shook her head. "No. I guess I dinna hate ye after all."

He touched her hair one last time, then rolled over and faced the fire, his back to her again. "Good. That makes me feel better. Now sleep, aye?"

She rolled her eyes. Heaven knows she wouldn't want the man to feel bad. She snuggled closer to Brodie, determined to get through this nightmare and wake up back home in her own bed.

HER HEART SANK when she opened her eyes and found herself still in the thirteenth century. Hard ground and a few hours of restless sleep while pinned between a sheep and a dog that had left her stiff and sore. She rubbed her neck and rolled her shoulders. God help her. She felt like she'd stayed too late at the pub and gotten hit by a car on the way home. If anyone crossed her this morning, they valued their life very little.

She crawled out of the lean-to, needing to pee, yearning for either hot tea or coffee and ready to be anywhere but here. Her teeth were coated in that goopy morning fuzz she detested, and her mouth tasted like someone had shite in it. Bhaltair's cheap whisky, along with the roasted birds and greasy ramps Eumann had cooked, created nauseating wake-up breath. She hated this century.

"Are ye ready then?" Mathias asked. His brilliant smile made her want to punch him.

"No, I am not," she snapped. Raking her fingers through her tangled hair, she swept it back and held it in place with an elastic band. "I need a little privacy, if ye dinna mind."

With a happy dip of his chin, he waved her crook toward the bushes and turned away. "Hie yerself, then. 'Tis time we crossed the river and got on our way."

"Hie myself," she muttered as she shoved through the thicket behind her shelter. "I'll hie myself all right." She barely controlled the unreasonable urge to run like hell in the other direction. Common sense won out. Not only would they overtake her in dawn's irritating light, but Mathias still had her staff. She wasn't about to abandon the precious crook that had been in her family for years.

After attending to the most pressing matter at hand and patting dry with a handful of last summer's leaves, she found a stick and frayed its end with her pen knife. It might not give her minty fresh breath, but at least if she scrubbed the gunk off her teeth and rinsed out her mouth with water, she might feel some better.

"Where d'ye think ye're going?" Mathias asked as she

stomped past him.

"To wash my face and brush my teeth." If anyone tried to stop her, she'd kill them.

"What's she doing?" Eumann asked as he kicked dirt over the hot coals of last night's fire.

"Something ye would all do well to do," she shouted at him. By jings, if she was stuck here for a while, she might as well improve the era—starting with hygiene. She knelt at the water's edge and washed her face, the back of her neck, then scrubbed her teeth as best she could with the frayed stick. It was a far cry from her rechargeable toothbrush and whitening paste, but it was better than nothing. She wished she had some mint to chew. Maybe once they reached the keep, there would be some growing in a garden of some sort. She assumed they had gardens. For the life of her, she couldn't recall reading much about life in a castle. When she rose, she turned to find all eight men standing in a line watching her. "Have none of ye ever cleaned yer teeth before?"

"Aye, but not with a stick," Eumann said as though he found the thought of such a thing ridiculous. He grabbed hold of his sleeve, scrubbed his front teeth with it, then gave her a toothy smile. "See? Clean enough without a splintered branch."

Kenzie wrinkled her nose. "Aye. That's much better than a stick."

Mathias waved her forward. "Ready now?"

"I suppose so since I doubt ye have any breakfast tea with cream and sugar." A drink of water after she cleaned her teeth wasn't the same, but it was better than nothing. All the men looked at her as though she spoke in a foreign language, and they hadn't understood a word she said. She shook her head and plodded over to Mathias's horse. With a look back at the men still clumped together, she arched a brow. "Well?"

"Is this what it's like to be married?" Eumann asked. "Except without the bed play?"

"How should I know?" Mathias pushed past the man. A

frown had replaced his irritating smile.

Good. If she had to be miserable, so should he. Before he reached her, she held up a hand and stopped him. "Dinna pick me up." There was something unnerving about him lifting her up into the saddle like she weighed less than a feather. "Just give me a boost. That's what Da and my brothers always did."

"What is *a boost*?" The furrow in his brow deepened, tightening his frown. "I dinna ken if we have one."

Kenzie rubbed her eyes. Considering they were both Scots, their inability to communicate was pathetic. She had no idea how they might have phrased *a boost* in the thirteenth century. "This." She laced her fingers together, then held her hands at knee level. "Ye stand like this so I can step into yer hands, and ye help me push up into the saddle instead of trying to jump with the stirrups so high."

Immediate understanding dawned in his eyes. "Let me show ye how we *boost* ladies in a more gentlemanly manner." He took a knee beside the horse and held out a hand. "Take my hand, then step on my knee, ye ken?"

While gallant in appearance, Kenzie doubted it would be as effective as her method. His monstrosity of a horse had to be at least eighteen to nineteen hands tall. It was the largest breed she had ever ridden. Mathias's knee wouldn't lift her much higher than the stirrup, and it would still take a healthy, jumping lunge to land her in the saddle.

Mathias wiggled his fingers. "Come. Trust me."

Trust him? She chose not to comment, just stuck her hand in his and stepped up onto his knee. Once sure of her balance, she latched hold of the lip of the saddle, then tried to hop and throw her leg over. The horse resettled its stance at the same time, breaking her hold on the saddle. "Shite!"

"I've got ye, lass." He caught her to his chest, cradling like a babe.

She smacked his shoulder, wriggling to stretch her feet to the ground. "See? Will ye try it my way now?"

With a rumbling chuckle, he held her closer and smiled down at her. "Now, why would I wish to try it yer way when mine ended so pleasantly?"

"Ye knew this would happen! Didn't ye?" She saw the truth of it gleaming in his eyes. *Trust him, he'd said. What a load of rot.* After a hard punch to his shoulder, she shook her fist in his face. "Put me down and do it my way. Now."

Mathias and the rest of the men roared with laughter. But he set her feet to the ground, laced his fingers together, and offered her the *boost* she had requested.

"Good man!" Eumann called out. "Best to heed the wee thing afore she thrashes yer arse for ye."

Wee thing. She'd show them a *wee thing.* Bouncing a leap off Mathias's hands, she landed in the saddle, took hold of the reins, and urged the horse into a trot toward the river's edge. The beast obeyed her just as it had followed its previous master's commands. She knew it would. Animals sensed authority and confidence.

But then a piercing whistle split the air. Her mount's dark mahogany ears perked, and the creature returned to Mathias, no matter how she tried to turn it aside. The man grinned. "Roch knows his true master well enough." He settled himself behind her with enviable ease. With a disturbing lean, he pressed his mouth close to her ear. When he spoke, it was for her alone. His warm breath tickled her neck, unleashing a chaotic mix of emotions. "Such loyalty and love is earned—with patience," he whispered. "'Tis the same between people."

This ancient man, this skilled flirt she should've never chanced upon, had an alarming effect on her. Made her toy with the thought of leaning back against that hard chest and enjoying the feel. Or resting a hand on one of his muscular thighs and squeeze. She wasn't immune to his charms, but she needed to be. Badly. With a stern inner scolding, she shook herself free of his dangerous spell. Her goal was to get back home. End of story.

She hitched forward as far as the curve of the saddle allowed and held herself ramrod straight. "Do ye wish Brodie to help with the cows again?"

A noticeable sigh came from him. Or it could have been the wind. Either way, it didn't matter. Nothing could happen between them. Not even a harmless flirtation.

"Aye, lass," he finally said, urging the horse to head down river. "There's a shallows up here a ways. We'll cross there."

They rode in silence the time it took to reach the strand where wide patches of smooth river stones peeped up through the bubbling water. Encouraged by their annoying canine herder, the cows sloshed across without issue, as did the men on horseback.

"Yer wooly beast doesna have a mind to cross," Mathias observed as he halted on the other side.

Kenzie looked back at poor Ramsay, pacing up and down the river's edge, bleating like a lamb in search of its mother. "He hates water." With all that had happened since they emerged from the cave, she had forgotten about the ram's greatest fear. He despised it so much, she had toyed with the idea of putting a shallow moat around the sheep pen to keep him corralled during the times she didn't want him wandering the fields. She shifted, glancing at the long descent to the ground. "I'll have to fetch him. See if Brodie and I can convince him to cross." She threw her leg over to dismount, figuring she could drop to the ground without issue.

"Ye're going to break yer fool neck, woman." Mathias grabbed hold of her by the arms and lowered her, releasing her once her feet touched the ground.

"We shouldha eaten that beast last night," Bhaltair called out.

"Get stuffed!" Kenzie shouted with a hard look back at him. Of all the men, she liked Bhaltair least of all and felt certain that for him, Mama would have broken her rule of not hating. She didn't trust that arrogant arse as far as she could throw him.

"Get stuffed?" Bhaltair repeated as though daring her to follow through on the strange threat. "What the hell does that mean?"

"From the look she gave ye," Mathias said, amusement and a hint of respect ringing in his tone, "I'd say her meaning is verra clear. Ye best heed her and shut yer maw."

After another narrow-eyed glare back at the men, Kenzie squatted down in front of the sheep, rubbing his ears and stroking his muzzle to calm him. "Come now. We'll cross together. It's shallow. Ye'll barely get wet." Taking hold of his shaggy jowls, she pulled. It was a wonder he didn't lower his head and bounce her into the water. Instead, the beast locked its legs and *baa'd*, refusing to move. She had a few of his favorite pellet treats left. Surely one of those would work. She pulled it from her pocket and waved it in front of his nose. "Come across, and it's all yers, pet. Come on. Ye know ye want it."

The animal looked at her, eyed the treat, then glanced at the water and backed up the few steps Kenzie had pulled him forward. The bribery had lost her ground rather than gained it.

A loud splashing pulled her attention from the frightened beast. It was Mathias, but he didn't seem angry—just determined. He gave her a polite nod, then looked back at his horse. "Join Roch, aye? I'll bring across yer wee ball of wool."

"Be patient with him, aye? He's just afraid." She stepped between Mathias and the ram. "If ye hurt him, I'll make ye sorry. Do ye hear me?"

Mathias didn't respond. Instead, the corners of his mouth tightened as though she had slapped him. Without a word, he shoved around her and lifted the sheep by wrapping one arm around its front and the other around its rear. He sloshed his way back across the shallows, then eased the animal to dry ground. "There ye go, lad." Standing beside his horse, he shot an irritated glance at Kenzie. "Now, come. We need to be on our way."

His tone bothered her. She couldn't decide if he was angry, hurt, or...or she didn't know what. Without a word, he bent and clasped his hands to help her into the saddle.

"Thank ye," she said when he settled in behind her.

"Aye." He urged the horse into motion behind the rest of the men herding the cattle.

"Why are ye mad?" She hadn't tolerated the silent treatment in her century and wasn't about to put up with it in this one. "Out with it. Now."

"Ye truly believed I would hurt yer wee pet?" he snapped. "After I've protected the three of ye since we came upon ye."

"I can also think of at least once where ye threatened to kill them." She twisted in the saddle, daring him to deny it. "Have ye forgotten about that?"

His nostrils flared like Da's old bull right before it charged across the pasture. He glared at her. "Ye knew I didna mean it."

"So, if I had entered the cave, ye wouldha let them follow me?" She called him on the lie. A man didn't become a leader by not following through on whatever he threatened.

"Nay," he growled, sounding like an irate guard dog.

"Then stop pouting."

"I dinna pout."

"Aye. Ye do. Worse than my three-year-old niece."

"God's beard, do ye wish me to make ye ride with Bhaltair?"

"Do ye wish *me* to have Brodie turn the herd? I promise he can do it in the blink of an eye, and yer inexperienced men willna be able to stop him." If she bounced her head back hard enough, she might split his lip. Maybe even bloody his nose. She had grown up with five irksome brothers and wasn't about to go soft now. If he thought to bully her, he better think again. "Well?" she goaded.

"Ye've a foul temperament, Mistress MacMartin. Foul temper, indeed. I pity the man who ends up saddled with ye."

He wasn't the first man to tell her that. Strange how the century didn't matter when it came to a criticism that stung. "Whatever." She squared her shoulders and made a show of supervising the collie's maneuvering of the herd. Never would she let him know he had scored a direct hit on an old wound. "Why dinna we just call a truce and ride in silence until we reach this keep of yers, aye?" She needed quiet to plan an escape, and the farther they traveled from the cave, the more complicated those plans became.

"Aye," he snapped again, hurting her feelings even more.

Funny how one word in a certain tone could speak volumes.

CHAPTER FOUR

"WHERE IS SHE?"

Eumann tipped his head toward a craggy mass of boulders farther up the rise. The mighty stones, squared off by the hand of God, stood stark and white against the sky's brilliant blue. Kenzie and her dog sat side by side atop the rocks, staring at the livestock grazing in the glen below.

"Bhaltair's getting bolder around her. Want I should tell him to mind his ways or else?" Eumann sounded ready to battle one of their own.

"I will handle Bhaltair," Mathias promised. "Ye keep an on eye Ruari. I would hate to have to kill my own cousin."

"Aye, that one's a problem, too." Eumann plodded toward the horses tethered to a nearby line stretched between two trees. "I dinna ken why that pair treat women like chattel to be used and tossed aside. Would they wish their mothers dealt with in such a manner?"

Mathias didn't bother answering. His friend nattered on about anything and everything unless silenced by eating or sleeping. Much of the time, the man talked to himself more than anyone else.

Mathias headed up the hillside, determined to make peace

with the vicious wee lass and her dog. She didn't acknowledge his approach, but he sensed she heard him.

"So, he's accepted the herd as his own?" he commented as though no cross words had passed between them. When she spared him a narrow-eyed glare, he nodded toward the ram meandering among the cattle. "Yer sheep there. With the cows. As if he's one of them."

"He's never been choosy about the company he keeps." She hugged her knees and propped her chin atop them. "What do ye want?"

"Want?"

"Aye," she said, her tone cold and defensive. "Ye came up here for a reason. I'm sure it wasna to talk about the livestock getting along."

"Are ye always so—" An apt description of this frustrating yet beguiling lass escaped him.

"So what?" she dared, bristling like an angry hedgehog.

"So damned hard to get along with." The words came out before he could stop them. So much for making peace. He settled down beside her, determined to vanquish the hostility between them, whether she liked it or not.

"Do ye always work so hard at befriending prisoners?" she countered. With a sharp sniff, she jutted her chin higher and rubbed her dog's ears as she stared at the glen below.

Then he noticed her eyes and nose. Red as could be. Not from sun or wind but from crying. Or at least, from wanting to cry. The sight made his heart hurt, and guilt pricked at him.

"Forgive me for my harsh words from earlier, lass. I should nay have said such things." He waited. No response. Not even a twitch. "And I shouldna have called ye hard to get along with either," he added.

"I am hard to get along with," she admitted in a quiet voice. "Ask anyone who knows me." A tear slipped down her cheek, and she swiped at it. Her jaw tensed harder. "How much farther to the keep?"

"None too far. Another day or so. Maybe more. Depends on the beasts. We dinna wish to drive them too hard." He nodded toward the herd. "Eumann says at least three will calve soon."

"Ye trust Eumann more than the others." Her mouth puckered with the observation, making her full lips even more tempting. "Why is that?"

"What?" Those lips of hers made him lose track of the conversation.

"Why do ye trust Eumann more than the others? Ye share a last name with two of them." She pointed at the riders below. "That pair. Are they yer brothers?"

While leery about her sudden curiosity, he grew hopeful since she was speaking to him without murder in her tone. "Cousins." He picked up a pebble and tossed it. "My only brother is dead."

"I'm sorry." The silence between them took on a life of its own, making the air crackle with tension.

"I trust Eumann because he has never given me cause not to," he said. Maybe, if he kept her talking, she might decide she didn't hate him so much. Such a bonnie lass. What a grand thing it would be if she developed a bit of kindness toward him.

"He does seem a decent sort." With a thoughtful frown, she eyed the men guarding the perimeter of the herd. "I wouldna trust the rest of them as far as I could throw them."

"And what about me?"

She shifted, directing her glare at him. "Why is my opinion of ye so important?"

"Because ye're different from any woman I have ever met. An intriguing mystery." He caught a hint of her smile, and it gave him more hope. "So, do ye trust me then?"

"A little. For now."

A promising start.

"Here comes one of yer wicked ones." Kenzie hopped to her feet. "Dinna bite him again," she instructed the dog. "There's no telling where he's been, and I dinna wish ye poisoned."

Mathias chuckled, but all good humor left him as Bhaltair rode closer. The lass was correct. If an unsavory thing existed, that man would find it.

"We should move on," Bhaltair announced. "All have rested, and we've plenty of daylight."

Mathias rose to his feet. "We camp here tonight."

"Why?" Bhaltair fired back, tightening the reins until his horse pranced to the side. "Do ye nay wish a decent bed?" His leering gaze settled on Kenzie. "And an agreeable lass to warm it?" With a suggestive smirk he added, "Or a disagreeable lass. They're even better for bed play."

In two strides, Mathias reached Bhaltair and yanked him down from the saddle. "Ye willna talk so rough in front of the lady." He twisted his arm behind his back and turned him toward Kenzie. "Apologize. Now."

"I meant no disrespect," Bhaltair forced through clenched teeth.

"Yes, ye did," Kenzie countered. "And that is not an apology."

He wrenched Bhaltair's arm harder, forcing the man to his knees. "The lass speaks the truth. Would ye care to try again?"

"Ye may be my commander," Bhaltair sputtered with an angry hiss. "But ye will rue this day. I swear it."

"Games again, Bhaltair?" Ruari mocked as he joined them. Wherever Bhaltair was, the backstabbing Ruari was never far behind.

"Nay," Bhaltair growled. "Just suggested we move on."

Mathias tightened his hold on the rogue. The pair had tested his authority more than usual this trip like young bucks attempting to oust the old stag. He kept Ruari in full view while he tended to the matter at hand. "Apologize. Now."

"Apologize? Bhaltair?" Ruari snorted. "Ye've gone daft, cousin."

Mathias noted with grim satisfaction that sweat now trickled down the sides of Bhaltair's red face. He twisted the man's arm to the point of almost popping his shoulder out of the socket.

Teeth bared, Bhaltair reared back his head and shot a glare of pure hatred at Kenzie. "Forgive my language. I meant no insult."

With a hard shove, Mathias sent him rolling. "Back to the herd. Both of ye. Stay there 'til someone relieves ye, ye ken?"

"This isna over, Mathias," Bhaltair promised again as he returned to his horse.

"Aye. It is."

Ruari didn't comment. His cold glare spoke for him.

"I dinna think ye should show yer back to those two." Kenzie stepped up beside him as the pair rode away. Arms crossed, she begrudged him a nod. "Thank ye for defending me." She stuck her hands in her pockets and pursed her lips. "Ye probably made things worse, though. Ye realize that, aye? Like when the teacher scolds yer classmates for bullying ye then leaves ye alone with them on the playground?"

"What?" He thought he understood what she meant but couldn't be sure. "I swear, lass, sometimes ye speak a different language."

"Ye've pissed them off," she explained with an exasperated huff. "Now, they'll be more intent on getting back at the both of us."

"Do ye expect me to ignore the man's insolence? He insulted yer honor."

"Trust me. This isna the first time my honor's been insulted, and I'm sure it willna be the last."

"As long as I am around, yer honor will be defended."

She stared at him for a long while, then smiled. A genuine smile that made him even more determined to keep her happy. "Thank ye, Mathias." Motioning to her dog, she headed down the incline. "I'm going to check on Ramsay. I dinna want him hurt or teased by those two."

The lass was right. Bhaltair and Ruari were capable of anything. "I shall accompany ye."

They meandered down the rocky hillside to the glen below. The meadow was already lush and green after but a few weeks of spring's coaxing. The gentle breeze held the fresh earthy scent of the ground's awakening. The dog bounded in front of them, leaping over the heartier tufts of grass and thick clusters of heather.

Mathias envied the dog his carefree happiness. "Not a worry in the world."

"As long as he's with me." Kenzie smiled, her gaze following the shaggy black and white beast. "Last time I vacayed, my father tried to keep him at his farm for me, and he kept escaping. Da always knew where to find him, though. He'd be on my doorstep waiting for me to come home."

While he had no idea what a *vacayed* was, he got the general gist. "He loves ye."

"Aye, and his love is unconditional. I'd be lost without him."

What would it be like if someone possessed such feelings for him? Not just any someone. But her? He decided such a thing might be very nice indeed. Life would never be dull. Her strangeness and fire guaranteed that. His conscience thumped him out of the reverie. Hard. Lilias and the clan came before all else. He wasn't a man free to harbor such thoughts.

"Hie to the sheep, lad," Kenzie sang out.

All playfulness disappeared from the dog. He shot across the remaining distance to the herd, weeded out the ram, and turned it back toward them.

Mathias caught sight of Eumann riding toward them. The man had a face dark as thunder.

"They've gone," he shouted before coming to a full stop. "Said they'd tired of cattle herding and serving as ladies in waiting."

"Who?" Mathias possessed a fair idea but needed confirmation.

"Ruari and Bhaltair, of course." Eumann spit as though the men's names left a nasty taste in his mouth.

Angered by the betrayal, Mathias looked to the west, the direction of the keep. "I'm nay surprised." Bhaltair had been trying to win the chieftain's ear ever since the Stronach had named Mathias his successor. "Who knows what lies the man will tell?"

"Shall I ride on and try to stop them?" Eumann's mount high stepped in place, ready to charge forward.

"Nay." Mathias scratched his jaw, scrubbing his fingers through the stubble. "If we gave chase, 'twould make us look as though we feared anything they might say. No wrong has been done here."

Eumann sidled a doubtful look in Kenzie's direction.

"What?" She stepped forward as though ready to fight.

"I'll watch the herd 'til time to cook supper." Eumann veered his mount away and rode off.

"What are the two of ye not saying?" Kenzie planted herself in front of him, as puffed up and defensive as a wee toad.

"Bhaltair's lies will center on yerself since he canna find fault with the regaining of the herd." He didn't add more. Clan Stronach's politics were not only complicated but also very troubling. Especially since the troubling part centered on him.

"What do ye think he'll say?" Oddly enough, she sounded more curious than upset or concerned.

"With Bhaltair, anything is possible." He didn't wish to worry her, but she needed to be prepared.

"Then that's even more reason for ye to let me go back to the cave."

So, that was the gleam in her eye. Canny woman. Turning Bhaltair's wickedness to her own benefit. In a way, he admired her but still wished she would accept her fate and be done with it. "I willna take ye back to the cave, so ye might as well leave off asking."

"Ye dinna have to take me back. I know the way."

He forced himself to keep his mouth shut for two deep breaths, else he might say something he shouldn't. She had to understand. A return to the cave would not happen.

"A woman shouldna travel alone," he chided with a gruffness

he hoped she'd take to heart. "It isna safe." He braced himself, knowing she would argue. It was the wee beastie's quarrelsome nature, and he expected no less. In fact, he enjoyed it.

Without further comment, she turned and trudged off through the lush grasses, disappointing him immeasurably.

"Kenzie!"

She ignored him and kept walking.

THE FARTHER KENZIE tromped across the field, the calmer she became. After a while, she realized why. It was the fresh, clean scent of tender young grasses crushed beneath her boots. That sweet aroma of spring triggered so many memories. Sunny meadows filled with wee lambs gamboling about. Granddad helping her train Brodie. Da working with her as she mended her very own barn. The knot in her throat swelled, chasing away her fragile calm and replacing it with unbearable sorrow. And anger. Anger at Mathias for his bullheaded refusal to release her.

"Kenzie!"

His shout only made her walk faster. If the fool man had any sense, he would leave her alone. A loud pounding coming up behind her proved he possessed no survival instincts. When Mathias ran, he sounded like a galloping horse.

"Kenzie, please."

She halted and stared at the ground, cursing her stupidity for following Ramsay into that cave.

"Why can ye not see that I am only trying to keep ye safe?"

He stood so close, the heat of him crept through her layers of clothing, daring her to draw closer. Maybe it wasn't his heat. But something else. A different teasing. As though he sought to wrap his strength around her like a security blanket. She rubbed her temples.

"I have lost my mind," she muttered.

"What say ye?" His concern and caring rattled her even more.

How could this man not know he wasn't supposed to act like this with a prisoner? Mean and callous—hated by all. Those were the traits of a kidnapper. If he kept this current attitude up, she'd end up liking him. In fact, she kind of already did.

"Kenzie? Did ye hear me? I only hope to keep ye safe."

"I heard ye just fine." She dropped her hands to her sides. "How can I make ye understand that I would be all right? I come from this land, and if ye give me back my staff, I can take care of myself. I promise."

"A woman, a dog, and a sheep would be no match for the MacPhersons in full force." The return of his chiding tone grated on her last nerve but made her feel cared about, too. He needed to stop doing that. Now.

After another step closer, he continued, "I guarantee that since ye thrashed Ellar's arse, he plans to retaliate and willna come alone."

How could a man's scowl be both ferocious and tender?

She gave the same uppity smirk that always irritated her brothers. "I handled him well enough the first time. It'll not be a bother to handle him again."

He resettled his feet like a bull about to charge. "Ye failed to overcome me. Has that escaped yer memory?"

"Because ye fought dirty."

"What?" His indignation charged the air to an explosive level.

"Ye fought dirty," she repeated, victorious at hitting a nerve. If the stubborn beast wouldn't release her, she'd make him regret it with a hearty dose of misery. "Ye held my animals captive to make me give over." She assumed a coy stance and batted her lashes. "Or has that escaped yer memory?"

"So, ye're saying ye couldha bested me?"

Her confidence faltered a wee bit, but she wasn't about to let him know it. Mathias fought like a panther. Powerful. Fast. Unrelenting. Ellar had bumbled about like a drunken fool. She lifted her chin, determined not to give an inch. "I feel I couldha given it a good shot—if ye hadna cheated."

"I didna cheat," he argued. "Have ye never heard of battle tactics?"

She waggled her head, amping up her righteous air. "Well, I call it cheating, and if ye hadna done it, me and my animals wouldha escaped."

"Eumann!" Mathias roared for the man without pulling his furious glare from her.

Coming in at a hard gallop, the guard almost unseated himself as he halted his mount. "Aye, Mathias?"

"Fetch the lass's wee stick," he growled as he resettled his footing and flexed his hands.

When Eumann returned, he dismounted and stood there, looking first at her, then Mathias. Seeing the commotion, the other riders came close enough to watch.

"Give it to her," Mathias ordered.

Kenzie caught the shepherd's crook, then held it between her knees as she stripped off her jacket. Speed and agility would be her only hope of coming out of this with any shred of dignity. Brodie appeared at her side, showing his teeth and growling. "Nay, lad. Not this time. This battle is mine alone." With a taunting grin, she added a little louder, "I dinna cheat, like some folk." Staff at the ready, she bent at the knees, ready to spring. Waiting. If he was like all the others, he'd charge like a raging bull. That's when she would step aside and whack him.

But he stood there with that infuriating, self-satisfied smile.

She danced from side to side, twirling the hardwood stick that had never failed her before. "Well, come at me. What are ye waiting for?"

"Ye are the mighty warrior queen. Wage yer battle, yer highness." With a cocky tip of his head, he motioned her forward. "Overcome me and win yer freedom. Or be ye scairt ye'll fail?"

She ignored the barb. He had offered high stakes indeed, but her starting the fight diminished her odds. And she felt sure that was why the arrogant fool had done it. She had taken self-defense classes. Not offense. Attacking people wasn't an art she possessed. But she had to do something. Honor demanded it. Suddenly, she wished she hadn't begged off those gymnastics classes her mother had tried to get her to take. At least if she could do a decent cartwheel or launch herself into the air, she might be like one of those superhero types and wrap her legs around his neck and bring him to the ground. As it was, if she attempted that, her arse would hit the ground before she ever reached him.

"Why do ye hesitate, my queen?"

The man's goading spurred her to action. She charged, determined to get in at least one good crack of her stick across his shins. Rather than knock her away or step aside, Mathias reached out a long arm and grabbed hold of her. His smirk enraged her even more as he crushed her to his chest.

"Let me go!" She kicked and punched to no avail. At this close range, her precious shepherd's crook was useless.

Muscled arms holding her tight, he looked down and twitched a brow. "I'll let ye go when ye admit I'm right."

"Never!" She twisted and bit into the rock-hard bicep next to her cheek.

He grunted, grabbed her by the hair, and yanked her head back. "Dinna bite. 'Tis cheating, as ye're so fond of saying."

"It's a tactic," she countered, pinching the underside of his arms hard enough to make him flinch. "Let me go!"

"Not until ye admit I am right, and ye are wrong."

"Never! Now, let me go ye goat-smelling son of a stoat!"

Eumann and the other men laughed, then returned to meandering their mounts through the grazing cattle.

"I dinna smell like a goat," Mathias argued in a slightly injured tone.

"Well, ye dinna smell like a rose," Kenzie countered. Of course, neither did she. Her antiperspirant and body spray had faded. But she had to admit, of all the Highlanders she had encountered so far, Mathias was the least offensive. She hadn't witnessed him washing, but he had to have done so at some time.

He smelled like a man minus any twenty-first century fragrances. The others ranged somewhere between rancid body odor and downright gag-worthy shite. She pinched him again. "Let me go."

"Who was right, ye wicked beastie? Say it, and I'll free ye!"

A counter plan came to mind. Mathias wasn't the only one who could fight dirty. She ceased struggling and molded her body tighter against him, noting with a great deal of satisfaction that her efforts caused an immediate reaction. A long hard rod that was impossible to ignore pressed against her belly. "Let me go," she repeated with a seductive wiggle.

"Ye're a vile, reckless woman. Ye know that, aye?" Instead of releasing her, he tightened his embrace and ground himself against her. "Who was right? Admit it, and I'll turn ye loose."

Unfortunately, this counter plan had a glaring flaw. While her physical reaction might not be as obvious on the outside as his, it was more than a little noticeable on the inside. Every nerve ending throbbed with an ache that begged her to go after more. At the current level of molten neediness coursing through her, she knew her cheeks had to be flaming.

Mathias brightened with a knowing grin. "Good. Ye should suffer from yer…" He tipped his face closer. "What did ye call it? Ah, yes. Yer cheating." He brushed the tip of his nose across hers. The heat of his breath tickled across her mouth. "Now, what say ye? Who was right about ye traveling alone?"

"Fine," she growled, arching to turn aside. That was a big mistake because as she twisted to keep her mouth out of reach, the rest of her wiggled harder against him. "Maybe I might have been overcome, but I could use stealth and canniness to keep from being caught in the first place."

"Ye are in my care until the chieftain decides what to do with ye." He sealed this declaration with a burning kiss. A kiss that made her forget what they were arguing about to begin with. As soon as she responded to the touch of his lips and exploring tongue, he plopped her butt down hard in the grass. Bending, he caught hold of her chin. "Accept it and stop being such a pain in the arse."

"I hate ye, and if ye dinna release me, I'll be a pain in yer arse forever!"

"So be it, my queen," he growled, then kissed her again. Hard enough to finish stealing her breath, but she'd be damned if she let him know it.

Then he released her and stormed away.

She rubbed her throbbing lips, hating him for not letting her go, but hating herself even more for finding it very desirable to stay.

CHAPTER FIVE

S HE HAD BEEN here before, many times. Stayed at a lodge alongside the River Loy. A lodge that didn't yet exist. Hiked the rugged mountain country. Picnicked and wandered among the ruins on this small parcel of land, an island in the middle of the river. Enjoyed the shade of the thick stands of trees along the waterway's banks. She had explored the tumbled-down walls and piles of rock that now stood fully restored.

The mighty skirting wall, complete with three enormous towers and one smaller one, protected the community inside. The thickness of the barrier amazed her as she peered through the entry tunnel closed off by a heavy portcullis of bolted iron. Invaders not slowed by the river, a river that somehow seemed deeper than it was in the future, would be hard-pressed to storm that gate. No wonder Mathias had spoken of the place with such pride. The fortification, with stone wedged upon stone that looked as though no mortar had been used, was breathtaking. The memory of what the place would become made her sad. It would all crumble away. Forgotten. A casualty of war, greed, and the relentlessness of time.

"'Tis a fine keep," she offered quietly, wishing he would stop being mad at her. His aloofness bothered her more than she liked to admit. Probably because of those kisses. He might be ancient, but the man knew how to kiss a twenty-first century woman and make her want more. A heavy sigh escaped her.

They hadn't spoken to each other any more than what was necessary. Just pouted and stomped around like bratty children in primary school. As they rode across the bridge that spanned the river, an uneasy nervousness wrapped icy fingers around her and squeezed. He had to talk to her. She'd make him. "Chieftain Stronach is kind, ye said?"

They came to a momentary halt in front of the main gate, waiting for the portcullis to be lifted. Just the two of them and her animals. The rest of the men had taken the cattle farther downriver to a field beyond the westernmost tip of the island.

"Mathias?" She turned and looked at him. The guards behind the arrow slits of the entry tower watched her. Their piercing stares drilled into her. "He is kind, ye said?" she nettled again. He might as well answer. By now, he should know she was relentless. "Kind and understanding?"

The stern set of her handsome captor's jaw softened, as did the tightness around his eyes. *Good.* Maybe he wasn't as angry with her anymore. She felt bad for the snappish way she had treated him. And now that they had arrived, she was too ill at ease to stay in a pissy mood. "Mathias?" she gently insisted. "Please talk to me. I am sorry for being so ratty. Forgive me?"

He snorted. She couldn't tell if that was acceptance of her olive branch or not.

"I said the chieftain was a fair man, lass. There is a vast difference between fair and kind."

Facing forward once more, she pulled in a steadying breath and let it ease out. "I suppose that's true." She glanced down at the dog and sheep, suddenly worried about what would happen to them if anything happened to her. "Promise me something, will ye?"

"I would hear it first," he replied in a clipped tone as they rode into the courtyard. He was still irritated at her. Did the man not realize that she never apologized to anyone? He should be honored.

She swallowed hard and stole a glance all around. "If anything happens to me, will ye promise to take Brodie and Ramsay back to the cave? Please?" Surely, both dog and ram could find their way home through the tunnels probably better than she could.

"I expected a more challenging request than that." He dismounted and helped her down as though he despised touching her.

She held onto his arm and kept him from turning away. "It may not be a big thing to ye, but it is big to me. I know I've been a pain in the arse, and I am sorry. What I ask of ye means the world to me. Will ye promise? Dinna take yer anger out on them. Please?"

He frowned down at her, appearing more annoyed and frustrated than she had ever seen him. "I willna let anyone harm yerself or them, ye ken? Ye should know that by now."

"Ye canna predict what yer chief will order, and whatever he says, ye must do or suffer the consequences." She remembered that much from family chats about the old clan system. At times, it had been known to be cruel and unyielding. "But if you could make sure my fur babies are kept safe, I'd appreciate it more than ye know."

"Yer fur babies?" he repeated.

"Aye." She smiled, wishing she was the charming, flirty type who could take men to their knees with a simple fluttering of her lashes. How could she make him understand? "None of this is easy for me because I dinna belong here. Surely, ye know that."

The longer he stared at her, the more his mouth slanted into the lopsided smile that always made her feel better. "Ye are quite the foreigner, and I will give ye that." He offered his arm, then leaned in close and whispered, "And it might do ye well to present yerself as a foreigner when Himself asks his questions, ye ken? For yer own sake."

His advice seemed sound. She nodded. "Aye. I'll do my best."

"Mathias! Mathias!"

"Yon comes Lilias." His arm tensed under her fingers. "The chief's daughter," he quickly added, then put a full stride of space between them before the lovely young woman made it to where they stood.

With her wild abundance of red curls bouncing, the wee slip of a lass skipped across the courtyard like a child, waving both hands high in the air. "Welcome to Stronach Keep," she sang out. Then her eyes went wide, and her mouth fell ajar as though she had just remembered something important. Giggling, she affected a curtsy, then stepped closer and whispered, "Forgive me. I always forget my curtsies." Her infectious smile reached all the way to her sparkling brown eyes. "My name is Lilias. What be yer name?" Before Kenzie could answer, the lass squealed, "A puppy! Ye have a puppy dog!" Dropping to her knees on the mud-encrusted cobblestones, she held out both hands. "Will he let me pet him? Please, would it be all right if I cuddle him?"

Kenzie crouched beside her. "Absolutely. His name is Brodie, and he loves attention." She gave the collie the hand signal for *gentle*. She had taught him the cue for the sake of little children to keep him from getting too rambunctious and knocking them down. The dog eased forward, sat in front of Lilias, and offered a paw. "See? He wants to shake yer hand."

The ram snorted and bumped Kenzie's back, almost knocking her to the ground. "And this is Ramsay. He likes scratches behind his ears, too."

The girl beamed even brighter and squealed again. "What fine wee friends ye have. A cuddly sheep and a braw comely dog." She lifted her chin to a proud angle. "I have a chicken. But Henny stays in my rooms most of the time. She helps the maids keep the floor weaves clean as can be. Pecks and scratches at them all the time. Finds every bug and dropped crumb. She is verra canny."

Mathias reached down and helped Lilias to her feet. "We must take Mistress MacMartin to meet the chieftain. If ye mean to come with us, ye best brush off yer gown, or Mrs. Kerr will be cross with ye again for not taking care of yer clothes."

"I pray for her a lot," Lilias announced as she dusted off her skirts. She fixed an earnest look on Kenzie. "Want I should pray for ye, too?"

"Aye, Lady Lilias. I always welcome prayers." Kenzie felt a sudden protectiveness for the girl, wondering what the poor lass's lot in life would be here in the thirteenth century. She was a fetching young thing, delicate as a porcelain doll, and of marriageable age, but she seemed more like a little girl than a woman. Would her father keep her safe from men who would destroy such innocence to claim the chieftainship of the clan?

"Folk are gathering," Mathias warned with a pointed glance at her boots and jeans, then a concerned sweep of the curious onlookers. "We should find Mrs. Kerr. 'Tis my hope she can help with…" With a pained flip of his hand in her direction, he continued, "Ye should dress proper to meet Himself. It would be best."

"I can help!" Lilias grabbed her arm and tugged. "Mrs. Kerr will help ye if I ask." With an excited bouncing, she patted Brodie's head, then rubbed Ramsay's black nose. "We must all go to my chambers. Ye can meet Henny. That'll be so grand!"

Unsure of the proper protocol to survive this meeting of the clan, Kenzie fixed an exaggerated stare on Mathias, hoping he would get the hint and give her a clue. Should she go with Lilias, or would that be a wrong move? Mathias gave an almost imperceptible nod, his glance pausing on Lilias before it slid to the massive double doors leading inside the main keep.

With her best smile, she patted Lilias's hand. "Wait a moment, Lilias. While I am anxious to meet Henny…" She paused as the ram *baa'd,* then dropped a pile of shite pellets on the cobblestones. The collie had manners for inside the house. The sheep did not. "I'm none too sure Ramsay would be welcome inside. Ye dinna wish yer chambers filled with manure, do ye?" But while she didn't think he belonged inside the keep, would he be safe if he wasn't at her side? "Mathias? I dinna want to insult anyone, but I dinna want him ending up on a roasting spit either."

"Rabbie!" Mathias strode across the courtyard, stuck his head through the wide arch of what looked to be a small stable, and shouted again. "Rabbie!"

"Here I be!" A young lad, probably in his early teens, popped out of a narrow doorway farther down the way. Barefooted. Breeks entirely too short for his long, gangly legs. Dingy tunic covered with clinging bits of straw. The ruddy-cheeked boy trotted over to Mathias. "Ye called, Master Mathias?"

Mathias pointed at the ram currently exploring the edges of the courtyard and weeding the cobblestones. "See that beast is fed, watered, and kept safe. He is…sacred." His voice dropped to an ominous whisper. "That animal crossed the River Spean without once touching the water."

"Truly?" the boy said in an awestruck whisper.

"Truly," Mathias confirmed with a serious nod.

Kenzie bit the inside of her lip to keep from smiling as the boy's eyes went so wide 'twas a wonder they didn't pop out of his head. The lad sidled close to the ram. He leaned over and studied the nonchalant animal munching on an uprooted sprout he'd just stolen from a pot beside the fencepost. With a glance back at Mathias, he shuddered with a nervous nod. "Ye can see it in his eyes." The poor boy's voice echoed with fear and wonder. "I shall see to him, Master Mathias. I swear it."

"Good lad. See that ye do."

Lilias pulled Kenzie toward the doors. "Come. Now we can go meet Henny. Rabbie's word be good as gold."

"Aye, go meet Henny," Mathias urged. His slate-gray eyes locked with hers. She almost heard him speak the warning to go straight to Lilias's chambers and not come out until she had changed out of her strange clothes. For the first time since she arrived in this era, she felt herself in a type of danger she might not be able to handle.

Taking care not to make eye contact with the increasing

number of men, women, and children milling about in the courtyard, she hurried up the wide stone stairway with Lilias. As soon as they pulled open one of the heavy oak doors, they were greeted by an elderly woman clutching a knobby walking stick. Her poor back was so bent, she had to strain and twist to see anything other than the floor. Something about the elder's smirking grin made the hairs on Kenzie's nape stand on end.

"Who be yer friend, Lilias?" the crone wheezed without removing the clay pipe clenched between her yellowed teeth.

Lilias turned to Kenzie, her brow furrowed. "I dinna remember yer name." Her gentle eyes troubled, she turned and looked behind them as though she had left her memories outside. "I canna remember." She stomped a foot and bowed her tousled head. "I am so verra sorry."

Kenzie's heart swelled. Poor distraught girl. Then it came to her that Lilias had been so excited about the dog, they hadn't finished their introductions. She scooped up the lass's hands. "I never told ye my name. Ye were too busy meeting my animals, remember?" Leaning down so she could peer up into Lilias's downcast face, she smiled. "I am Kenzie MacMartin. Ye wouldha remembered that had I told ye. I feel sure of it."

Lilias's infectious smile reappeared, and she lifted her head. "Kenzie MacMartin," she repeated carefully. "Aye. I wouldha remembered such a pretty name."

"Kenzie MacMartin," the old woman echoed. Her grizzled head tilted and one eye squinted shut as she cradled the bowl of her pipe in her palm and puffed harder. "Came from the caves east of Loch Lochy, did ye not?"

Another chill rippled through the hairs on the back of Kenzie's neck, then zipped down her spine. "How did ye know that?"

"Annag knows everything," Lilias volunteered with a hearty nod. "She be Stronach's wise woman. Father listens to everything she advises."

"Pleasure to meet ye, Annag." Kenzie shuffled in place, uncomfortable under the old woman's beady-eyed scrutiny.

"Get yer clothes changed and mind yer tongue," Annag ordered, then continued her painful hitching out the door without another word.

"We best make haste and do as she says." Lilias tugged her deeper into the high-ceilinged common room.

A flurry of activity filled the large chamber. While some servants pushed the long trestle tables and benches over to the walls, others swept up the soiled rushes scattered across the flagstone floor. A cheery fire crackled in the broad hearth. Its stone mantel was framed with woven banners of crimson, blue, and yellow. Kenzie assumed those must be the clan's colors. A parade of iron sconces, their black curves gleaming as though greased, ran the length of the hall, one attached to each side of every column. Some of the candles sputtered and popped with stubby wicks nearly spent.

Kenzie noticed a pair of servants at the far end of the room cleaning the sconces of their drippings and replacing the burnt-out stubs with fresh tapers. She wondered if they ever finished the task or had to do it all over again as soon as they worked their way back to where they had started.

A coughing fit overtook her as they passed the young lads sweeping out the old rushes. She shielded her mouth and nose with her lapel, squinting through the dust and debris filling the air. How could such a thing be healthy? Why didn't they just leave the floors bare? Or weave carpets or something. She tried to remember if rugs existed in the thirteenth century but found herself at a loss. Did they even mention furnishings in any of her history classes? She doubted it. All the professors had seemed more intent on wars, politics, and power rather than the everyday life of the people. She crooked her arm over her nose and mouth and exploded with a series of ferocious sneezes.

Lilias, oblivious to the choking cloud, tugged her through an archway to the left and down a narrow corridor. The farther they traveled through the torchlit passage, the stronger a mouthwatering aroma became. Bread. Freshly baked bread. Kenzie had foolishly declined the oat cake offered this morning, and now she was starving. Her stomach gurgled and growled at the rich, yeasty scent, scolding her to be smarter and accept food when it was given from now on.

"Is that bread that smells so heavenly?" she hinted, not too proud to weasel an offer of at least one slice hot from the oven and hopefully slathered in butter.

"Baking day," Lilias responded, skipping along even faster. The lass lifted her nose and sniffed. "Cook's best bannocks for sure. The one's she bakes special for Father."

They burst into the kitchen, nearly jostling the maid balancing a platter of steaming brown skillet bread. Another young lass followed, carrying a tray of golden loaves, their tops dusty with the flour from the rolling benches. Both servants stared at Kenzie's attire, then glanced at each other in an unspoken promise to meet and gossip about it later.

"Mrs. Kerr!" Lilias sang out as she rounded the long center worktable. She stretched on tiptoe to see over and around the kitchen girls busy with the day's food preparations. "Mrs. Kerr?" she called again.

"Coming, child, coming," came from a doorway off to the right. An older woman emerged. Her silver hair peeked out where her linen barbette joined the fillet across her brow. A self-conscious chill ran through Kenzie as she remembered seeing those sorts of head coverings in a Medieval documentary. She raked a hand across her bare head and tucked her ponytail down inside the back of her jacket. The lady would probably think her some kind of floozy. Or a whore. Or whatever they called loose women in this century.

As the veiled matron strode across the kitchen, she tapped a finger against her palm while scolding a red-faced lass trotting along beside her. "If I find that root cellar or cook's larder in such a state again, ye will find yerself in charge of a shovel in the stables. Do I make my meaning clear, Jeanette?"

The girl bobbed a series of nervous curtsies. "Aye, Mrs. Kerr.

Aye, ye most certainly do."

As Mrs. Kerr turned away from reprimanding the maid, her stern gaze settled on Kenzie. One hand flew to her chest while she made a hurried sign of the cross with the other. "Saints preserve and protect us," she whispered as she crossed herself twice more. Her lined mouth puckered as she leaned to the side and gave Kenzie a closer up and down perusal. "What on earth have ye brought into my kitchens, Lady Lilias?" Her strained tone conveyed a great deal more than her inquiry.

Kenzie forced herself to stand tall. She had never been a shirker. There was nothing to be done about her clothes. At least, not yet. With a step forward, she offered her best smile. "I am Kenzie MacMartin, and it's a pleasure to meet ye. I imagine heaven smells just like this kitchen. Ye've made my mouth water, Mrs. Kerr."

The housekeeper eyed her as though she feared Kenzie might reveal a weapon at any moment. Without responding, she turned her attention to Lilias. "Lady Lilias," she began in a placating tone. "Where—"

Lilias looped her arm through Kenzie's and hopped in place. "Mathias found her. She is my new friend. And she has a puppy, too. See?"

Brodie flicked an ear and leaned against Kenzie's leg.

"Master Mathias," Mrs. Kerr repeated. Her wrinkles settled into a disgusted scowl. "I shouldha guessed." She turned to Kenzie. Her upper lip twitched into a slanted curl that matched her flaring nostrils. The woman looked as though she smelled a stink. With a sweeping gesture toward the door they had just used, the matron forced a polite grimace that Kenzie assumed was meant as a smile. "Perhaps it would be best if ye went with the Lady Lilias to her chambers. I shall see that food and drink are sent to ye there, aye?"

Lilias's easy friendship had spoiled Kenzie. The more people she encountered, the more it became obvious that none of the others would welcome her so readily. Come to think of it, most of Mathias's men had acted as though she should be handled with a long pole and a thick pair of gloves, too. Except for Eumann and the Stronach brothers, who apparently didn't worry about strangeness as long as it didn't stand in the way of eating or getting laid. They should have gone straight to Lilia's chambers just as Mathias suggested. Turning back toward the door, she whispered to Lilias, "We shouldn't have bothered Mrs. Kerr. Remember how Mathias said we should go to yer rooms without talking to anyone?"

"But I had to," Lilias argued, pulling her back around to face the housekeeper. "She needs garments, Mrs. Kerr. All she has are these…" She fluttered a hand at Kenzie's jeans and jacket as though searching for what to call them. "Strange things," she finally said. "Can ye help, Mrs. Kerr? I dinna think I have a single shift or kirtle that might fit her. She's much too tall and filled out for any of my clothing to offer her any decency."

"Aye, ye speak the truth of it there, child." Mrs. Kerr circled them, a hand pressed to her cheek. After a complete circuit and a repugnant look directed at the dog, the housekeeper shooed them toward the door again. "Take her on now. I shall see what I can find."

"And the food?" Kenzie reminded. In for a penny, in for a pound, Da always said. If the lady would be sending her clothes, she didn't want her to forget the food, too. She was starving.

"Aye, food and drink as well." The matron fiddled with the prayer beads pinned to the shoulder of her kirtle. "On wi' ye now. The both of ye." Then she pointed at the dog still sitting beside the table. "And dinna forget yer beast."

"Brodie, come." With a wicked smile intended for the frustrated matron, she motioned him to her side. "I feel sure Mrs. Kerr will send ye a fine meaty bone. Will ye not, Mrs. Kerr?"

With a tight-lipped look, the woman gave a curt nod. "Aye. Now off wi' ye."

Rather than go back through the large common area that was being prepared for the next meal, Lilias took her through a different arch and up a twisting tower staircase. Kenzie had to slow her pace to manage the narrow stone triangles forming the steps. With her hands pressed against both the walls, she followed the lass round and round, wondering how many levels they would climb. The steep stairs were deadly, and she couldn't imagine anyone surviving a tumble down them. Even rambunctious Brodie maneuvered the things with extra care.

Right before Lilias pushed open a heavy oak door at the landing, the lass smiled and patted the dog's head. "Be kind to Henny, aye? She hates cats, but that's because they always try to hurt her chicks. But ye will be kind, I am sure."

Kenzie signaled the dog to heel, hoping he wouldn't disobey when he saw the chicken. There had been an unfortunate incident back on the farm while he was still a pup before he had completed his training. Her poor birds hadn't laid eggs for a month after he'd herded them around the yard, then made several galloping laps through their coop. She had fenced them off after that, so he wouldn't be tempted. This would be the first canine versus fowl encounter since that experience. "Let's enter slowly, Lilias, so as not to frighten Henny."

Lilias nodded and eased open the door. "Come, Henny. We have friends a'visiting."

As soon as the short-legged bird waddled into view, Kenzie smiled, recognizing the black and white speckled breed as the same kind her Da kept. "She's a Dumpy. What a lovely girl!"

"A what?" Lilias scooped up the plump hen, cradling her under one arm and stroking her feathers.

"A Dumpy." Kenzie flagged Brodie forward, betting this pampered bird could hold her own with the dog. "It's what we call chickens that look like her back home. Because of their short legs."

Lilias frowned at Kenzie. A troubling uncertainty shadowed her lovely eyes for the first time since they met. "Ye should take care about saying such things. Like Annag said. Mind yer words lest some take offense and demand ye locked away or banished."

She crossed the rich crimson and blue weave covering the floor, gently rocking the hen as she made her way to a pillowed bench in front of a window. "Annag knows all about such risks. I remember Father talking about a terrible tower and how they had saved her from it to bring her here." She settled the bird down in the pillows, then peeled away an oiled cloth from the arched window set waist high in the stone wall. "I dinna like the window covered. I like the air and all the smells it brings."

A sharp rap on the door interrupted them.

"Ye may enter," Lilias called out.

The door swung open, and in came a parade of servants with Mrs. Kerr in the lead. The matron pointed to the hearth. "Set the trunk there, then fetch another pitcher and bowl. There'll be a need for another chair, too, I think. I willna have Lady Lilias nor her guest having to make do with the one."

The maids toting the large worn trunk between them placed it where instructed, then scurried back out the door.

"And now the bed. Come, come." She clapped her hands. "We dinna have all day. We've still the meal to attend to."

A pair of boys, gangly teenagers, hurried in with a wooden bed frame. A plump, albeit lumpy looking, mattress was draped over the side. Kenzie couldn't imagine how the poor souls had managed the stairs with such a cumbersome load. A young girl scurried in behind them, her arms overflowing with linens and blankets. As soon as the boys had the bed in place, the lass set to making it.

More servants rushed into the room, one bearing a tray of food, another an earthenware pitcher in each hand. A third appeared, the red-cheeked lass who had taken the scolding in the kitchen. She took something bundled in a cloth for Mrs. Kerr's inspection, all the while stealing fearful glances at the dog.

"It is just a mongrel," Mrs. Kerr said with stinging curtness. She flicked a hand in Kenzie's direction. "If ye fear to approach it, ask the mistress if she would mind feeding the beast herself."

"Of course, I dinna mind." Kenzie stepped forward, but the

nervous maid backed up, staring at her with as much anxiousness as she had looked at the dog. "I willna hurt ye." Hands held out, she smiled. "Ask Lilias."

"There is nothing to fear," Lilias said with a reassuring smile. "She is verra kind."

The lass shoved the bundle into Kenzie's hands, then fled.

"That one will be shoveling shite in the stable afore a sennight passes," the housekeeper observed, her narrow-eyed glare locked on the door. "Heed my words." She turned back with a stiff nod. "Ye will see I am never wrong about such things."

Deciding it best not to comment, Kenzie unbundled what turned out to be a meaty bone fit for the king of dogs. She strode over to the corner where the floor was bare and motioned Brodie forward, giving him the signal that it was okay to eat. The dog complied, his tail happily thumping against the floor as he enjoyed his treat.

"So, she has manners," Mrs. Kerr observed in a low tone, but Kenzie heard her. Still fiddling with her prayer beads, the matron spun about, marched to the trunk, and lifted the lid. She paused, giving Lilias a pained frown. "Lady Lilias. These were the only garments on hand, but…"

Lilias stepped forward with a sad smile and rested her hand on the lid. "I remember Mama was considered a tall woman."

Kenzie's qualms about the day shot to an epic level. She couldn't wear those clothes. Not if they had belonged to the chieftain's late wife. The one killed in a Norse raid. It wouldn't be right to stir such painful memories among those who loved the woman. "I dinna mind wearing servant's clothing. Do any of them have anything to spare? It doesna matter if things are a bit short. Ye shouldha seen me sometimes when I was little. I outgrew things so fast, Mama struggled to keep up."

Acting as though Kenzie hadn't said a word, Lilias reached into the trunk and drew out a dark green kirtle. Its hem, sleeves, and neckline were trimmed with burgundy and gold ribbon. "I think this one would be lovely for her. Bring out the green in her eyes. Do ye not think so?"

With a kindly smile, Mrs. Kerr nodded. "I agree. We shall have her dressed proper in no time, m'lady." She turned to Kenzie, and the kindly smile shifted to the determined glare of a war general. "If the mistress will remove her things, I believe there to be enough water left from earlier if ye would like a good wash before ye dress."

"She doesna smell bad enough to need a washing, lest she wishes to refresh her face," Lilias volunteered as she pulled more garments from the trunk and draped them over one arm.

Kenzie appreciated the observation, thankful that her long-lasting deodorant hadn't completely spent itself. Personally, she considered herself a little gamey, but very little could be done other than scrub and hope for the best. Deodorant appeared to be another modern convenience she would have to learn to do without until she made it back home. "Uhm…so, I'll be changing right here?"

Two maidservants were still busy at the other end of the room, sorting out the food on the table, refilling pitchers and jugs, and bringing in additional furniture and supplies from the stairwell. The lads had left, but Mrs. Kerr, Lilias, and the two servants remained. Kenzie wasn't all that keen on stripping down in front of an audience, even if they were women. As the only girl with five brothers, she had always enjoyed her privacy.

"She has the right of it, Mrs. Kerr." Lilias hurried to the open door and looked out. "Where be Sorley? Mistress Kenzie and I can share her."

"Sorley?" Kenzie repeated. That was all she needed. Another person added to the audience.

"Here I be, m'lady. Ne'er ye fear." A bouncing lass with plump cheeks aglow appeared with a basket of tidy, linen-wrapped bundles and small cloth-covered crocks. "I had to fetch more soaps and such for yer table." She came up short when she spotted Kenzie. After a moment's hesitation, she hopped a curtsy and bobbed her head. "Forgive. I didna realize ye had company, m'lady." Even though the maid did her best not to react to Kenzie's appearance, she appeared quite shocked.

"'Tis good that ye've come," Lilias reassured. "This is Mistress Kenzie. She is my new friend and is kind as kind can be." Her voice dropped to a loud whisper. "But we need yer help with her clothes, ye ken? She canna verra well go about the keep dressed as she is."

After clearing her throat, Sorley charged forward like a hound released at the races. Kenzie wanted to run, but instead, edged backward slowly with both hands held up to ward off the determined maid. "If ye'll just leave the clothes on the bed, I'm sure I can figure them out."

"Nay, m'lady." Brushing Kenzie's hands aside, Sorley latched hold of her jacket and had it peeled away before she realized what was happening. "Ne'er ye fear. We'll be sure to fold yer…" The maid paused, her head tilting as she reached in one of the pockets of the jacket and drew out the phone and penknife. "… yer…uhm…things and store them away in the trunk for ye." She held up the phone. "Might ye wish to keep this with ye?"

"Aye, my charm." Kenzie snatched it away. "It's for luck. I need to keep it with me at all times, please. And my wee knife there, too."

Sorley pursed her lips, then turned to Mrs. Kerr. "She'll be needing a belt for certain so's we can tie on a purse for her things."

"Aye, there's one right here." Mrs. Kerr added it to the pile of articles Lilias had placed on the bed.

"Do ye need a washing?" Sorley asked as she frowned at the plastic buttons on Kenzie's denim work shirt. "Will ye look at these things?" She waved Mrs. Kerr closer. "What a craftsman it must ha' took to shape and polish these wee bits of ivory."

"I can undress myself." Kenzie whirled around, giving them her back and bracing herself for the reaction they would have to her silky black bra and panties. She leaned on the end of the bed, removing her knee-high rubber boots and wool socks first. After a deep breath, she stripped away the shirt, her thermal, and shucked off her jeans. Arms crossed over her chest, she turned back around. "Ready now." Her voice squeaked like a rusty hinge.

"What in Heaven's name are ye wearing, lass?" Sorley asked, tracing a chubby finger along the satiny shoulder strap of the bra. "Such tiny stitchery, too. Amazing."

"And such fine threadwork on her—" At a complete loss for words, Mrs. Kerr pointed at the lacy panties that weren't as skimpy as thongs but were still quite sparse in their coverage.

Chill bumps not brought on by cold rippled across her body. "What do I put on first," she interrupted, ready to be dressed and out of the limelight.

"Take off the rest first," Lilias instructed as she handed what looked like a plain white linen nightshirt to Sorley. "Then ye'll don this chemise."

Kenzie contemplated arguing but realized she was outnumbered. Besides, judging by the size of the pile, she'd be wearing so many layers, no one would know she was braless and bare bummed underneath. Teeth clenched, she stripped the rest away, deciding that privacy and self-consciousness must not have been invented yet.

With a nod of approval, Sorley placed the chemise over her head and yanked it down in place. "Now the kirtle," she said, holding up the deep green gown made of a lightweight wool. "Fine color for ye, mistress. Brings out yer eyes."

"That's what I thought," Lilias agreed, beaming with approval. "Here's her belt and purse for her wee charm."

Sorley snugged the articles in place then pointed at a lighter green garment still on the bed. "'Tis a warm day. I dinna think she needs the surcoat 'til later, ye ken?"

"I agree," said Mrs. Kerr. "But after ye finish with her stockings and shoes, something must be done about that hair of hers. 'Tis improper and lacks modesty."

"Are ye married?" Lilias asked.

Still dazed from being stripped down then re-dressed like a favorite doll, Kenzie blinked. "What? No. I'm single."

"Single?" Lilias repeated slowly.

"Unmarried," Kenzie clarified.

With a nod at both Sorley and Mrs. Kerr, Lilias pointed back at the trunk. "Just the circlet for her hair then. She doesna have to wear a veil if she doesna wish it since she's still a maiden."

"Do ye wish to wear a veil?" Sorley asked.

"No, thank ye." Kenzie wondered what sin she had committed to be sent to the thirteenth century. Before she realized it, they had shod her with wool socks secured with strips of fabric tied just below the knee and brown leather shoes that were surprisingly comfortable. All three women had a turn at running the wide wooden comb through her long hair and picking out all the tangles and bits of debris collected on the way to the keep. They pulled it back in a single braid, making it even longer still by adding extensions of what looked like horsehair that was close to the same shade. After finishing a braid that dangled clear to her rump, they wrapped it in a strip of pale yellow satin then placed the simple silver circlet on her head. All three women stepped back and smiled.

Kenzie forced a smile in return, feeling like she had just been crowned the queen of time travel.

CHAPTER SIX

"**H**E'S WORSE EACH time I see him," Mathias observed in a guarded tone behind the safety of his tankard.

"Some say it's the feud," Eumann said, his voice just as hushed. He snagged another full cup from a passing tray, flashing a charming smile at its bearer. "He fears for the clan. For the Lady Lilias. Everything. He knows his days are numbered." After a deep draught of his drink, he smacked his lips and added, "I think he's just ready to be done with it all."

Ailbeart Stronach, respected chieftain of the clan, slumped sideways in his chair with his head propped in his hand. No others had yet joined him at the table. That would happen after his daughter arrived. The chief no longer attempted grand entrances or meandering among those gathered. He had ended that custom months ago, bitter at its loss but knowing that soon, he would be absent from the hall altogether.

Mathias turned away from the pitiful sight. The feud with the bloody MacPhersons had almost finished the man off. What in God's name had possessed him to make such a fool decision to steal those feckin' cows?

"It isna yer fault," Eumann said as if reading his mind. "If ye hadna ordered that prized herd lifted, we wouldha done it on our own to impress yerself and the chieftain." His snorting chuckle echoed in his empty tankard as he drained it. "Braw beasties, them there coos are. That bull for certain. Prized animals, indeed. Ye should take Lady Lilias to see them once they settle and the calves come. She loves coos. 'Specially them wee ones." He nudged him as he waved down a servant to fetch another drink. "Ye know we wouldha lifted that herd with or without ye. See sense, man."

"Maybe so, but I shouldha thought through the whole of it better."

The MacPherson chief was known for his unreasonable temper. The man embodied his clan motto, *touch not the cat bot a glove*. He had taken the thieving of his fine fat cows as a direct insult to himself, his clan, and every MacPherson ancestor since time began. Just an ordinary lifting of a few cattle, and the man had declared full on war against the Stronachs. And so, Mathias had ordered them returned to ease his ailing chieftain's troubles.

That infuriated the crazed MacPherson even more, so they stole them back again. By the time the shaggy beasts finished shifting back and forth between Stronach and MacPherson lands, they'd be twenty stone lighter and have shorter legs.

"That canna be our Mistress MacMartin," Eumann said, his latest full tankard relaxing to a dangerous angle. His voice dropped to a wistful tone. "And there be the lovely Lady Lilias."

"Mind yer drink, man." Mathias turned and decided the greatest force on earth wasn't lightning, gale force winds, or fire. Nay. Neither Heaven nor Hell nor anything in between possessed the power of a beautiful woman. He swallowed hard. How could this regal beauty be the annoying wee hellcat they had taken prisoner?

Entering the room with her head held high, she carried herself with the grace and surety of a queen. Those strange clothes of hers had failed to do her lithe form justice, but the proper clothing she now wore showed her at her finest. The deep green of her kirtle brought out her eyes. Shadow and light shifted them from green to golden, filling them with mystery. Her soft curves dared a man to look at another. She could be a fae queen or mistress of the wood. Even though her hair was ebony rather than flaming red, she was the embodiment of the goddess Brid herself. Canny. Fierce. Comely. Her gaze flitted across the room as if noting her subjects and finding them lacking.

Sweet, innocent Lilias walked to her right, and her dog guarded her left. He had never seen such loyalty in an animal. That rare woman was not of this world. She was magical and had bespelled him for certain.

"We should seat ourselves," he said abruptly, needing to be closer to this precious mystery fate had placed in their midst. As commander of the guard and Eumann, his second, their places were at the head table with the chief and his daughter. For that, he was very thankful.

"Mind yerself, old friend," Eumann warned. "Himself might be weakened, but he isna blind. The Lady Lilias is yer intended, remember?"

When Chieftain Stronach had first named Mathias war chief and *tanist* to the chieftainship, the sly old fox had attached a condition to the honor. When the time came, he would relinquish the role to Mathias as long as he had taken Lady Lilias as his wife. The chief knew his sweet, childlike daughter could never manage the monumental task of leading the clan by herself. He also knew Mathias would treat her with the gentle kindness she deserved.

With Eumann's reminder still ringing in his ears, Mathias pulled out Lilias's chair first. "M'lady, yer seat."

"Nay, Mathias!" The smiling girl patted Kenzie's shoulder. "Ye must help Mistress Kenzie first. 'Tis only proper." Leaning closer, she beamed up at him. "Is she nay fetching in her new garments? Pretty as pretty can be?" Lilias sounded like a child delighted with a new doll.

"Lilias!" Kenzie gave her a teasing nudge. "If ye have to milk it out of him, it doesna count."

"Milk it out of him?" Lilias repeated, then caught her bottom lip between her teeth. Her troubled gaze flitted to those nearby as though fearing they might overhear and make a jest of her ignorance. "Forgive me, but I dinna understand."

Mathias noted how Kenzie's teasing nature immediately disappeared. Remorse tightened the lass's features. She scooped up Lilias's hand and whispered, "Forgive *me*, Lilias. I worded my thoughts poorly. They made no sense at all. Not even to me now that I think about them." She stole a glance around the room and twitched a tiny shrug. "It's because I am so nervous here where I know so few. Will ye help me?" The tender words she gave the worried chieftain's daughter softened Mathias's heart. At least this feisty, stubborn lass came with a hearty helping of kindness.

Lilias didn't respond, just stared downward.

Kenzie hugged closer to the lass and kept her voice low, but Mathias heard every word. "Please? I mean it, Lilias. I'll need yer help during dinner, so I dinna make such an error again. Will ye help me? I canna do this without ye. I'm nervous as can be."

Lilias lifted her head, and her relieved smile bloomed like a flower warmed by spring's coaxing. "Aye, Kenzie. Dinna fear. I shall help ye."

"And have the lot of ye forgotten yer chieftain?" The Stronach's once booming voice quivered with the hollowness of age and poor health. "Who be this fair lady in our midst?"

Mathias held out a hand to Kenzie. After a noticeable deep breath, she took it and stepped to his side.

"I present the Mistress Kenzie MacMartin, my chieftain. Not only did she put Ellar MacPherson on the ground with naught more than a wee stick, she granted us the help of her animal ye see there at her side. The cattle go wherever that lad takes them." Mathias waited, hoping he had not misinformed the lass about the chieftain helping her. The man looked to be in a foul mood. His suffering appeared worse this evening.

With weary eyes shadowed by his bushy gray brows, the chief's head tilted. He studied her so long, the entire room fell silent.

Kenzie stood tall with her chin lifted, unflinching beneath the chieftain's scrutiny. Mathias admired the woman's strength, even though she had been quite the trial since they found her.

The Stronach struggled to sit straighter, then leaned forward and latched hold of the table's edge. With a strained, gasping groan, he hoisted his wasted form upward. Mathias knew better than to help the man stand. He would grant the once powerful chief as much dignity as he could.

"I am Chieftain Ailbeart Stronach," the chief replied with a regal nod. "We are grateful for yer aid against the bloody MacPhersons, and welcome ye to our table." Then he eased himself back into his seat and lowered his gaze to the dog. "Fine looking beast ye have there. What piercing eyes he has."

"His name is Brodie," Kenzie volunteered. At the sound of his name, the dog's black ears perked, and he stood at attention as though waiting for her next order.

"Brodie," the chief repeated, then managed a faint smile. "He only has eyes for his mistress, even though I spoke his name as well."

Kenzie made an almost imperceptible fluttering of her fingers, and the animal went to the chieftain's chair, sat, and offered a paw.

The Stronach's smile disappeared. "Obedience without hesitation. Almost as if they are one. A familiar." He lowered his hand, placing it in front of the dog's nose. Brodie rested his paw atop it, then looked back at Kenzie. The chief jerked away, rubbing the back of his hand as though the animal's touch had burned him.

"Come, lad." Her smile disappeared, and she resettled her stance as though preparing to run.

Mathias watched the interplay between his chief, Kenzie, and the dog. He was at a loss as to what had just happened. The Stronach liked dogs. His own were long since dead, and he had refused to replace them. Perhaps that was the problem. Maybe

Kenzie's wee pup made him miss his own.

"Seat the ladies, Mathias," the chief ordered. He kept his stare locked straight ahead. "At the farthest end of the table. I dinna wish them near." He tapped a trembling finger on the place beside him. "Sit yerself to my right and Eumann to my left, aye?" He resettled himself in his seat, sitting taller and looking about the room. "Bhaltair!" Shaking a bent finger toward the last empty chair, he nodded at the man. "Ye will join us at the chief's table this night."

Both Eumann and Bhaltair looked to Mathias as they moved to where their liege had ordered. Mathias arched a brow and gave the slightest shake of his head. He had no idea what had put the chief so ill at ease. The man seemed almost fearful. Usually, Lilias sat at his right, but he had shuffled the women as far from himself as possible.

"I'll sit at the end," Kenzie hurried to say when Mathias tried to seat her next to him. "I'm certain that would be best."

"As ye wish." He helped her into the other chair, then seated Lilias between them. "What is wrong?" he asked, glancing between the two women, hoping one of them could tell him. He had felt sure the chief would warm to Kenzie and help her and her kin. He had not foreseen such a strained meeting.

"I'm not sure what went wrong," Kenzie murmured, refusing to meet his gaze.

Hands in her lap and her head bowed, Lilias closed her eyes. Her lips moved in silence. After a few moments, she crossed herself, then leaned over until her shoulder rubbed Mathias's. "I dinna ken for certain, but I prayed all will be well. Dinna fash yerself. Our Lord Almighty shall address it."

While Mathias appreciated Lilias's faith, he would feel more at ease with something he could see or touch.

With everyone seated, servants rushed in bearing boards of roasted ptarmigans, smoked fish, and boiled beef. Bowls of gravy for sopping came next. Breads. Root vegetables. Cheeses. Boiled eggs. Freshly baked trenchers were placed in front of each person, ready to be filled. After the chieftain speared a bit of meat, everyone set to eating.

Mathias selected a few bits of meat. Although, the tension at the table chased away all thoughts of filling his empty wame.

Kenzie picked at a chunk of bread and stole occasional glances around the room. Her self-assured air from earlier had disappeared like morning mist burned away by the rising sun.

He decided to steer the conversation to the Stronach's growing herds. Riches measured by the number of Highland cows wandering their glens always lifted the chieftain's mood. Maybe that would help chase the tension from the air. "With the new bull, there shall be many calves next season."

The weary chief slumped back in his chair. He clutched his tankard to his chest while his meal sat untouched. He took a deep drink, then hugged the mug close once more. "I visited Strona again today," he said as though Mathias had never spoken.

Too weak to ride, the Stronach rarely left the keep, but when he did, he rode in an enclosed cart built for him by a craftsman who lived in Strona, the largest village on the clan's lands.

"With the improved weather, the people will rebuild," Mathias reassured. The part of the village troubling the chief lay north of the River Loy. The MacPherson clan had razed it. Several houses, the kirk, and worst of all, the mill had been burned to the ground. Two had died, and several were injured in the late-night siege that caught them all by surprise. No one expected such a reaction to the thievery of a few cows.

The chief's unkempt head rolled from side to side on the pillow tied to the back of his chair. "This has become more than a mere feud between clans." He paused for a deep drink. The wine dribbled from the corners of his mouth, its red droplets catching in his gray beard. "This is war."

"We shall quell it," Eumann said with a sympathetic glance at Mathias.

"Aye," Bhaltair assured, thumping his tankard on the table. "MacPherson villages burn just as easy as ours. I can ride as soon as tonight and lead a raid."

The chief held up a hand for quiet, then turned and fixed a sour gaze on Mathias. "Travel to Brittany. Bid them send us help." His hard look softened as his attention slid to Lilias. "Her mother, my dearest love, was cousin to the duke's mother through the mighty bloodline of the Scottish kings Malcolm and William. Tell them if they render us aid, we shall help them recover the young duke from Rouen. We are known for our stealth and have successfully recovered prisoners before. They know this about our clan."

Brittany again. Mathias drained his tankard and banged it on the table for a refill. While he pitied Arthur, the Duke of Brittany, he grew sick of hearing about their politics that seemed to preoccupy the Stronach so. Young Arthur, little more than a lad, had been doomed since birth. Used as some sort of distraction by his uncle, King Richard of England, who had named him as his heir. Then on his deathbed, Richard had changed his mind and placed his brother, John, on the throne instead, saying Arthur was too young—or so it had been rumored. Now that the lad was grown, or nearly so, he was feared and despised by his cowardly uncle, King John. As far as Mathias was concerned, they were better off forgetting about England and Brittany and concentrating on Scotland. They could handle the MacPhersons. Eventually. "We can quell the MacPhersons, my chieftain. I swear it. There is no need to involve Brittany."

The Stronach didn't respond. Just scowled at him. Which always meant that what he suggested had fallen on deaf ears. He tried a different tactic. "Besides, I thought the duke still imprisoned at Falaise?"

"He was moved to Rouen." The chieftain glared at him fiercer, finding strength in his anger at being denied. "Ye shall go to Brittany as yer chieftain bids ye. Hear me, I say!"

Loud whispering to his right distracted him. Mathias turned to find Kenzie shielding her mouth while leaning close to Lilias's ear. She spoke with such fervor, her words had to be dire. Lilias nodded and held tight to Kenzie's other hand. The longer Kenzie talked, the wider Lilias's eyes became.

"How do ye know this?" the young girl asked, forgetting to whisper.

"How does she know what?" the chief growled before Mathias could intervene.

"She says the hour is too late, Father. The poor duke already be dead." A wave of shocked gasps and murmurs rippled through the room.

Kenzie cringed and dropped her gaze to her lap. She looked ready to crawl under the table. And well, she should. This news would not bode well. The ailing Stronach had become obsessed with Brittany because somehow, he felt it a last connection to his beloved wife.

Mathias cleared his throat and gently took Lilias's hand in his. "Now, lass, calm yerself. With all the noise in the room, I'm sure ye didna hear Mistress Kenzie proper."

Color flared across Lilias's cheeks. "I did so hear her proper. I am nay deaf." She yanked her hand out of his and turned to Kenzie. "Ye said Mathias shouldna go because Arthur be dead and canna help him. Did ye not just say that?"

"Something like that," Kenzie mumbled, brushing her fingertips across her mouth as though wishing she could seal it shut. She shifted with a wincing shrug. "It happened earlier this month, I think. They think King John did it in a drunken rage. Maybe like the first week of April. I've never been really good with dates." She fixed a pained look on the chieftain. "I am verra sorry. I probably shouldna have said anything, but I didna want ye to stretch yer resources so thin for nothing. Especially not since ye said the MacPhersons burned one of yer villages and killed some folk."

"Ye lie." The man pounded a shaking fist on the arm of his chair. "Ye be a spy for that vile demon, John. He has tormented our kin for years. Distant kin they may be, but kin they are to us just the same. I shall have ye thrown in the pit for such wickedness."

Kenzie sat taller. "I didna lie, neither am I a spy. Arthur's fate is one of the few history tests I actually made a good score on." Her eyes flared wider. She bit her bottom lip and turned to Lilias. "I am not feeling well. Could I please go back to yer rooms? I think I need to lie down."

"Nay." The chieftain pummeled his chair arm again, then raised his fist, but before he could speak, there was a commotion from the great double doors at the front of the room.

"Back! Out of my way, I say! I bear grave news for Himself." Ferguel, the informant the Stronach had irrationally placed in France, waded between the crowded tables and made his way to the dais. Bedraggled, filthy, eyes red-rimmed as though he hadn't slept in days, the man snatched off his tam and dipped his chin. "My chieftain, 'tis glad I am to find ye in such good spirits, but I fear the news I bear shall end yer happiness."

"Good spirits, my arse," Mathias muttered, scrubbing a hand across his mouth. *What else could go wrong this evening?*

"What ill has befallen us now?" the Stronach asked with a heavy sigh.

"A fisherman's net brought in the young Duke of Brittany's body. From the Seine." Ferguel shook his head, crossing himself over and over as he spoke. "His life was taken from him. The bastards tied him to a stone and dumped him in the river." He clutched his hat to his chest. "Thanks be to the saints that good people found him and buried him proper. He lies at Notre Dame de Pres." He sagged onto the nearest bench. "Forgive me, my chieftain. I came straight away and have rested verra little."

A chill that no blaze could ever dispel took hold of Mathias. He turned to Kenzie, who sat with one arm hugged around her middle, and her fist pressed to her mouth. "Ye heard of this, aye? Before we found ye?" That had to be how she knew. What other explanation could there be?

She sat straighter and bobbed her head. "Aye. I heard of it. Before."

"That isna possible," Ferguel said. The offensiveness he found in their conversation sharpened his tone. "This has all been handled with the greatest of secrecy until this verra moment out of fear that the body might be stolen."

"Then she possesses the sight," Bhaltair said before Mathias could quell the wild murmurings in the room. "We've found us a new seer for the clan. 'Tis high time. Old Annag is nearly spent."

"Enough!" Mathias roared, toppling his chair backward as he stood. A charged silence fell over the hall as he offered her his hand. "Ye said ye were unwell. Allow me to escort ye to yer chambers, Mistress Kenzie."

"I am nay done speaking with that woman," the Stronach bellowed, sounding stronger than he had in months.

Mathias faced the chieftain he had always respected, but of late, had begun to doubt. "Aye, ye are done, my chief." Feeling everyone's stares, he sought to spare the elder as much embarrassment as he could. "I feel sure ye would rather speak to her in the privacy of yer solar, ye ken? If ye were nay so weary and overwrought by the troubling news, I am sure ye wouldha said so yerself."

The chieftain's furious scowl softened. "Aye." His chin dropped to his chest, and he sagged back in his chair. "I am verra overwrought."

"Get yerself food and drink, Ferguel. The chief appreciates all ye did to bring this news to him so quickly." Mathias shot Bhaltair a damning glare for his outburst. "We shall speak of this later." Turning back to Kenzie, he extended his hand again. "Mistress Kenzie?"

Kenzie slid her hand into his, her relief apparent. "Thank ye," she whispered.

"Forgive me." Lilias looked up at them both, her eyes filling with tears. "I didna mean to cause ye such trouble."

Kenzie bent and gave the fretting lass a hug. "This is not yer fault."

"Ye will stay and dine with yer father, Lilias," the chieftain ordered. He bounced his fist on the place beside him, then his voice softened to the loving tone he always used when speaking to his daughter. "Here, child. I beg ye. I feel the need to have ye close since yet another connection to yer beloved mother has left us."

"Yer father is troubled, lass." Mathias could tell Lilias would rather come with Kenzie, but he needed to speak with her alone first. "Sit with him a little while longer, would ye?"

"Aye, I will." She gave Kenzie a sorrowful look. "Feel better soon, friend. And again, I am sorry."

Resting a hand on Lilias's shoulder, Kenzie bent and looked her in the eyes. "It is not yer fault, and we're still good friends. I promise."

"I am glad," Lilias whispered as she moved to sit beside her father.

Kenzie looped her arm through Mathias's and motioned for the dog to follow. "Get me out of here before I say anything else I shouldna," she ordered under her breath. "I could really use some air."

"I, as well." Mathias led her from the room, using the private hallway reserved for the chieftain and those of his personal council. He didn't miss how the guards' eyes followed them when they passed through the arch. His lovely Mistress Kenzie had branded herself a thing of strangeness more surely than if she had taken a red-hot poker and seared her flesh. Some would call her a seer. Others a witch. Still, more would say she was a spy. Rumors could be dangerous things. They often became living, breathing monsters that destroyed everything in their path.

He lengthened his stride, moving faster until they nearly ran down the hall. When they reached the small side door he sought, he halted. "Here. This leads to the parapet walk."

Hand to her chest, Kenzie leaned back against the wall, gasping for breath. "Give me a minute. I'm not used to running while swaddled in yards of linen and wool."

Her comment gave him pause. She said the oddest things,

and he feared this trait would be her undoing. He yanked open the door. "Come. We shouldna be followed, but at this juncture, I dinna wish to take any chances."

She looked up and down the passage, then eyed the steep set of narrow stone steps rising in front of them. "So, no one else should be around?"

"No one." He braced himself, unsure as to what she intended.

"Come on, Brodie." Gathering her skirts up to her knees, she charged forward and began climbing. The dog wiggled around her and took the lead.

Mathias found himself watching her ascent with his mouth ajar. A flash of bare leg as she trudged upward made his trews uncomfortably snug. Noise from the great hall, sounds of heated discussions yanked him from his stupor. He hurried forward, pulling the door shut behind him before vaulting up the stairs.

When he emerged from the stairwell, Kenzie had disappeared. A possessive panic took hold. "Kenzie!"

"Here," she called out, stepping out from behind the corner. "I went this way to see the river."

Relief flooded through him. "Ye should stay close to me, lass," he scolded. "For yer own safety." She needed to heed his words whether she cared to or not. After the incident in the hall, her life depended on it.

Without comment, she turned and stared over the battlement. Silent. Brooding. She hugged herself tight as though fearing she'd crumble to pieces. The soft curve of her jaw hardened as she scowled at the river sparkling beneath the starlit sky. "That did not go well at all, did it?" she observed quietly.

He didn't miss the faint tremor in her voice. Her fear filled the air. Good. She needed to be afraid. 'Twould keep her alive. He decided not to comment, knowing that silence could sometimes be the best way to get questions answered.

She gave him a sideways glance, rubbing her arms as she moved to the wide crenel in the battlement. "Well?" she prodded. The chilly evening breeze fluttered the wispy curls escaping her braid and framing her face.

He should've thought to get her a cloak or a plaid, but urgency had kept it from his mind. He stepped closer, blocking the wind as best he could. "Nay," he said. "It didna go well at all." Standing at the crenel, he rested a hand on the cold, hard grittiness of the stone and tried to understand this unusual woman. "Explain how ye knew of the duke."

She twitched a shoulder, never once taking her gaze from the river. "I told ye. I heard it. From before."

"Ferguel seemed to think that impossible, and I must admit, lass, I feel the same." He waited for her to comment, but all she did was resettle her footing and lift her chin to a more defiant angle.

"We came upon ye but a few days ago. How could ye know of something that happened in France? It takes most nigh a *month* to get to Rouen. Ferguel only managed to make it back quicker because the man pushed himself hard."

Her eyes flinched at the corners, narrowing the slightest bit.

"I would hear the *truth*, Mistress Kenzie."

"If I told ye, ye would never believe me."

Depending on what she said, the lass was probably right. "I would hear yer answer, anyway."

She fixed him with a look that repeated the chill he had felt earlier. Without a word, she gave the slightest shake of her head and turned away, walking down the aisle with her dog trotting beside her.

"I canna protect ye, if ye dinna confide in me," he called after her. He felt a responsibility for her, but it was more than just a matter of keeping her safe. He needed her. There. He finally admitted it to himself. Whether witch, or seer, or one of the fae, he needed her in his life, and against his better judgment, needed her to need him, too.

She halted but didn't turn, just stared straight ahead. "The only way ye can protect me is to get me back to that cave."

"That, I willna do." He caught up with her, took hold of her arm, and forced her to face him. "Ye must tell me how ye knew the duke to be dead, what really happened to yer home, and why that bloody cave is so important to ye."

Fire flashed in her eyes.

"Fine," she snapped. "I read about the duke in a history book, my home is just fine—or was the last time I saw it, and that cave is how I get back to it." Yanking free of him, she stormed onward, but not before he spotted her tears.

The dog stayed behind, looked up at him, and growled.

"Come on, Brodie!" Her voice cracked. With a stomp of her foot, she buried her face in her hands.

Mathias strode forward and gathered her into his arms. His heart swelled when she sagged against him, trusting as a child. But then, like a mighty beast awakening, she came back to life, clutching his tunic and fighting to shake him. He tightened his hold as she pounded his chest with both fists, then exploded into keening sobs.

"My chickens need feed. The sheep are out. I promised my brother a cake for his birthday." She froze, stared up at him, her lips moving without a sound. "Oh no!" Her face crumpled. "I missed it! Ari's birthday was yesterday!" Her piercing cry reached a higher pitch. "I missed it!" she repeated. "All because of that stupid ram!" Her wailing grew in ferocity until her words were barely intelligible. "My truck payment's due. They're supposed to install the new heaters in the barn on Friday." She squalled out another ear-splitting cry. "I'm going to lose my deposit on all the renovations for the breeding house!"

"Now, now, lass. All will be well." He gently rocked her back and forth while awkwardly patting her shoulder. "Hush now. All will be well." He hadn't understood half what she said, but whatever it was, he would find a way to make it better.

"No, it won't," she bawled even harder. "On top of every-thing else, I think I left the coffee pot timer on."

Coffee pot timer? What the hell was a coffee pot timer? No stranger to holding a beguiling woman in his arms, he felt at a complete loss when it came to this one. "Calm down, *mo nighean donn*. I canna help ye if I dinna understand ye."

That only succeeded in making her bawl harder and shake them both with her hiccuping gasps for air. When the dog threw back his head and howled, Mathias knew something had to happen—and with haste.

Taking hold of her shoulders, he bent 'til they stood nose to nose.

"Cease," he ordered with a firm shake. "Ye must overcome one battle at a time. Ye canna fight the entire war at once, and all this panicked caterwauling doesna help ye, ye ken?"

"Take me back to the cave," she hitched out between sniveling hiccups. The flickering torchlight reflected nothing but truth and sorrow in her eyes. These tears were not some sort of ruse. This was not a game. "Please," she begged. "Please take me back so I can go home."

"Why the cave?" he asked softly, hypnotized by the teardrops quivering on the ends of her long dark lashes.

"Because the cave will send me back to my time. 2019. Back where I belong."

CHAPTER SEVEN

S HE HADN'T MEANT to say that, but at this point, she no longer cared.

Coughing and sniffing, she wiped her face on her sleeve, then tried to find the square of linen Sorley had sprinkled with rose water before tucking it inside the front of her dress. *In case ye have a need or wish to offer a favor to a warrior,* the maid had said with a suggestive wink.

Kenzie found the cloth, dried her eyes again, and blew her nose. Hard. She doubted a warrior would want her favor now.

Mathias remained silent. Just stood there. Staring. Silhouetted by the moonlight. She couldn't see his expression, but she had a pretty good idea of what she'd find. He was probably calculating how long it would take to gather enough firewood to burn her at the stake.

Her conscience kicked her. Well, maybe he wasn't actually plotting to get rid of her, but still. Something in her heart told her he was the only real ally she had in this time. Deep down, she knew she could trust him. What a shame she would never see him again once she went back to where she belonged.

The thought of leaving him disturbed her. Made the center of her chest all achy, as though a dark emptiness had taken hold. She tried to ignore the hurting as she moved to the battlement and lifted her face to the wind. She leaned farther through the opening and stared down at the overgrown patch of ground between the wall and river. Crenels and merlons. The memory of the words threatened more tears, triggering a case of hitching sniffles. The spaces cut into the top of the battlement were crenels and the upright bits were merlons. Funny how she remembered that from playing *storm the castle* with her brothers when they were little.

She swallowed hard and blew her nose again. No more tears. If she kept at it, she'd soon be heaving. She stole a glance back at Mathias. "Well? Say something."

He joined her at the wall. The moonlight illuminated his utter bewilderment. She understood completely. She felt the same. "Would ye please tell me what ye're thinking?"

"2019," he repeated. The poor man looked pained.

"Aye. The twenty-first century." She wished she had her shepherd's crook. Not to fight with Mathias, but because the worn, twisted wood in her hands somehow always brought her comfort. Kept her family close instead of centuries away. "I dinna really know how it happened. I just know when Brodie and I were trying to catch Ramsay, I felt kind of funny in the cave, and then here I was." She huffed out a bitter laugh. "I thought it was some kind of underground gases making me sick. Not traveling through time."

"Yer farm. Yer kin. Everything ye know waits for ye back in the year of our Lord 2019?"

"Well…not *back* really, but *ahead* since it's the future." A minor technicality, but the situation was confusing enough without garbling the semantics. "But yes. The future is where I belong."

Silent again, he leaned against the wall and stared out at the land. The longer he remained quiet, the edgier she got. She felt sure he wouldn't cause her harm, but what would he do? After all, the man had loyalties of his own.

"Ye've mentioned a father and brothers before," he finally said. "Did ye also leave a husband behind? Children?" He spared her a glance that struck her as almost accusing. "Ye never said. After all, ye are of a marriageable age."

"I didn't *leave* anyone willingly, so mind yer tone, aye?" The man made it sound like she had deserted her responsibilities on purpose. What did he think? She'd done this because she thought her life boring? When he didn't comment, she continued. "I have never married because I have yet to meet a man who not only passes my tests but also wins the approval of my Da and five brothers."

"Tests?" He spared her a side-eyed glance, then returned to staring at the river. "Feats of strength or battling, I suppose? Swords or fighting against ye with yer wee stick?"

"I wish it were that simple." She fisted her hands atop the crenel, remembering a string of short-lived relationships that had proved too frustrating to continue. "My farm takes a lot of hard work and sacrifice. Not all men in the future are up to rising before dawn for milking, gathering eggs, shoveling shite, and making sure all is as it should be with the animals and the land." Her conscience and the truth of the matter poked her. "But the fault of my single state is mine as well. I didna make time for them or give them half a chance."

"So, ye remained alone?"

"Aye." She tucked an errant strand of hair behind her ear, wishing she could remove the circlet digging into her scalp. The thing would trigger a migraine if she wasn't rid of it soon. A pang of sadness squeezed at her heart, threatening to unleash more tears. Mama had suffered from migraines. She had inherited them from her.

"Five brothers, ye said?"

"Aye. Ari, Barkev, Levon, Rusa, and Gavrel." Saying their names made her want to cry again. "Da is Balfour, and Mama was Nazani. A braw, fiery Scot and a feisty Armenian." She closed her eyes, seeing her mother's face. "Nazani is Armenian for *delicate.*"

Another tear escaped, joined by her quivering smile. "Mama might have been delicate, but she kept Da and the boys in line. That's for certain."

"Might have been?"

"Aye, she passed away last year. A stroke." She pressed the wad of damp linen to her mouth, determined to get her emotions under control. All this crying had to stop.

"I am sorry for yer loss," he said with a gentleness that made her miss the tenderness of his arms around her. A strong protective tenderness she had never known before.

She swallowed hard, giving herself another stern internal shake. She needed to stop being ridiculous. What good would it do to have feelings for a man in this century? "Thank ye," she said. "At least she passed quickly and didna suffer."

The minister had preached those useless words over and over at the funeral, but it had taken a while for Kenzie to realize their truth. Mama had always been a force of nature. If her sharp mind had ended up trapped in an unresponsive body, it would've been torture. At least this way, Mama's spirit soared free.

With her mother's fiery strength stoking her own, she touched Mathias's arm. "I have to get back to that cave. If ye canna find it in yer heart to take me there, then at least stall yer guards and give me as much of a head start as ye can. I'll leave tonight once everyone is asleep. That way, they willna hold ye responsible."

"I think it best ye stay here, lass." He took her hand and cupped it between his. "Yer journey has wearied ye to the point of weaving far-fetched tales ye have yerself believing." He gave her the smile given to a person not in their right mind. "I'm sure it canna be easy being such a talented seer."

He didn't believe her. She stared up at him, unable to accept that she had been so wrong about how he would understand. How could he not believe her? He had seen her clothes. Her phone...her phone! That was it. She'd show him the pictures saved on her phone. Pulling it free of the drawstring bag knotted on her belt, she powered it on, thankful its battery looked to be holding fast. "Look. Look at these pictures." She held it in front of him, swiping through the photos of her farm, her family, her animals, herself. "See? From the future." He remained silent as she showed him one after another. Finally, she shut the phone down, disheartened that once the battery finally gave out, those memories would all be lost. "If I were a seer from this time, how could I have this?"

After a glance up and down the path, he lowered his voice. "'Tis clearer to me now. So, ye're a witch then. Able to call up images on yer wee brick of onyx." An ominous chill rang loud and clear in his tone. "Take note, lass. Never show that to anyone else. They would surely kill ye for it, ye ken?"

"But ye're willing to let me live?" she snapped, frustration at the unreasonableness of it all making her ready to scream. "What makes ye so generous to grant me such favor?" How could he *still* not believe her?

With a hesitant touch, he brushed his fingertips across her cheek. "Because I like ye, Kenzie MacMartin. Verra much so. I fear ye've bewitched me."

Before she realized what he was about, he kissed her. Not fierce like before, but just as all-consuming. The warm softness of his lips nibbled her into a state of wonderful breathlessness. His calloused hands cradled her face, and he deepened the kiss, making her realize some things were unaffected by date or time. Some things surpassed everything, no matter the century.

She pressed a hand to the center of his chest. Not to stop him. But to feel the strong beat of his heart. Why? She hadn't a clue. All she knew was this needed to be real. She needed a safeness she couldn't explain, and deep in her soul, she knew Mathias could provide it.

He broke the connection, but stayed close, his gaze locked with hers. "I couldna help myself," he whispered. "I have wanted ye since I first laid eyes on ye."

Tears threatened to set in again. She didn't need this. A man she would never see again if she went back to where she belonged? What a cruel choice. Him or her life that some strange rippling of time had stolen away?

She stepped back and turned away. "Ye won't believe anything I say, but ye have no problem stealing kisses?"

"Ye are overwrought and unsure, lass. I understand, and ye should be leery." He closed the distance between them again. "But I swear to keep ye safe if ye'll but let me."

"Dangerous words for a man betrothed to another." Bhaltair stepped around the corner. "How strange, Mathias. I knew ye for a thief, but I never took ye for a liar or a cuckold."

Hackles raised, the collie bared its teeth and growled. Kenzie agreed completely. She didn't like Bhaltair either. Then what the man had said sank in.

"Betrothed?" she repeated. She turned back to Mathias, waiting for him to deny it. The longer he took to answer, the angrier she became. The only other women, other than Lilias, she had seen him interact with were servants. A man of his status wouldn't be betrothed to a maidservant. She thought back to the sea of faces in the room. Wouldn't his intended have been at the banquet? Sat at the head table with him? And then it hit her. "No. Sweet little Lilias?"

Bhaltair moved closer, flashing his teeth like a shark going in for the kill. "Aye, ye've the right of it, my lovely seer. If Mathias wishes to gain the chieftainship, he must marry the Lady Lilias."

"Ye should be ashamed," she hissed, sounding like her scolding Sunday school teacher. This wasn't the first time a man had tried toying with her, treating her like she was too stupid to catch on to his games. But what about poor Lilias? That girl might physically be a woman grown, but she still seemed like a child and needed to be treated with all the love and caring that required.

What a disgusting, two-timing arsehole. She wadded a fist. "Come near me again, and I'll skin ye with a rusty knife."

Scrubbing a hand across his mouth, Mathias shot a narrow-eyed look at Bhaltair. "This is none of yer affair. I suggest ye be gone. Now."

"There is no affair here," Kenzie interjected as she put more space between them. A sense of betrayal, of being played for a fool, made her blood boil. How had she misjudged him so? Usually, her instincts warned her about lowlife connivers. The century must be throwing her off. What kind of man married a childlike lass just to get a leg up in his clan? Disgusting. She motioned for Brodie to heel. "In fact, we are done here. I was just leaving."

Mathias visibly flinched, then his scowl hardened even more. He took a step toward Bhaltair. "Were ye no' assigned to the guard tower this evening?"

"Oh, aye," Bhaltair said with a snide smile. "But are tower guards not expected to walk the wall once every hour?" He caught up with Kenzie, snaked an arm around her waist, and yanked her close. "Ye'll find I'm nay betrothed to anyone, m'love. At least, not until the chief speaks with ye and makes the announcement. Care to join me as I walk?"

The last thing she needed right now was another arseworm. She pushed away, brushing off his touch as though it soiled her. "I willna be joining anyone, thank ye verra much." Not only was the man a jerk, he also wasn't making any sense.

"Wait," Mathias growled as he stepped between them. "Explain yerself."

The cocksure fool gave Kenzie a look that made her feel like she needed a bath. "Since the lady stated her family scattered and lost, I asked the Stronach for her hand. To protect her." His mouth took on a belligerent slant as he gave them both a regal nod. "He approved the match. Of course, it will nay be announced until he has spoken with Mistress Kenzie, but since she is now the Stronach seer, I am sure she already knows all I have just told ye. D'ye not, m'love?"

"What I know," Kenzie said, doing her best to tamp down a rising panic, "is that I can never marry. Not if I want to keep being a seer." Thankfully, several old movie tropes sprang to mind. "If I marry, I lose my ability to foretell the future. It's how it's been with all the women of my line." She held her breath, praying both men would swallow the lie.

She couldn't read Mathias's expression, but Bhaltair's was unmistakable. The man was not happy. He shoved around Mathias and snatched hold of her arm. "Then our daughter shall become the next seer," he growled. "I am certain the chief wouldna mind as long as our clan lays claim to such a powerful bloodline." His grip tightened to the point of becoming painful.

Kenzie twisted around, stomped his instep, then tried kneeing him in the groin but was foiled by the infernal layers of clothing. "Let go," she demanded. "Ye're hurting me!"

Brodie attacked, but Bhaltair kicked him away, hard enough to send the dog bouncing into the wall.

"I'll kill ye for that!" Nobody hurt her fur babies! She'd make him pay if she had to cling to his back and claw out his eyes. Just as she sank her teeth into his hand, he tore away, stumbling backward.

Mathias had charged into him like a raging bull, hitting his chest at full force. "Touch her again and die," he bellowed.

Kenzie ran to Brodie. Her sweet pup lay so still, she feared the worse. She glanced back at the fools, hoping they'd kill each other.

Bhaltair fought back but was clearly outmatched. Even though he was near the same size as Mathias, he didn't possess the man's massive build nor his prowess at hand-to-hand fighting. "The Stronach shall hear of this!" he threatened as he broke away, swiping blood from his hand.

"Aye," Mathias agreed. "He shall at that. Last I knew, we didna force our women into a marriage they dinna wish."

"We shall see," Bhaltair said. Hatred rolled off the man in waves. "We shall see," he shouted again as he stormed away.

MATHIAS WANTED TO touch her, make her know the truth of his heart but held himself back. "Are ye all right?"

She crouched over the dog, murmuring as she ran her hands across him. He lay too still against the wall. If Bhaltair had killed it, he'd beat that insolent bastard bloody. "Is he… Is yer pup all right?"

Without answering, she lowered herself to sit with her back against the wall. She gently pulled the dog into her lap and cradled his head in her arm. It was then that Mathias noticed the beast's eyes appeared to be open and as clear and bright as always. Relief filled him as the tip of the dog's tail weakly thumped against the floor.

"I am glad to see him all right," he said as he knelt down in front of them.

"Get the hell away from me," she said without taking her gaze from the pup. She stroked the animal's face, caressing his muzzle and whispering words that Mathias couldn't hear. The canine hugged its front paws around her arm.

Heart heavy as stone, he had to explain. She had to understand that he had not meant to deceive her. Nor would he dishonor or hurt Lilias in the manner she supposed. "Kenzie—"

"I said," she paused, finally looking up, "get the hell away from me." Teeth bared like an enraged beast, her eyes flashed with disgust and hatred. "I have no time for a lying pedophile."

"A what?" He didn't know that word but figured it to be an insult by the way she had spat it.

"A pedophile," she repeated. "A lowlife scum who molests children."

"Never!" How dare she say such a thing. He rose and backed up a step, repulsed by the very idea. "Why would ye disparage me in such a way?"

"Lilias?" Still hugging the dog, she glared up at him as though wishing he'd fall dead on the spot. "She's as innocent and trusting as a child in her first year at primary school. Ye know that, and yet ye still plan to marry her so ye can be chief? Ye should be ashamed." Her eyes narrowed. "I suppose ye planned to consummate the marriage to make it official, then take a few mistresses on the side to keep yerself amused." She shook her head. "Ye disgust me." With one last hug of the dog, she patted his side. "Up now, lad. Ye're better, aye? Merely a little stunned."

The collie wiggled to his feet, his tail swishing back and forth.

Mathias held out a hand to help Kenzie stand.

She scowled up at him. "Get stuffed." She rose without his help. "Get stuffed and go straight to hell!".

"Let me explain." Her hatred burned worse than any wound he had ever known.

"Why?" Loathing dripped from her tone. "Ye dinna owe me an explanation. I'm just passing through here, remember?"

"Ye are nay just passing through," he corrected. She needed to understand that above all. "The Stronach will never agree to yer leaving. Not after tonight." He moved a step closer, but the growling dog backed him up again. The last thing he wished to do was incense her even more by fending off her beast. "I beg ye, please calm down and hear me out."

"Are ye, or are ye not sworn to marry Lilias so ye can become the next chieftain?"

"I am, but—"

"*But* nothing. Either ye are, or ye're not, and ye just said ye are." She motioned to the canine and headed toward the stairway.

"I intend to marry the lass, but that doesna mean I will ever touch her," he said as he hurried to catch her.

Kenzie halted, then turned and gave him a look that called him a liar. "If ye dinna consummate it, it willna be valid. Dinna ye have to show bedsheets or something in this godforsaken age to prove you did it and that ye're married?"

"A wee vial of sheep's blood will make the marriage official."

A heavy sigh left him. He had planned it out long ago when forced with the choice of either marrying Lilias or turning his back on caring for his clan.

"If ye go near my ram, I'll kill ye."

"Not yer sheep, ye thick headed woman. Credit me with having a bit a sense." Eyeing the dog with its teeth still bared, he risked another step closer. "Ye think I'd threaten the pet of a woman I care about?"

Whipping the circlet off her head, she massaged her temples. "I dinna ken what I think anymore." She dropped her hands to her sides and blew out a disgusted huff. "I just want to go home."

The way she stuck to her unbelievable tale of the caves made him wonder if it was true rather than just some strange tale to make folk forget about her gifts as a seer. Whatever it was, he had to make her understand it did her more harm than good. "Guard yer words, lass. I beg ye."

"Why will ye not believe me?"

"Because what ye say isna possible."

"Ye believe in seers and witches, but time travel is out of the question?"

The lass made a valid point. If futures could be told and spells cast, why couldn't folk travel to a time other than their own? "Even if I believe ye, ye must still guard yer words, ye ken? After what happened earlier, this keep is now yer home. The Stronach willna suffer ye to leave." Remembering the intensity of her kiss, he held out a hand. "But I swear to keep ye safe. If ye'll but let me."

She rolled her eyes and waved the dog forward. "Come on, Brodie. Let's go down and visit Ramsay before bedtime."

"I shall accompany ye." Whether she wished it or not, he would stay at her side. After Bhaltair's behavior, he didn't feel comfortable with her moving about the keep alone. And by this time, who knew what sort of rumors that bastard had started? Also, at some point, she would have to have a private audience with the chieftain.

"Save yer attentions for yer child bride. I can find the way m'self." Head held high and twirling the silver circlet around her finger, the woman charged forward as though heading into war with her trusty beast at her side.

He snagged hold of her arm and whirled her around to face him. "I told ye how it will be between myself and Lilias. I intend to protect both her and my clan."

She jabbed a finger at him, spearing his chest with her nail. "That's fine. But dinna think I'll be a part of yer mean-spirited games. I like Lilias and would do nothing to hurt her—which includes sneaking around behind her back and making her look the fool. Ye know how she worries about what others say about her. Ye've seen her upset when she doesna understand."

How could he argue with that? He dropped his hand from her arm and stepped back. "I would do nothing to hurt wee Lilias either. She's a dear lass who deserves better." He wished he could make her understand. "If I dinna marry the poor girl and protect her, what do ye think will happen to her?"

Kenzie shrugged. "How should I know what'll happen in this godforsaken time? I assume she'll go on as she does now."

"Nay, woman." He leaned closer. "Her father will force her to marry another who might not be so careful with her as I intend to be."

Her face tightened in disbelief. "Is the man blind? Can he not see how she is?"

"He knows how she is," Mathias assured. "But he must protect the clan's future. Lilias could never be a chieftain. So, she must marry a man who can be."

"Even at the cost of her innocence?" Kenzie's tone had gone cold again, as though she thought the Stronach little more than a monster.

"A leader must sometimes make hard choices. Sacrifices for the well-being of all." Mathias's heart ached. He wasn't speaking of the chieftain but his own sacrifice. Aye, he would marry Lilias, and in doing so, condemn himself to a life of loneliness and no children of his own.

Kenzie frowned. "There has to be some other way. Can't he just name a successor with the stipulation that Lilias be taken care of as long as she lives?"

Mathias found it amusing that this beguiling woman had just restated the very argument he had once suggested to the chieftain. "Nothing would be as certain as a marriage contract with Lilias. Anything else could be easily overthrown once the Stronach was gone."

"Maybe Lilias needs to come home with me." Even though her face was still dark as thunder, at least she seemed somewhat calmer. "I could keep her safe on my farm. She'd like it there."

"I plan to keep her safe." The stubborn woman had no right filling Lilias's head with such impossibilities. Although he'd never loved the innocent lass, he cared about her as though she were a little sister. "Dinna be confusing her with yer talk of the caves. When she gets confused, she often frets herself into a sickness, and her head pains her something fierce."

Kenzie went still, then graced him with the hint of a smile. "Ye do care about her, do ye not?"

"Have I once acted as if I didna?" Her assumptions hurt his pride.

"No," she agreed softly. Tilting her head, she studied him until her stare burned his flesh.

"What now?"

"So, ye're saying ye plan to live yer life married but alone. No children. No lovers. Nothing but leading the clan all the rest of yer days."

"What choice do I have?"

"Ye dinna strike me as the celibate sort," she observed with the arch of a brow.

"Aye, well." He blew out an uncomfortable breath and glanced around. He agreed with the lass, especially since he wanted her with a fierceness that bordered on frightening. But he daren't admit it to her. She no longer acted ready to gut him, but he wasn't foolish enough to think that couldn't change. Best stay the course and keep to the topic at hand. "As I said, what choice do I have?"

She shrugged. "Ye could come with me to the future, too. Ye and Lilias both. I'm sure my brothers would like ye, as long as ye let them win at arm wrestling."

That tale again. And what the hell was *arm wrestling*? He ignored all of it for now. "I must protect my clan along with Lilias." He offered his arm, "What would happen if Bhaltair's leadership were unleashed upon them? The Stronach favors him, ye ken?" Some of his tension eased when she took his arm and stepped to his side. She possessed the power to soothe him as well as inflame him.

"Bhaltair is a loose cannon," she observed as they made their way around to the stairs that descended closer to the stables.

"Cannon?"

She frowned, remained silent for a moment, then held up a finger. "He is an out-of-control weapon," she explained, choosing each word with care.

"Aye." That he understood and heartily agreed with.

Rabbie stopped them just inside the stable door. With a sharp shake of his head, he held a finger to his lips, then motioned for them to follow. With his lantern held low, the lad led them to a corner stall at the very back where the ram stood contentedly munching grain from a wooden trough.

Kenzie took the lantern and went to the ram, looking him over as though she feared him injured. "He seems all right," she whispered. "Why the warning to keep quiet?"

"'Cause Master Bhaltair done said he'll be telling the Stronach to slaughter the beast if ye dinna agree to marry him." Rabbie craned his neck and looked toward the entrance. "So's I moved him back here. Soon's he's finished with his feed, I know a place to hide him in the woods behind the keep." He gave Kenzie an apologetic bob of his head. "He'll have to be tied, but Bhaltair willna be able to find him."

"I'll kill him," Kenzie said through clenched teeth. She shoved the lantern back in Rabbie's hands. "I'll be back later to help ye move him." She gave the lad a look that backed him up a step. "Dinna ye dare take him until I've joined ye, ye ken?"

Eyes wide, the boy gave a quick nod.

"I dinna think that wise," Mathias warned. The lass had more in mind than hiding the sheep. He could smell it.

"I dinna care what ye think." She scratched the ram's ears one last time, then pushed around them and headed toward the door. When she passed by the tool rack, she backed up and stared at it, then took down the knife used for chopping hay. "I'll be taking this one."

Mathias grabbed hold of her wrist. "Why?" If she meant to kill Bhaltair, she'd need more than that.

"Because I want it."

"Ye canna kill Bhaltair with that wee bit of iron." He eased his grip but didn't let go. The woman had to see reason.

"Fine." She let the weapon drop. "Now, let me go."

Any alliance, any forgiveness or caring found since their words on the wall were now lost. He felt it as surely as the sudden chill in the air. Releasing her arm, he blocked her path. "Rabbie willna let the ram be hurt. Ye heard him say so yerself."

"I'm tired of depending on everyone else for the safety of me and mine. That isna how I operate." She lifted her chin to that defiant angle he knew so well. "Step aside. I'll be going to my rooms now." Her eyes narrowed, and her tone mocked him. "If that meets with yer approval, Master Mathias."

Bowing his head, he stepped aside. "Kenzie please," he whispered as she passed him.

She paused but stared straight ahead. "Go to yer betrothed, Mathias, and dinna worry after me. I can take care of myself."

CHAPTER EIGHT

"KENZIE? WHY? WHY are ye wearing those things again?" Candlelight danced across the floor, tickling back the hushed darkness. Barefoot, her hair braided and hanging over one shoulder, Lilias stood in the doorway. Her shift glowed a ghostly white.

"Go back to bed, Lilias. Ye'll get a chill if ye dinna take care." She would miss Lilias. Even though they had just met, she had taken an instant liking to her. The sweet lass was like the little sister she had always wanted.

"Ye are nay coming back to us, are ye? Ye are running from us forever." Lilias crept closer, her bottom lip trembling into a pitiful frown. "Is it because I repeated what ye said about the duke and caused such a stir?" She clutched a fist to her chest. "I am so verra sorry. I…I know I should think afore I speak, but it seems I never remember until it's too late." Her worried look grew more pinched as she eyed Kenzie's jacket and jeans. "Please dinna leave us," she whispered. "I shall make everything right again. I promise."

Kenzie stepped into her rubber boots and forced a kindly smile. "I have to go home, Lilias. Not because of anything ye said, but because…" How could she explain it so the dear lass would understand? "Because if I dinna leave, Bhaltair is going to cause trouble for me." She attempted a lighthearted air. "Besides, I have to hurry home to feed my chickens and take care of my sheep. Just like ye take care of Henny."

"Mathias will protect ye from Bhaltair," Lilias argued. "He likes ye." Her chin tucked as the golden glow of the candle revealed her shy smile. "I can tell by the way he looks at ye, ye ken? If ye stay, I feel sure he shall ask for yer hand. Would ye nay like to be his wife? He is so verra kind." A quiet giggle escaped her. "And he is quite handsome. More so than many of the others. Do ye nay think him so?"

Lilias's argument hurt like a physical blow. Did the poor girl not have a clue about her fate? "He is verra handsome and kind," she agreed, already missing the stubborn medieval warrior who had wormed his way into her heart no matter how angry he made her. "But I'm pretty sure he's promised to another."

"I willna marry him," Lilias stated, sounding a great deal more mature than before. "I dinna love Mathias. Well, I love him like a brother, but nay like a man I would wish to marry." Her frown shifted to a stern scowl that was very much out of character. "Father willna hear of a match with the man I truly feel a warmth for. Swears he's beneath me." She lifted her chin. "I know I am not quite…right. But I still know who I love and dinna love. I'm also nay so daft as to think Mathias truly wishes to marry me any more than I wish to marry him."

"I am not sure what to say here," Kenzie admitted as she took a candle off the nightstand and lifted it to better see this new Lilias that didn't sound like herself at all.

The lass held her candle closer to Kenzie's. She leaned into the light, her smile gentle and understanding. "I am a little slow, but not so simple and childlike as everyone likes to think." She stole a glance back at the door, then lowered her soft voice even more. "But ye must never say a word to anyone, aye? Please? It must be our secret. 'Tis all a part of my plan."

"But—" At a complete loss, Kenzie stared at the girl, then

realized she stood there with her mouth hanging open. She snapped it shut, then tried again, "Are ye telling me ye are—that it's all an act?"

"Most the time." Lilias rubbed her forehead as though it pained her. For the first time since they met, Kenzie noticed a silvery scar running up the girl's temple along her hairline. "Sometimes I get a mite confused, and the ache in my head becomes so fierce, I canna see, but I am nay the addled, half-wit as rumors describe me." Her smile faded. "It took me a long while to come out of the darkness after all that happened. Mama's murder." A bleakness came across her, making her seem trapped in something only she understood. "And the other things those men did after they killed her. I still struggle with it at times." She closed her eyes and bowed her head as though praying for strength. "It is Father's wish our bloodline always leads this clan. So, I play to the rumors of being simple as much as I can, hoping Mathias will refuse to marry me. He could still be chief. I feel sure I might eventually convince Father to make it so, even without us marrying. After all, Mathias is a distant cousin, so the bloodline would still be true." She rested a hand on Kenzie's arm. "I have had visions, Kenzie. Angels. The blessed Virgin. They saved me from my horrors of long ago. I pray every night for guidance to walk the proper path and be true to the Lord. I know the man I love, and I know in my heart, the blessed Virgin has given me her blessing and will make it so."

"Who do ye love?" Kenzie whispered.

With a shy smile, Lilias tucked her chin. "Forgive me. But I canna say his name aloud. 'Tis the oath I made to Father so he wouldna kill him or banish him from the clan."

Kenzie wished she could help but didn't have a clue how. "Yer father seems verra set in his ways. And also, verra afraid of me." She glanced around, making sure she had left nothing behind. Even with Lilias's revelation, she couldn't stay. She didn't belong here. Though some things in this time made it tempting. "Your father favors Bhaltair and is sure to grant his request to marry me. Are ye not worried about that jerk?"

"Jerk?" Lilias repeated, frowning at the strange word.

"Arsehole," Kenzie said. The girl should understand that word.

"Ah." Lilias nodded. "Never fear, God will handle Bhaltair." She took hold of Kenzie's hand. "If ye promise to stay, I shall tell Mathias all I just shared with ye. Then the two of ye can be together. I have seen it clear as day."

"I dinna think it will be that simple." The chieftain wasn't the only one set in his ways. Mathias was loyal to his clan. He would still marry Lilias just to make sure Bhaltair didn't wrangle his way into the chief's seat. "I must go, Lilias. Please forgive me." Gently, she pulled her hand free. "I will never forget ye. I swear." There was much she would never forget about this time. Too much, in fact.

"Old Annag told me ye would refuse to stay." Lilias moved to the bed, running her fingers across the garments Kenzie had left there. "She said some canna settle no matter the welcome they receive. They canna accept the differences and adapt, she said."

"Canna accept the differences and adapt?" Kenzie repeated, chill bumps rippling across her flesh. "What did she mean by that?"

With a shake of her head, Lilias shrugged. "I am nay certain." She turned and studied Kenzie as if seeing her anew. "She merely spoke as if she understood how ye think and feel about living among us." Her braid slid off her shoulder as she tilted her head. "Are ye one of the fae?"

Muffled footsteps out in the hallway reminded Kenzie she needed to get moving. The cloak of night would only last a short time. "I am not one of the fae," she assured, then gave Lilias a quick hug. "Ye're a dear friend. I hope everything turns out as ye wish."

Lilias responded with a quivering smile, then gave her a tighter hug. "I willna tell anyone of yer leaving. I promise." She made the sign of the cross. "Go with God, my precious friend.

And may He bless ye and keep ye safe."

Kenzie nodded, then hurried out before they both ended up crying. She would weep later. Once she was back home. Silent as possible, ducking into the shadows whenever servants passed, she and Brodie made it out of the keep without being discovered. Watching the top of the wall for the guards, they darted across the courtyard and slipped into the stable.

She helped herself to the glowing lantern hanging on the post beside the door and crept down the path separating the stalls. Rabbie was fast asleep beside the ram. Ready to cover the lad's mouth in case she startled him, she gently nudged his shoulder. "Rabbie," she whispered. "Wake up."

The boy jerked awake but didn't squeak a sound. Just scrambled to his feet, slipped a rope around the sheep's neck, and handed it to Kenzie. He motioned for her to follow along the rear wall of the stable.

She fell in step behind him, wondering what the lad had in mind. The back of the building was actually part of the stone skirting wall with the front doorway its only exit. Or so she thought.

Rabbie came to a halt and revealed a short door hidden behind a wooden pallet. "For when I shovel out the shite from the stalls," he whispered. Latching hold of its large iron ring with both hands, he yanked it open. "Mind the guards," he whispered, pointing upward. He frowned at her clothes, as though realizing for the first time that she no longer wore her kirtle.

"These are easier to sneak around in," she hurried to explain. "Skirts get snagged on bushes, ye ken?" Kenzie hoped the lad would accept the lie. She and the animals would have to stick to a fast pace to get as much distance between themselves and the keep as possible before either Lilias or Rabbie tipped off Mathias. Neither of them seemed capable of keeping a secret for very long.

The boy shrugged. "Leave the lantern here. The moon'll light our way." He eased out the door, glancing upward all the while.

Kenzie, the ram, and the dog followed. The ram tossed his

head, not liking the rope around his neck. The fool thing would start his loud grumbling soon if she didn't remove it. She slipped it off and signaled the dog to herd the stubborn beast forward. Rabbie's eyes widened, and he stared at her as if he thought her barmy. "Just head on," she urged quietly after a glance back at the wall. "Brodie'll take him wherever we wish to go."

The boy frowned. His doubt clear as the moon in the sky. But he trudged onward, and they followed.

She didn't have a clue how to rid herself of Rabbie once they reached wherever he intended to hide the ram. He'd have to be knocked out for a wee bit. Not hard enough to *really* hurt him, just solid enough to send him off to dreamland for a while. Aye, that's what she'd do. She resettled her grip and prepared to deal the blow.

"Master Mathias!" Rabbie's greeting warned her that getting rid of the boy wasn't her only problem.

"So, ye took me for a fool," Mathias accused her as they stepped into the clearing.

"No more than ye took me for one." She wouldn't give an inch. She couldn't afford it.

"Back to the stables wi' ye, lad. Afore ye're missed." Mathias clapped a hand on Rabbie's shoulder. "And I thank ye."

"Aye, master." The lad had the decency to grant her an embarrassed glance, then took off at a fast lope.

"On foot. The three of ye. All the way back to cave." He shook his head and blew out a disgusted snort. "No supplies. No weapons to speak of. How in hell's name did ye think to make it?"

"Quite successfully, thank ye verra much." She had walked the land all her life and knew how to glean its treasures to survive. "I'm nay as stupid or as helpless as ye like to think."

"Ye canna leave here," he growled, stalking toward her, her wee stick strapped to his back. He wanted her to have it.

"I am sick of this game." She braced herself, knowing she'd lose in hand-to-hand battle but determined to win her freedom somehow. "Go back to yer clan. And Lilias," she added, noting with sad satisfaction that he flinched when she said the girl's name. "I have no choice. Let me go back where I belong."

"Ye belong with me." He offered her the weapon she seemed to love.

She had never seen such pain and longing in a man's eyes before as she accepted her staff. Especially not a man looking at her. "Ye dinna even know me," she reasoned, feeling defeated even before she escaped. "Go back to Lilias. Talk to her, Mathias. I think ye'll be pleasantly surprised."

"I love Lilias like a sister." One corner of his mouth twitched higher, and in that moment, Kenzie realized he already knew Lilias's secret. "And her heart belongs to another. As does mine."

Horns blared loud and long, joined by clanging metal and drums. An alarm. Kenzie recognized the noise without being told.

Mathias stiffened and turned a fierce look back in the keep's direction. "The warning. We must return. Now."

"All that noise because I escaped?"

"Nay, woman." He grabbed her arm and urged her forward. "It signals we're under attack. MacPhersons, I'd wager. Come! We must hie to the safety of walls."

"Ye're the leader of the guard. Hurry on ahead! I'll follow." She signaled Brodie to turn the ram. "Ramsay's slow. Ye know how stubborn he can be."

"Ye swear it?" Already at the edge of the clearing, he stopped and stared back at her, wanting to believe, but doubt filled his eyes. "Ye swear ye'll follow?"

"Aye," she lied, making an 'x' over her breaking heart. "Cross my heart and hope to die."

"I want to believe ye." In one determined stride, he was back in front of her. Without a word, he yanked her into his arms and kissed her long and hard. His fingers cradled her head, lacing into her hair and tightening as though he'd never let her go. She couldn't breathe. Couldn't think. All she could do was wish. Wish he would come with her. Wish they could be together. Wish she had never met this man she could never have. He finally broke the breathtaking bond, lifted his head, and stared down at her for a long, painful moment. "Dinna make me regret placing my trust in ye, aye?" Then he was gone, charging back to protect the people he loved more than her.

Kenzie touched her lips, savoring that last kiss she would never forget.

The noise from the keep grew louder and more chaotic, shaking her from her daze. She spun about and ran in the opposite direction, tears streaming. Choking back a sob, she signaled her faithful friend. "Brodie! Hie to me now, lad. Home, now. We're going home."

"GONE?"

The way the Stronach barked out the word, he almost sounded like his old self before the long months of ailing had diminished him. "Ye're telling me that woman escaped ye? Mathias Stronach? Next in line to lead this clan?" The frail leader sagged back into the pillows of his couch, shutting his eyes as if this latest problem was more than he could bear.

Mathias bit back the excuse of placing the safety of the clan first, of trusting the conniving beauty to follow as she promised. Excuses did naught but weaken a man. Instead, he squared his shoulders and endured his chieftain's rancor. "As soon as I leave yer presence, I shall recover her. Fear not."

His liege dragged open his eyes and gave him a damning glare. "Yer father, my cousin who died fighting the same Norse bastards who took my wife and ravaged my daughter, is wailing in his cairn right now. Wailing over yer ever-growing string of failures." He counted off on trembling fingers as he railed. "The MacPherson feud ye canna seem to quell. A feud started by yer poor choices!" He sucked in a deep breath and took hold of the next finger. "Strona's destruction." His red-rimmed eyes narrowed, and he pointed at Mathias. "Those deaths are at yer door. Not mine!" Floundering to sit taller in the pillows, a frustrated growl strengthened his tone. "Ye brought that witch into our midst, then let her slip away to cast her spells against us now that she knows our secrets." Thin chest heaving, he jabbed the air again. "And ye have yet to marry my poor defenseless Lilias! Dinna think I failed to notice how attentive ye were to that sorceress."

"Mistress MacMartin is nay a witch, and I have done nothing to dishonor the Lady Lilias or our agreement." Mathias shoved the matter of the kisses to the back of his mind. Or attempted to. Those kisses were of the like he had never known before.

"She is a seer, ye ken?" He remembered the lie she had told while they stood on the wall. "And she can never marry. For when she does, she says the sight will leave her." He jerked a nod, affirming the words he recognized as a pitiful ploy to escape Bhaltair. "The woman said it has been that way with all the seers of her line."

"And ye believed that weak tale?" The Stronach rolled his eyes. "Bhaltair shall have her as he has asked." The lines of the elder's sallow face tightened. "I promise ye that warrior will control her spell casting and train her up to behave proper even if he has to keep her chained to their bed. She willna escape him!"

The thought of Bhaltair with Kenzie set fire to his blood. Teeth clenched, Mathias struggled to keep his inner fury from surfacing.

The chief's eyes narrowed again. "That witch—beg pardon— that *seer* is not for the likes of yerself. Lilias is to be yer wife, ye ken?" He reached back and grabbed his tankard from the table behind his couch. After a deep draught that left a trail of pale glistening droplets down his front, he shrugged. "My daughter may be tetched, but she can still breed. Her maid reports she bleeds regular like any other woman."

Mathias found the chief's words disgusting. Lady Lilias was not some bitch in heat waiting to be serviced by a stud. "By yer leave, I shall be off to recover Mistress MacMartin."

"Take Bhaltair," the chief ordered.

"Would it not be better if Bhaltair stayed to watch over the keep? After all, 'twas he who sounded the alarm when he thought the MacPhersons had descended upon our glen." Mathias knew exactly why Bhaltair had ordered the horns blown. The bastard had discovered the ram missing. Bhaltair was not a fool to be underestimated.

The Stronach grew quiet, frowning as he hugged his tankard close. "He did at that," he muttered.

It took every ounce of self-control Mathias possessed not to smile. He had suspected it before, but now he knew the truth for what it was. The Stronach feared the MacPhersons. "Bhaltair willna allow any ill to befall yerself or the keep," he assured the cowardly chief. "The man lives for battle and bloodletting." With a disinterested shrug, he added, "and the seer is but one woman with a dog and a sheep. I'll nay make the mistake of trusting her again. I shall return her to ye trussed up and thrown across my saddle."

The Stronach blew out a relieved breath and nodded. "Aye. Do that. Bhaltair will keep us safe whilst yer gone." He waved him away, then returned to hugging his ale. "Go now."

Mathias left the chieftain's solar, snorting to clear his nostrils of the fetid air. With each passing day, he found it more and more difficult to respect the man he had once thought a noble leader. It was more than a little obvious Bhaltair had labored hard to burrow his way into the Stronach's good graces. 'Twas a wonder their liege hadn't named the man the next chief instead of him. That thought sickened him. Lilias would never survive a brute such as Bhaltair.

Another wave of bitter jealousy set fire to his blood. Neither would Bhaltair ever touch his Kenzie. He would see to that even if it got him banished from the clan. Storming out of the keep, he headed to the stable. "Rabbie!"

The boy emerged with Mathias's horse in tow. "Fed and

watered. Provisions in the bag tied to the saddle. Old Annag brought them and said to get yer mount ready."

The old woman always knew. He settled into the saddle. "Good lad."

"Shall I clean the stall for the ram?"

Mathias toyed with the idea of telling the boy the truth, then decided against it. "Aye. Ready the stall."

Rabbie bobbed his head, then hurried back inside the stable.

"Open the gate!" he bellowed to the guards atop the wall as he urged his mount forward.

Chains rattled, and gears groaned as the portcullis lifted.

After thundering across the bridge, Mathias turned his horse northward, following the river. He felt certain she would stay in the tree line along the waterway's banks. The canny lass knew better than to take to open ground on foot. She'd be easily spotted and overtaken.

The sky pinked, growing ever lighter with the rising sun. Mathias slowed, wondering if she would bed down during the day and only move at night. She hadn't slept since the night before. A body could only move so long on the initial rush of energy her escape would give her. A few hours had passed. Enough time to get her down the river a bit, but not that far with the slow ram in tow.

His mount sloshed across the shallows. Kenzie and the animals would more than likely travel along the far bank. 'Twas more overgrown. He dismounted and studied the ground, unable to tell very much until the sun lit the day better. With the ground soft from the spring rains, it would be most nigh impossible for her to move without leaving tracks to betray her.

"Where are ye, my love?" Nothing answered but the wind and the water gurgling across the rocks.

Mathias returned to the saddle, still unsure whether he'd kiss her first or thrash her arse for lying to him. He wished she had trusted him to keep her safe. A snort escaped him. Why the hell should she trust him when he hadn't even known *how* he'd keep her safe? Well. He hadn't known before, but he knew now. The only way to keep her safe was to find her and take her back to that damn cave.

If the fantastical tale she had told was true, that place would take her to safety. Back where she belonged, she said. The thought of it made his chest ache. She would go where he could never follow. God's beard, he wanted her to belong with him. To stay here. And he meant to tell her so. Make it clear before she left him for all time. A tiny part of him hoped she would choose to stay. Choose a life with him over the life she had once had. If she did, they would leave Glen Loy forever. Make a life together. Somewhere.

And then he remembered innocent Lilias. Back at the keep. Depending on him to keep her safe. If he left Lilias behind, it would be like tossing a lamb to wolves. Her fool of a father would marry her off to Bhaltair. He scrubbed a hand across his face and growled like a frustrated beast. How had life gotten so complicated?

He urged his horse to a faster trot, scowling at the scrub growing along the riverbank, pausing now and then to search through the trees and study the ground. Her odd footwear left strange tracks with ridges across the soles. Dog and sheep left their signs as well. It appeared she intended to keep moving through the light of day. Stubborn woman.

But then he came to tracks that made his heart pound harder. Boots. Horses. Several. All mixed with Kenzie's prints. He knelt at a patch that looked like a struggle and the dent of a body on its side. Whoever it was had hit the ground hard. Trailing his fingers across the muddy ground, he gritted his teeth. Too slight for a man. And surrounded by dog prints. It had to be Kenzie. He felt it as sure as he breathed.

Something at the edge of the bushes caught his eye. Kenzie's shepherd's crook. The gift from her grandsire that she cherished as much as she loved her animals. He picked it up and stared at it, wishing the bit of wood could speak. *What had happened here?*

Who had come upon her?

A familiar *baa* made him look up. The ram and the dog stood in front of him as if brought forth by witchery. Mathias shook aside the eerie chill. "Crazed notion," he muttered to himself.

The dog cocked its black head and eased another step closer.

"Who took her, lad?" He didn't care that it seemed foolish to talk to a wee mongrel. This beast was his only hope.

With an imploring whine, the dog turned north. *North.* MacPherson land lay to the north. If Kenzie wasn't among the Stronachs, MacPhersons had to have taken her. Mathias felt certain of it. No other clan ever encroached upon their land. Not since the Norse raids nearly two decades ago. And more than likely, Ellar MacPherson was still thirsty for revenge for the thrashing he had taken at the hands of the woman. His father nor his clan would let the man live that down.

He saddled up, then paused, staring down at the sheep. Alone, the animal would fall prey to wolves, or more likely, Stronach hunters. For Kenzie's sake, he had to see the creature safe before setting out to find her. "Brodie, lad. Herd him this way. Back to the keep." He turned his horse, then waved for the dog to follow. A glance back revealed both animals trotting northward. "Brodie! This way."

The dog didn't slow or look back, just continued northward, nipping at the ram's heels whenever the creature slowed.

Mathias tried the sharp whistle that always worked on his horse. His hopes rose when the dog paused and glanced back at him. He tried to mimic one of the hand signs he had seen Kenzie use. The animal ignored it and continued on its way.

"Shite!" he hissed through clenched teeth as he wheeled his horse around and took off after Kenzie's animals. The fool things were as stubborn as their mistress. A sad realization came to him. They also loved her. That he understood more than he cared to admit.

He toyed with the idea of hoisting the ram over his saddle and carrying it back to the keep but dismissed it just as quickly.

He feared if he did so and lost track of the dog, he'd be sore pressed to find the wily beast again. The Highlands could be a vast place when hunting a wee animal, and he knew in his gut he didn't have that kind of time.

Following close, he noted how the dog occasionally paused and ran its nose along the ground. It didn't follow the river. Instead, he cut across the glen, moving ever northward. The farther they traveled, the more Mathias knew the MacPhersons had taken her. If he rode on without veering from the direction the dog headed, he would find himself at the MacPherson keep by nightfall tomorrow, which brought him to the next problem. How in every blessed saint's name would he recover her by himself? Soundless stealth was a lost notion since that infernal sheep kept up a constant stream of noise. The fool thing sounded like a grumbling old washerwoman bemoaning everything under the sun.

Perhaps he could distract the MacPhersons with the animals. He pondered this tactic, weighing the risks. If anything happened to either the dog or the ram, Kenzie would never forgive him.

They made their way across the land. Watching the signs. Traveling steadily throughout the day until the sun dipped low and almost touched the land. It amazed Mathias that the kidnappers had covered so much ground in such a short amount of time. They must have snatched hold of Kenzie sometime last night. Perhaps not too long after he had left her—and it had been many hours before he was able to go after her…

Without warning, the dog ran in front of the sheep and walked it back, bringing it to a halt. Ears perked, he crouched down, his long slender nose pointed at a copse of trees up ahead. The woods lay nestled in the center of the valley below.

He dismounted, deciding it worth the risk to walk up to the dog.

"Is she there, lad?" he whispered, noting it would be the perfect place for the kidnappers to make camp for the evening.

The beast ignored him, just remained locked in place, his

nose aimed at the trees.

Mathias studied the surroundings. From the higher ground, he had a full view of the valley, even the land rising beyond the large stand of trees. A burn trickled down the far hillside, glistening like a silvery vein that disappeared into the woods. The breeze brought him a faint scent of wood smoke. Arrogant bastards. So sure of themselves. They lit a campfire on Stronach land.

He glanced upward. No sign of clouds. That could be both good and bad. Whenever he stepped out of the shadows, he would be easily discovered. Then there was the matter of the beasts. The cave lay not far to the west, after crossing the valley below. If he expected to rescue Kenzie and take her to it, the animals would have to accompany him rather than wait for him here. He also couldn't properly plan his rescue until he discovered how many MacPhersons he faced. According to the tracks back at the river, there appeared to be only two. But during the journey, it looked like a third had joined them. He could overcome three MacPhersons, as long as he handled the overcoming with care, silence, and surprise. He'd know more once he found their camp.

An eerie quietness, the first he had experienced since taking up company with the dog and sheep, made him look around. The ram had settled against an outcropping of boulders at the edge of a stand of good-sized pines. Generous boughs not only sheltered the animal but also provided a soft bed of needles. The dog perched atop the squared-off top of a rock and stared down at the valley below. It appeared Kenzie's animals had decided to stay where they were.

"Perhaps, that's best," Mathias said quietly as he climbed into the saddle. Before starting down the rise, he looked back and held up a hand. "Stay," he ordered.

Brodie remained seated on the stone but acknowledged the order with a huffing growl that Mathias took as an urging to stop wasting time and get on with saving Kenzie.

He gave the dog a nod. "I shall return with her soon."

CHAPTER NINE

S HE REFUSED TO let them see her cry.

Seated in front of a stump, hands tied behind her back, Kenzie lifted her chin and gritted her teeth. *Live to fight another day.* She silently repeated Da's favorite phrase about not giving up. Stay calm. Plan. Escape and run like hell. "It could be worse," she comforted herself under her breath, barely moving her lips. And it could be. Aside from a few bumps and bruises, she was whole, healthy, and pretty much untouched.

Thank goodness, she had developed the habit of keeping her cell phone powered off whenever afield. Her eldest brother, Ari, had taught her that to conserve the battery while out with the herds, when calls were impossible because of no service. That little trick had saved her life. Or at least, extended her existence in this hell a little longer.

When Ellar MacPherson and some irritating dobber whose name she hadn't caught, surprised her beside the river, if not for the camera on her phone, who knew what those two might have done. Kenzie was ashamed of how easily they had overpowered her, ripping away her staff and tossing it into the brush.

But they had been too afraid to touch the strange brick of onyx, or so they called it. To build on their fears, she had powered it up, taken their picture, and informed them she had just stolen their souls. Now, neither of them would look her in the eyes, and when a third MacPherson joined them, they warned him about her, too. Unfortunately, they had found the courage to tie her hands behind her back before plopping her onto Ellar's horse and riding off with her.

She hoped Brodie and Ramsay were all right. Worry for her animals threatened to choke her. Even though her dear collie would have fought to the death, the faithful Brodie had obeyed her shout to *hide the sheep*. A herding game they had often played when he was a pup learning his first commands. If he and the ram hadn't disappeared into the scrub along the riverbank, she knew the MacPhersons would have slaughtered them both just to get back at her. Gutless bastards. She wished there was such a thing as magic so she could turn all three of them into toads and toss them into the fire.

"Here, witch." The roughest of the trio, a grizzly, gap-toothed man who appeared old enough to be Ellar's father, dropped the charred carcass of a rabbit in her lap.

She glared up at him. "How am I supposed to eat with my hands tied behind my back?"

"Let her starve," Ellar growled from his spot beside the fire. "Da said fetch her. He didna say feed her."

"Dinna be such a coward, Ellar." The deliverer of her supper pulled a dagger from his boot. "I shall cut ye free to eat, but dinna think to run." He pointed the knife at the other man, refusing to acknowledge her. "My son, Lanner there, not only runs like a deer but is mighty accurate with throwing a blade."

"He'll have a hard time chasing me or throwing a knife when he's so gutless he canna even look at me." She couldn't resist. Tact nor the ability to keep her mouth shut had ever been one of her superpowers.

The old man wheezed out what appeared to be a chuckle. "Old Lanner might seem so at first." He fixed her with a hard glare, and the lines of his weathered face tightened into a chilling scowl. "But he fears me and his chief more than he fears yerself, I grant ye that." He cut her hands free and nodded down at the rabbit. "Eat or starve. I dinna give a damn which ye choose."

As unappetizing as the burnt meat appeared, she forced down a bite. To survive and escape, she needed strength and stamina. "What about water?" she asked before her server lowered himself to the ground beside the others. He moved with such stiffness, she figured once the man sat, he wouldn't be inclined to get back up.

"Old Garlan MacPherson, maidservant to a witch," Ellar taunted.

Garlan booted the man in the face, hitting him hard enough to roll him backward. Apparently, the elder wasn't as decrepit as she thought.

"Ye broke my nose!" Ellar scrabbled out of the old man's reach while holding a hand to his face. Blood streamed from between his fingers.

"Good," Garlan said as he picked up a bulging water skin. "Mayhap, it'll improve yer looks."

Lanner snickered. "Nothin'll make that face better."

Ellar glared at them both from where he cowered on the other side of the fire.

Garlan tossed the bag within her reach, then returned to his spot, seated himself, and tore into his food.

Kenzie retrieved the bag, cringing as she lifted it to her lips. The first time she had drank from it, she gagged. The soured thing smelled rancid as spoiled meat, and the nastiness of the tepid water within escaped description. Careful to hold her breath, she gulped quick to avoid both the taste and odor. She failed at stopping a shudder as she shoved the cork back in place.

"Wha's wrong wif ye, witch?" Garlan gave her a grin that showed how few teeth he had left. "Ye dinna care for water from the MacPherson well?"

"Spring water is better." She rose to her feet, holding the water bag in one hand and what was left of her meal in the other.

"Speaking of which, how about I refill it after I wash my face and uhm...?" She inclined her head toward the bushes.

Personal business had been a royal pain in the arse. Her captors didn't trust her any more than she trusted them. At first, they had threatened to stand at her side, denying her any semblance of privacy. But when she pulled out her phone again and said she'd make their souls disappear, they relented by tying a rope so tight around one of her wrists that it cut off the circulation. Thinking to escape, she had tried untying it a time or two, but suspicious about the extra time she took, they yanked her out of the bushes, almost dislocating her arm. She came to accept that escaping her toilet leash was not the way to achieve freedom.

"Fetch the rope, Ellar," Garlan ordered as he gnawed the last of the meat from a bone, then flung it into the woods.

"Why always me?" Ellar whined, his nose still bleeding.

"Do as yer told," the old man growled. When his son laughed, he pointed a finger at him. "Go with him and fetch more wood whilst she has a piss and gets the water."

Lanner's levity disappeared just as quick as it came. "Aye, Da," he grumbled, forcing his long, lanky body upward.

"Ye can tie my hand once I've filled the water bag and washed my face, ye ken?" Hurrying toward the spring, she took care not to get so far ahead as to make the men suspicious. A stolen glance back told her that Garlan had risen to check the horses and could mount and give chase in no time at all. She needed time and distance. Her escape had to be handled so the two younger men would stall about telling Garlan she was gone until they had no choice but to return for their mounts. That would give her the chance to run and find a place to hide.

Lanner tripped over an exposed root, cursing it when he fell face-first into the leaf mold. She had watched him stealing gulps from a small flask when Garlan wasn't looking. From the way he acted, it must have been something a lot stronger than water. Especially since his father didn't share it. With Ellar still bleary-eyed from his broken nose, Lanner finding it a challenge to walk a straight line, and Garlan breathing like an asthmatic in the night air, she felt sure a run for it would work as long as she delayed them using their horses. As soon as possible, she'd head back to the river for Brodie and the sheep. They would all hide until it was clear, then they'd set out for the cave again. Her chances might be slim, but they were better than none.

"Some cool water from the burn might ease the ache of that nose," she suggested to Ellar. The man had shown himself to be whinier than a spoiled bairn. She had no doubts he'd be more interested in taking care of his throbbing face than he would be in guarding her.

"Dinna drown yerself," Lanner jeered as he stumbled off in the other direction, dropping as many sticks of wood as he picked up. "And dinna forget to tie her afore she goes off in them bushes, ye ken?"

Ellar glared at the man but didn't comment. His actions screamed *coward*, which made sense since he had behaved like such a bully on their first meeting. Jumping an unarmed woman. With a sword. As if he feared a fight with his bare hands.

Kenzie made a show of emptying the water bag, taking note of Lanner's movements deeper in the woods. Enough trees were between them now that he'd never get off an accurate throw of his knife. She waited for Ellar to kneel beside the spring. Right next to her. She might not have her staff, but she had her boots, perfect aim, and a thirst for revenge. Breath held, she tensed as he dropped to his knees and leaned forward over the gurgling water.

She spun and kicked him in the face, rolling him back just as Garlan had done. Both hands clapped to his face, the man howled in pain. She leapt across the spring and ran for dear life, zigzagging through the trees just in case Lanner had enough sobriety left in him to attempt a throw of his dagger. She had to put enough space between them to give her time to climb the densest pine in the woods. The night was her friend, but the moon was her enemy. If she hit open ground, the three fools would spot her in a heartbeat. Her only hope was to hide up in a tree and wait for them to decide the witch had disappeared into thin air. Scanning the woods as she ran, she searched for a trunk with low enough branches to give her an easy leg up.

The approach of thundering hoofbeats from behind filled her with a fresh surge of adrenaline. Somehow, Garlan had reacted faster than she calculated. The old fool must be smarter than she gave him credit. She didn't take time to look back, just ran harder and faster, swerving under low-hanging branches every chance she could. But the dreadful pounding grew louder, closer. A powerful hand grabbed the back of her jacket and yanked, swinging her up over the horse. Head down, arse in the air, she bounced in time with the horse's gait. She struggled, trying to squirm free. Better to risk injury falling from the horse, then become their prisoner again.

A hard smack across the arse enraged her even more. "I'll send yer soul straight to hell! Ye just wait and see!" she yelled.

"Ye already have!"

That voice. Deep. Familiar. Wonderful.

She twisted around, trying to see her captor's face as they pounded through the darkness. "Mathias?" she called out.

"Shut it!" he barked as he leaned across her and spurred the mount to run harder.

They exploded out of the tree line, crossing the valley at a full gallop.

Bouncing on her stomach, Kenzie felt sure she would puke soon but didn't care. Mathias had ridden in like a white knight and helped her escape the bloody MacPhersons. She slid, almost falling off as the charger pounded up another rise. He grabbed hold of her by the seat of her pants and yanked upward, making her squeal as she went air-born. His arm snaked around her waist and caught her to his chest. She twisted, wrapped both arms around his neck, and held on tight. When they reached the summit of the hill, they swerved behind a wall of jagged boulders and came to a halt in the center of a thick stand of pines.

Even though they had stopped, she didn't let go, just hugged him tighter. Tears broke free, but she didn't care. Just buried her face in the warm crook of his neck. "Ye came for me. Even though I lied to ye and ran away, ye still came."

He crushed her closer, holding on as though he feared she'd escape him again. "Never lie nor run from me ever again," he said in a ragged whisper. He gave her a hard shake without relaxing his embrace. "D'ye hear me, woman? D'ye hear what I'm telling ye? Never again!"

"Aye." She lifted her head and touched his cheek. So much churned within her, she could barely breathe. Wants and needs. Hopes. Dreams. Fears. All she felt, the frightening revelations, charged the air between them. 'Twas a wonder lightning didn't strike.

"Slate gray," she whispered, unable to bear the crackling silence any longer.

"What?"

"That first day. I couldna decide the color of yer eyes." Running her thumb along the ruddy stubble of his beard, she stared at the curve of his mouth. Those unforgettable kisses. He had poured so much into those glorious kisses.

A curt bark shattered the moment. A loud grumbling *baa* followed.

Another surge of emotions blew away the last of Kenzie's control. "My babies! Ye saved my babies!" Sobbing, she half slid, half fell off the horse, rolled to her knees, and pulled her animals close. Mathias had saved her precious dog and cantankerous ram. At that moment, she admitted what she had been too afraid to acknowledge all along. She had fallen in love with this thirteenth-century man. Loved him with a dangerous fury. She twisted around and stared up at him through her tears. "I'm so afraid I love ye, Mathias. Love ye more than I should."

He jumped from the saddle and pulled her to her feet. Clutching her shoulders, he brought his face so close she couldn't escape the ferocity of his glare. "Dinna toy with me," he warned soft and low.

Even though she knew they could never be, she bared her soul. "Ye heard me," she said. "I've never said those words to anyone. Not ever."

"Then say it again." His eyes narrowed, making it hard to read all that lay within them. "I would have ye say those words again."

"I love ye, Mathias. I fear I always will."

"That sounds like a farewell." Releasing her shoulders, he gathered her into a tender embrace and tipped back her head. "So sorrowful," he whispered with a caress of her cheek. "Why does yer declaration of love, the words I longed to hear, why do ye make them sound so sad?"

"Because we can never be." The blasted tears returned, and she didn't bother to stop them. She forced out the reality she wished she didn't have to say. "I belong in another time, and ye must stay here and protect Lilias. Save her and lead yer clan. Ye know that as well as I."

The lines at the corners of his eyes tightened. He flinched as though she had struck him. But she saw the realization. He knew every word she said was true. "There has to be a way," he argued, then brushed the softest of kisses across each of her eyes. "There has to be," he repeated, pressing his forehead to hers.

Brodie growled and leapt to the top of the boulders. Hackles raised, he crouched and growled low again while staring down at the valley they had just escaped.

"They've found us." Panic filled her. Three MacPhersons against the two of them, plus a dog and a sheep. What chance did they have?

Mathias hoisted her back into the saddle and led the horse deeper into the pines. "If they come up here, ride fast as ye can to yer cave, ye ken?" He glanced back toward the valley, then put the reins in her hands. "Ye must save yerself. Swear that ye will." His look hardened. "And dinna lie to me this time."

How could he ask such a thing of her? Leave him to die? She caught his hand before he pulled it away. "I willna leave ye. Not like this."

"I pray ye dinna have to," he said quietly, then swept a kiss across her knuckles. "Stay still and quiet unless they come, aye?"

"Aye." she whispered, then added a silent prayer to send the MacPhersons searching in the other direction.

"DOWN, LAD," HE ordered in a stern but hushed tone.

Amazingly enough, the dog obeyed. Perhaps the canny animal had finally realized Mathias had their best interests at heart. The beast eased his way around to another spot at the base of the boulders and returned to watching the MacPhersons searching the valley below.

Mathias peered over the top. Two on horseback. One on foot, stumbling around like a fool with his mount following him. They all kept to the edge of the woods, searching back and forth and paying little mind to the open space beyond. Thankfully, the thick sedge hid all signs of his horse's hoofprints. At least, it did in the moonlight. Once daybreak came, the clots cut loose by sharp hooves would be easy enough to discover. The moon had yet to reach its zenith. Surely, the MacPhersons would give up soon and head back to their clan, making up lies to explain their failed kidnapping.

After a long while of riding around the border of the wood, the two returned to the man on foot. The three appeared to be deciding what to do next. Not once had they ridden across the valley or explored any of the surrounding hills or woodlands. The one on the ground attempted to mount his horse, failed, and fell on his arse.

Mathias frowned. Was the man drunk? What self-respecting warrior weakened himself with drink while guarding a prisoner?

The stumbling devil tried again, and this time, succeeded. Riding at a slow pace, the trio headed north toward the MacPherson border. At last. Mathias exhaled but remained watchful until they had ridden out of sight.

"Are they finally gone?" Kenzie whispered from so close it startled him.

"Dammit, woman! Will ye never listen and do as yer told?"

"I agreed to be still and quiet," she retorted with a defiant look. "I never agreed to stay on the horse, and I told ye plainly I would not ride away and desert ye."

He yanked her close and kissed her hard, fueling it with all his fears and frustrations. He needed her safe. More simply, he needed her. Forever. When she clung to him, matching his fire with hers, he made up his mind. Time to wage the most important battle of his life. He broke their connection and stared down at her. "Stay with me." It was more an order than a question.

"I did," she said, looking dazed.

He shook his head. "Ye dinna understand my meaning. Stay with me. Here. In this time."

Regret shouted from her, stabbing more painfully than any dagger.

"Dinna refuse me," he argued before she could deny any hope of a future together. "We will think of a way to get Lilias to a nunnery where she will be safe."

"And yer clan?" she asked. "Ye expect me to believe ye're willing to abandon yer clan to the likes of a dying chief who listens to Bhaltair?"

At least she hadn't refused him outright. His determination grew. "I can live with that as long as we get Lilias to safety. She is an innocent in all this."

"And what of my family back home?"

Even as dark as the shadows were beneath the trees, he could tell she was close to tears. He could hear the sorrow in her voice.

"My Da. Five brothers? Their families. All my nieces and nephews?" She paused and turned away, refusing to face him. "I'm their favorite auntie, ye ken? Buy them all the toys they're not supposed to have. Give them all the sweets they want, then send them home."

"But I love ye, Kenzie. Please tell me that matters as well. Say ye'll stay and be my wife." With a gentle pull on her chin, he forced her to look at him. A subtle breeze helped his cause. Stirring the pine boughs so moonlight slipped through and chased away the shadows. "We will have bairns of our own to love. Lots of them. And we shall have each other." Brushing his thumb along the satin of her cheek, he tightened his embrace. "I swear to spend the rest of my days striving to make ye happy. Swear it with everything in me."

"Ye are making this so difficult." Her cheeks glistened in the moonlight, wet with fresh tears.

"I'm glad I'm making it difficult." He gave her a fierce smile. "'Tis my hope to make yer leaving impossible." It was time for another kiss, more tender than before. She had to realize all he felt for her. "I love ye, *mo nighean donn*. Forever and a day, I shall always love ye."

"Ye know I love ye the same."

Her whispered reply made his heart swell. But he didn't miss the sadness or the regret in her tone. He still hadn't convinced her to stay. Sweeping her up into his arms, he moved deeper into the trees. The pines became so thick that barely a sliver of moonlight made it through them. Years of pine needles covered the ground, offering a pallet softer than any pillow. He knelt and lay her down, settling beside her to hold her as long she would allow.

"I love ye," he whispered. Yet even in the shadows, he could see more tears shining in her eyes. "Please dinna cry."

"I canna help it." Her attempt at a smile failed. Reaching up, she touched his face with such a gentleness he shuddered. Her smile finally appeared, but it held no joy. Only a sad wistfulness. "Ye know the truth as well as I. Please accept it."

"I accept nothing. We will find our way." He caught hold of her hand, pressed a kiss to her palm, then held it to his heart. "I swear it. We will save Lilias and the clan, then spend the rest of our lives together." She had to know he meant it. Somehow, together, they would forge their way ahead.

"I must go back." She leaned up and nibbled a soft kiss across his bottom lip. "But we have tonight," she whispered. "And will have it to remember always."

For now, he would accept whatever she offered, then pray that by the rising of the sun, her mindset would change. She had to stay. Anything else would be unbearable. Without another word, he covered her mouth with his and fueled every touch, every precious caress, with the aching he felt that went far beyond the physical.

Her beauty, her scent, everything about her inflamed him. Except her modern clothes. Their strange fastenings infuriated him. Had women of the future devised these things to protect their virginity?

"Let me do it," she finally said, gently pushing his hands aside. Rising, she kicked off her boots and shucked her jacket. As she undid her shirt, she turned her back to him. "Do ye have a blanket?" she asked without turning around.

"Aye." How could he be so thoughtless? They might tolerate bare skin on pine needles for a bit, but not long. He fetched a blanket. While he was about it, he gave each of the animals an oatcake, knowing Kenzie would like that. Horse, ram, and dog accepted their meager feast. A small burn trickled nearby in case they needed water. The lass would appreciate that, too. He had to make her see that he would always take care of her and anyone or anything she cared about. She had to stay. No matter what.

When he returned, the sight of her naked and waiting for him struck him mute. Her long, lithe form. Skin like cream waiting to be tasted. For several beats of his heart, he forgot to breathe.

Kenzie folded an arm across her breasts, and the other crossed her body much lower. "Ye're staring, Mathias."

He spread one blanket across the ground and tossed the other close by. "It is yer beauty…" His words trailed off. He knew all he felt when he looked at her tempting form, but damned if he could put it into words. "Ye are a beauty like I have never seen," he finally said.

With a shy smile, she ducked her head, then knelt on the blanket.

Ridding himself of his own trappings, he joined her, kneeling in front of her. He framed her face with his hands. "I know we have no witnesses other than our beasts and the creatures of this wood," he breathed. "But on this night, I take ye as my wife. To love and protect. Honor and cherish. All the rest of my days."

Her bottom lip trembled. More of her tears threatened to overflow.

"Dinna cry, *mo nighean donn*." He slid a hand down the silkiness of her back, then nibbled the lightest of kisses across her quivering mouth. "I swear all will be well, my love," he whispered against her mouth. "I beg ye. Grant me the joy of accepting me as yer husband."

"Here in this wood," she whispered, halting when her voice broke. She started again, smoothing her hands up his bare chest and leaning in to wrap her arms around his neck. "Here in this wood, as all living things in this place and time shall witness, I take thee, my beloved Mathias, as my husband." Tears escaped, tumbling down her cheeks. "I swear to take yer memory and yer love with me now and forevermore. Whether we be separated by time, space, life, or death. I swear to always love ye and know myself to be yer wife."

"Such a sad vow," he rasped as he tightened his embrace.

"Love me, Mathias," she begged so softly he barely heard.

Without another word, he lowered them both to the blanket and did exactly as his lady bade him.

CHAPTER TEN

S HE HAD NEVER imagined that spending the night on a bed of pine needles could be both so wonderful and terrible at the same time. Mathias lay spooned against her back. The warm protection of his arm curled around her as she watched the sun peep above the horizon. Its golden beams slipped through the trees like a thief coming to steal away the last few moments of the night she would never forget. The night she had spent loving a man who, once she returned home, would have been dead for over eight hundred years. Suddenly, she very much hated time and its cruel ways.

He shifted, tightening his hold as if overhearing her thoughts. They had loved, argued, then loved some more. A sad smile came to her as she smoothed her hand across the worn plaid he had spread across the ground for their bed. She would remember this pattern for the rest of her life. If she couldn't find this tartan in any shops or online, she would find a weaver and have them recreate it. No matter the cost. It would be something of his, and she would cherish it forever.

"Be still, woman," he murmured, nuzzling through her hair until he found her bare shoulder and started nibbling. "If ye insist on wiggling," he rumbled between nips and bites, "ye force me to take matters into my own hands." And then he did, fondling her breasts as though he worshiped them.

The man had the power to make her want him again, no matter how recent their lovemaking. She would be so lonely once she left. *Not now,* she silently scolded, knowing if she dwelled on what lay ahead, she risked breaking down again and ruining what would be their last bit of loving. Instead, she wiggled her backside against the long, hard length of him and pressed his hands tighter to her breasts. "Dinna make promises ye're not willing to keep," she dared, trying to sound as lighthearted as she could.

With a groan, he countered her dare with a thrust that returned him to where he belonged. Slow and artful, he slid in and out with more intense caressing that made her forget everything except him. She surrendered to the wonderful, fiery bliss. Legs entwined, their ancient dance increased in fervor until they both shouted with delicious agony, frightening the birds singing their morning songs.

Still breathing hard, Mathias trailed more kisses along her shoulder. "I canna think of a more delightful way to start the day. Every morning will be just so. I swear it."

She pushed up on her elbows and tried to shame him with a scolding look. "Ye promised. Ye promised me ye understood."

All joy left him, leaving behind a pained scowl, an expression that tore at her heart and made what she had to do even more difficult. "A man will promise anything when he hopes to keep his dear one in his life."

"I messed up yer life when I stepped out of that cave," she reasoned for what had to be the hundredth time. "If I stay here and we canna protect Lilias or save yer clan or both, ye will grow to hate me. Resent me for destroying all ye once cherished." She shook her head. "I could never bear that." She touched his face, willing him to understand. "I could never bear looking in yer eyes and seeing nothing but hate."

"I could never hate ye."

"Aye, ye could." She rose from their woodland bed, scooped

up her clothes and boots, and turned toward the spring. "We should go soon. There's no telling what the MacPhersons might try next."

"Ye are killing me, m'love. Ripping my heart from my chest and grinding it to dust."

"We must go soon, Mathias." She ignored his pleas, fighting to harden herself against anything he might say. She had to leave. For so many reasons. Lilias and the clan. The bloody MacPhersons who wanted her dead. And she felt certain they wouldn't stop at her. She knew they would do their best to kill Mathias, too. Her family and friends back home. They were probably searching for her all over the Highlands by now.

But most of all, she had to go back because of the last argument she had given. If she stayed and it all went wrong, she couldn't bear watching their love sour and seeing nothing but resentment in his eyes every time he looked at her. She had seen that happen to a friend who had tried to change the one he loved and mold her into something she wasn't. Their relationship had turned very bad.

"Nothing I can say will change yer mind or make ye see reason?"

A sigh escaped her as she scrubbed with the icy water from the burn. "No, Mathias. Ye will find I am a verra stubborn woman once I make up my mind." Yanking on her clothes, she made it a point not to look at him. She didn't need to. She knew what she'd see. A wonderfully fierce, glowering man who she loved more than she ever thought possible. For his sake and the sake of those he cared about, she had to leave.

Mathias shook the woods with the throaty roar of an enraged beast, then stomped off deeper into the woods.

The dog leaned against her and whined.

"He'll be fine," she whispered. "We all will." She crouched down and hugged him. "It's going to take a long time and hard work, but we'll be fine." Rubbing the animal's silky black ears, she kissed the top of his head then stood. When she turned around, she almost bumped into Mathias. "Bloody hell!" She punched him in the chest. "Are ye trying to startle me to death?"

"If ye insist on going back to that damned cave and leaving me, then I will take ye," he said through clenched teeth. "But know this—" He shook a finger so close it nearly hit her nose. "If ye enter that cave, I will know ye lied to me yet again and played me for a trusting fool. I will know ye never really loved me."

"That isna fair, Mathias."

"Neither is it fair for ye to make me love ye, then leave me forever."

She had never seen him like this before, and she hated it. He was heartbroken, bitter, and madder than hell. Even though her intentions were noble, his suffering made her feel lower than sheep dung. But she had to stay the course and remain strong. For his sake as well as hers. She prayed he would forgive her someday.

With a tip of her head toward the horse, she forced a calm she didn't feel. "Are ye ready to go, then?"

His shoulders sagged, and he bowed his head. She wanted to hold him, make him understand everything would be all right. But she didn't. In her heart, she doubted the truth of that herself.

Without another word, he strode to the horse and secured the rolled blankets back in their place behind the saddle. With one hand on the saddle and his gaze locked on the ground, he waved her forward. "Come."

"Hie, Brodie. Hie the ram," she forced out as she allowed Mathias to lift her up and set her in the saddle. He mounted behind her without a word and urged the horse northward at a fast clip that had the sheep and dog running to keep up.

She rested a hand on his arm. Her heart broke when he tensed beneath her touch. It didn't matter. This had to be done. "Would ye slow a bit, Mathias? Ramsay canna run the rest of the way to the cave. I know 'tis close, but it's still too far for him to run."

"As ye wish, m'lady." He slowed the horse's canter. "I figured the faster I got ye there, the happier ye'd be," he added with a coldness he'd never used before.

She decided she deserved that, so didn't rise to the bait. Just blew out a heavy sigh and forced herself to sit taller. Low, jagged mountains rose in the distance on either side. They stood like dusky blue sentries against the brilliance of the clear sky. The surrounding land rolled with gentle hills like the soft curves of a woman. Thickets of pine filled the area, along with bountiful clusters of gorse everywhere. At the sight of the spiny bushes, Kenzie bit her bottom lip and blinked against the threat of more tears.

Da's name for the gorse was *whin*. He had always teased Mama with the old saying, "when the whin is in bloom, kissing's in season." Mama would bring in a prickly branch or two and coax the yellow blooms into opening early, then kiss Da whenever he walked past them.

Kenzie pulled in a deep breath, remembering how she loved the blossoms' powerful fragrance that smelled like sweet coconut. It always made her think of Mama. From the abundance of swollen nubs on every bush they passed, the gorse would soon bloom of its own accord. She swallowed hard against a knot of emotions about to choke her. No matter how many of the yellow flowers filled the Highlands, there would be no more kissing for her. Not for a very long time—if ever.

Her heart fell as they arrived at the cave entirely too fast for her liking. She stared at it and failed at stopping the tears. A hitching sob shook her. Brodie and Ramsay took their places inside the opening, staring deeper within as if they knew it was finally time to go home.

Mathias dismounted, helped her down, then stepped back. Jaw tight and head bowed, he stood with both hands fisted so tight, his knuckles whitened.

She wanted to hold him one last time. More than that, she wanted to be held. But she didn't. Couldn't. She knew in her heart he would refuse. And that was his right.

"I do love ye," she managed to say. "I swear it." Tears choked off the possibility of saying anything more.

He didn't look up. Didn't speak. It was as though she hadn't said a word.

She understood. Hated it but understood. Joining the animals at the mouth of the cave, she motioned toward the narrow passage that was almost hidden behind a large slab of stone. "To the house, Brodie," she ordered, the command trailing off into a sob. "Hie to the house, lad," she repeated to ensure the dog understood she meant it.

The collie sprang into action. Ramsay then Brodie disappeared into the passage.

Kenzie took a step forward, then stopped and looked back.

Mathias had lifted his head. Her mighty warrior had come no closer, but he stood with a hand outstretched. "Stay, my love. I beg ye."

"I can…not," she sobbed. "I love ye." Her heart shattered into bits as she forced one foot in front of the other, deeper into the cave. Closer to the entrance of that damned tunnel. She rested a hand on the boulder that almost concealed the opening. Once she stepped through, there was no turning back.

Footsteps pounded behind her. Mathias spun her around and yanked her into his arms. "I had to hold ye one last time," he rasped. "One last time."

She clung to him, her keening sobs echoing through the cave and beyond.

With more tenderness than she had ever known, he held her as she cried. Then, gentle as a caress, he set her out of his arms and stepped back. "I will love ye 'til time is no more." With a jerk of his head toward the passage, he said, "Now go. God be with ye."

She forced herself to do as he said. It was best for both of them. One hand on the boulder, the other on the edge of the tunnel's wall, she paused. Brodie and the sheep were probably already back in the twenty-first century by now. At least, she hoped so. What if the cave didn't take them back? Closing her eyes, she fought away the terrible thought. No. It would take them back to the safety of home. They would find their way. Animals always knew what to do. They were so much cannier than people, relying on instinct and what they felt. No matter what. They didn't give a whit what anyone else thought. They did what they did, and all else could just whistle in the wind. It sometimes cost them their lives—especially when the people they loved and trusted turned out to be ignorant fools. But they still did what their hearts bid them.

Then it hit home. The stark realization. The truth.

"I canna do this," she whispered. Hands sliding down the stone walls, she sank to her knees. Now, not only was her family forever gone but so was her precious wee dog. "I canna go," she sobbed, bowing her head and rocking forward and back like a lost child.

Mathias knelt beside her and pulled her back into his arms. Stroking her hair, he shushed and rocked as she mourned all she would never see again. "Thank God," he whispered when she finally quieted. "Thank God in heaven above that ye stayed."

"At least they will be safe, aye?" With a hitching sniff, she pressed her cheek harder against his chest, his tunic soaked with her tears. "My brothers are probably at my house. They'll find Brodie and Ramsay and take them in. D'ye not think so?"

"Aye, m'love." He kissed her forehead. "I feel certain of it."

Drained as if she had chased sheep all over the Highlands, Kenzie plopped to her bum, sitting with her back against the rock wall. "Can we rest here for a bit?" she asked, leaning forward to cradle her head in her hands.

"Aye, lass." Mathias settled down beside her. "We can stay here as long as ye like." He brushed her hair out of her face, then pulled her over to lean against him. "Try to sleep, dear one. Escape the pain for a while, ye ken?" After another kiss, he added, "Ye're safe now, love. Here in my arms, I will keep ye safe forever. I swear it."

IN ALL HIS days, he had never known such happiness. He trailed Kenzie's soft, dark tresses through his fingers, smiling down at the precious woman, so exhausted from the battle she had just waged with herself. Curled up against him, her head propped on his thigh, she dozed. Just as he had bade her. He almost laughed out loud. This was the first time since they had met that she had actually done as he asked.

Leaned back against the inner wall of the cave, Mathias stared outside, not seeing anything but his wonderings. What should he do now? Kenzie's safety came first. He doubted they had seen the last of the MacPhersons. And then there was the weak-minded Stronach and power-hungry Bhaltair to deal with. Lilias must be saved as well. He wasn't certain he could protect his clan from their failing chieftain or Bhaltair's greed. His people might have to tend to those matters themselves. But Lilias, he would save. Kenzie would demand it, and so would his conscience.

Apt at stealth and battle, especially when it came to thieving, Mathias sorted through all that had to be done. A solid plan fell into place. An abandoned croft lay within a day's ride from here. Still on Stronach land, but long since forgotten by anyone in the clan. Southwest of the cave, it was. A decent cottage, deserted but solid. Located close to the northern tip of Loch Shiel. The last he'd seen of the place, it wouldn't take much to make it bearable. They could live there for a little while. Kenzie would hide there while he stole back and kidnapped Lilias as easy as lifting a weaned calf from its mother. Then Lilias could stay with Kenzie and himself until it was safe to take the girl to an abbey. She'd be safe taking sanctuary on holy ground. He prayed the girl knew of one not too far away.

Kenzie shifted in her sleep, emitting a soft groan as she tried to get comfortable on the hard floor of the cave. Her eyelids fluttered open, but she didn't rise or look up at him, just lay there staring straight ahead.

"Are ye all right, lass?" he whispered, fearing to speak too loudly lest he startle her.

"Nay," she responded ever so softly. "It will be a little while before I am all right again." She pulled his arm across her and hugged it tight. "I have to wrap my head around losing everything and yet gaining so much in one fell swoop."

He hadn't understood all that she said but got her general meaning. "How can I help, dear one?"

"Just love me."

"That will always be so."

She rolled and pushed herself to her feet, rubbing her shoulder as she walked outside the mouth of the cave. "What do we do now?"

His heart ached at the forlorn despair in her tone. The poor thing sounded like a lost bairn.

Hands shoved in her pockets, she turned to him. "We canna return to the keep. That madman will have me married to Bhaltair faster than grass through a goose."

"Grass through a goose?"

She gave him a sad smile. "Sorry. It's an old saying my father always used because soon as ye feed geese, they shite it out."

"I see." Mathias joined her in the sunshine, scanning the area to ensure all was still as it should be. They were too close to the MacPherson border for his liking. "Ye are right, though. We canna return to the keep. At least, not yet."

"What do ye mean *not yet*?" Scuffing the toe of her boot in the dirt, she shielded her eyes from the sun and looked up at him. "I smell a plot cooking. What's our next move?"

If he told her straight out, she'd fuss about being left behind at the cottage while he fetched Lilias. He'd stall a bit. Maybe a convincing argument would come to him. To put her off, he fetched some provisions old Annag had packed for them. Oatcakes and a small leather flask rather than the water bag. They had yet to toast their union. Digging deeper in the sack tied to his saddle, he discovered several small loaves of horse bread. "Forgive me, Roch, I didna see these last night. Looks as though Annag thought of ye, too." His horse accepted the offering with a grumbling of thanks.

Oatcakes in one hand, flask of whisky in the other, he returned to Kenzie. "We must toast our union before we do anything else."

Her lovely eyes narrowed, their hazel coloring shifting to a deeper green. "Why do I think ye're avoiding giving me an answer?"

A happy contentment tightened his chest. So, this is what life would be like with a woman who knew his every move before he even thought to make it.

"An oatcake for ye," he offered, then uncorked the flask with his teeth. He poured out the barest bit of the golden liquid on the ground. "An offering to bless our marriage, ye ken?"

Her lopsided smile encouraged him as she held up her oatcake. "And how shall we word our toast?"

"To a life filled with love and contentment for all our days." He bumped his oatcake to hers, then held the flask so she might drink.

She licked her lips after she swallowed. "That's much better than Bhaltair's swill."

Mathias grinned. "Old Annag's known for her whisky. The woman has the touch."

"Now, the details of your plan," she prodded while munching on her oatcake.

"I know of a place near Loch Shiel where ye'll be safe." He could already see the denial sparking in her eyes. It wouldn't be long before those sparks crackled into a blaze. "An abandoned cottage. It willna take too much toil to make us a temporary home of it." He shrugged. "Perhaps even a permanent one."

"And what about Lilias?" she asked, reaching for the flask.

"While ye remain hidden at the cottage, I shall return to the keep and fetch her. Slip her right out from under their noses." He braced himself for the full force of her storm.

She shook her head. "That willna be happening, and I canna believe ye even dreamed I'd go along with it. I willna cower away like a frightened lamb, while ye ride into danger and may or may not make it back to me." She pinned him with a furious scowl. "Are ye daft? One man against an entire keep? Sneaking Lilias away willna be like lifting a few cattle from an open glen. Did it not occur to ye that ye're sure to meet resistance?" She shook her head. "They willna trust ye when ye return without me. They'll be watching yer every move. We must come up with a better way."

Determined to remain patient and calm, he kept his tone even. He had to make her understand this plan was the *only* way. "Many in the guard are my close kin. They willna fight me with the full force of their vigor. Remember, I am their commander."

"How can ye know they willna fight ye?" She stared at him as if she thought him tetched. "Ye've no idea what they've been told while we've been away. Ye know Bhaltair. Would ye doubt he'd spread lies to win their allegiance? And that cowardly chief of yers would do the same. Ye know that as well as I."

Frustration mounted until he snorted. The woman made a fair point, but there was still no other way. He had to try it. "Have ye any better ideas?" Whilst it chafed him to even ask, he realized that his new wife was not some meek woman willing to go along with whatever he ordered. Not that he wanted such a mild-mannered lass, but it wouldn't hurt if she agreed with him at least part of the time.

"Well?" he prodded, noting with some satisfaction that she appeared perplexed.

With a quelling slide of her eyes, she held up a hand. "Give me a minute. I'm thinking on it."

"Well, best be quick about it. We've tarried here as long as we dare. This isna far from the MacPherson border, ye ken?"

A calculating slyness curled her lips, sending a chill across him. "How about we head toward Loch Shiel? I'll think as we ride."

"So, ye accept the part I said about the croft?" He wanted to ensure he understood. 'Twas a rare thing for her to agree with him, especially with so little a fuss.

"Aye," she said, heading for the horse. "At least, for now."

That smacked of a future battle of wills, but he'd worry on that later. He lifted her into the saddle and seated himself behind her. Her warm curves pressed so close made him want her all over again. The aching filled him with lusty anticipation. *As soon as we're safer*, he promised himself. They had the rest of their lives to enjoy each other's embrace.

The farther they rode from the cave, the quieter Kenzie became. Mathias feared she was having second thoughts about staying. God help him if she changed her mind. He didn't think he could bear that. His worries increased when he hugged her tighter, and she didn't respond.

"What is it, love? Good or ill, troubling or not, I would hear it."

"I miss Brodie." She jerked a quick shrug as if ashamed of the confession. "I keep looking down and expecting to see him trotting along beside us." She ducked her head. "But he's not there."

He could tell by her breathing she was trying to shed her tears without his knowing. "He is safe now," he reminded quietly. "With yer brothers. Remember?"

"I hope so." She drew in a hitching breath and shuddered it back out.

Clouds rolled in, blotting out the sun as if mirroring his dear one's sorrow. Thunder rumbled in the distance. With no cover to be seen, they would both soon be soaked. He didn't worry about himself. But it had been a hard few days for Kenzie. A hearty drenching from a cool spring rain might inflict a chill upon her.

A copse of thick pines up ahead looked promising. It might not be perfect, but it would provide some shelter. With a little urging, the horse broke into a full gallop, then came to a halt in the center of the small wood just as the deluge started.

Mathias dismounted, helped Kenzie down, then grabbed his plaid from behind the saddle. Even though Kenzie had the cover of her odd surcoat's hood, he draped the cloth over them. The tight weave of the woolen cloth stood up well to the rain, slaking off most of the wetness. They huddled close under the drooping branches of the largest pine, watching the treetops sway in the wind. The horse stood near, skittish with all the thunder and lightning. Mathias patted its flank. "It's all right, lad. Hold fast. We've been through worse."

"It's midday. Surely, it'll blow itself out soon?" Kenzie shouted.

Mathias answered with a nod as the wind and rain raged even louder. At least it had come about during the day. If such a storm had struck at night, finding the tree cover might have been next to impossible. He watched his mount more than he watched the sky. The animal's agitated fidgeting would end as soon as the worst of the weather had passed.

"Yer horse—he's getting calmer."

A smile came to Mathias. Kenzie knew to watch the beasts, too. Within moments of the horse settling, the wind and rain both slacked to the regular spattering of any normal day in Scotland. Easy enough weather to endure while traveling.

"We can be on our way now, I think." He helped Kenzie back into the saddle, mounted behind her, then covered them with the plaid to shield them from the rest of the rain.

Huddled together in the folds of the weave made him even more aware of her warm, inviting scent—the beckoning fragrance of the woman he had enjoyed all last night and couldn't wait to enjoy again. It drove him mad. God's beard, he needed her, but he stayed the course and urged their mount onward. His self-control had to hold until they reached the cottage. They daren't stop out in the open. Not during the day. The need to protect his lady love far outweighed his unbearable yearning for her.

Kenzie tilted her head, turning toward him. "What is that? Behind us. Listen."

He pushed the plaid aside and inclined his head, then wheeled their mount around. Urgency and dread shot through him. "Damnation."

Even through the foggy haze of the drizzling rain, he made out several riders headed toward them at full gallop. At this distance, he couldn't make out who they were, and it didn't matter. He spun about again and spurred the charger onward. He wasn't vain enough to think he could fight that many men and win, but, by damn, he might outrun them. At least, he hoped to pull far enough ahead to find a place to hide. Roch was a fine warhorse, but carrying two, speed would not be their advantage for long.

"Who is it?" Kenzie shouted.

"I canna tell." He scanned the countryside, praying for some sort of cover. The River Lochy was to the right. The mighty Ben Nevis, its snow-capped peaks barely visible in the day's grayness, loomed in the distance to the left. He'd planned on crossing the river up ahead before reaching Loch Linnhe. But with the unknown men giving chase, he decided to cross now. They splashed over, then picked up speed again.

Kenzie pointed toward Loch Eil. "A ravine. Not too far. Just there beyond that tree line."

Mathias could tell his mount's stamina was waning. He allowed the horse to slow, steering him into the brush. The scrub would be more difficult, but it would also provide a bit of cover until they could shelter in the nearby ravine.

"If we walk alongside him, they willna see us so easily." Kenzie stole a frantic look back. "I dinna see them, but they're sure to be following. They werena so far behind. If we dismount, we willna be so high above the bushes, ye ken?"

Not convinced, Mathias jumped to the ground rather than argue. It was worth a try. He pulled Kenzie down, then shoved the plaid beneath the rope behind the saddle. His head still well above the tangle of saplings, bushes, and clusters of sedge, he kept watch. Hope left him as the outline of the riders became visible through the misting rain. Crouched as low as possible, he peered through the tangle of branches, tall grass, and weeds. His gut tensed.

The approaching men drew close enough to reveal themselves. It was Bhaltair and the guards who followed him like dogs trained to heel. Not a one of them would hesitate in killing Mathias if given half the chance. He pulled Kenzie down beside him, held the horse still, and prayed they would ride on past.

"There!" one of them shouted.

It appeared today was not a day for answered prayers.

CHAPTER ELEVEN

"WHY DID YE flee, Mathias?" Bhaltair called out. The taunting wickedness in his tone said he already knew.

"In the rain, I couldna see if it was friend or foe giving chase." It wasn't a lie, and Bhaltair understood which he was. Mathias had never liked the man nor had Bhaltair ever liked him. Peace between them had never been an easy thing.

With both hands resting atop his pommel, Bhaltair leaned and inclined his head toward Kenzie. "I see ye recovered my bride. For that, I am grateful." After an exaggerated scan of the area, he gave Mathias a quizzical tilt of his head. "But why have ye ridden so far south? Did the storm blow ye off course on yer way back to the keep?"

"Maybe she clubbed him and knocked his sense of direction off," one man suggested. Another snickered.

"Bring her to me," Bhaltair ordered. "A wife should ride with her husband. Not with another man."

"I am not yer wife," Kenzie said.

"Dinna rise to his bait," Mathias warned under his breath. "'Tis what he wishes."

"Ye are not my wife *yet*," Bhaltair corrected. With a flick of his hand, he again inclined his head in her direction. "Fetch her to me. Now."

"Run!" Mathias unsheathed his claymore from its scabbard at the front of his saddle.

Kenzie turned and dove, disappearing into the bush.

"After her!" Bhaltair barked. Two of his men dismounted and gave chase, giving Mathias and his weapon a wide berth.

"Leave her be," Mathias ordered Bhaltair. "She isna for the likes of ye."

With a laugh that smacked of malice, Bhaltair unsheathed his own two-handed sword and pointed it at Mathias. "She is to be mine just as Lilias will be yers." He motioned the remaining four men forward. "Take him and tie him to his horse." A devious smile quirked a corner of his cruel mouth. "Beat him as much as ye like, but dinna kill him. The Stronach has yet to realize this one isna the best choice as our next chieftain. We must not hurt our chief's wee pet—at least not just yet."

The guards eased down from their saddles. One hefted a battle-ax. The next a club. The last two advanced with swords raised. They spread out, creeping toward him like hunters going in for the killing of an injured beast.

"Afraid to fight me?" he shot at Bhaltair. Five men to one were slim odds. He preferred one-to-one. But knowing Bhaltair's explosive temperament, he hoped to goad the man into action. Once he bested Bhaltair, the man's traitorous guards would yield as well.

Bhaltair gave him a chilling smile. "Nay, my friend. We will have our own battle in due time. Ye will see."

Off in the distance, a man screamed in pain. "Help!" came his pitiful cry. "She…she's broke my leg! I'm caught in the rocks!"

The guards advancing on Mathias stopped and looked back at Bhaltair.

"Leave him to die," Bhaltair snorted out. "I have no use for a lame warrior."

"Ye follow a man who thinks so little of ye?" Mathias taunted. "One who willna even carry his men from the battlefield?" Seeds of doubt planted in Bhaltair's men could work to his advantage. "I am yer commander. Not that cold-hearted bastard ye follow. Ye waste yer fealty on him."

The man who had chased after Kenzie howled out a string of obscenities, making the rest of the guards pause again. Mathias seized the opportunity. If five against one were the odds, then so be it. He took down the closest man, then swung the mighty blade and slashed through the next. Their deaths were regrettable but necessary. His beloved Kenzie came first. Dodging a blow from the battle-ax, he kept the man with the club in his peripheral vision. The bastard thought to work his way around and knock him in the head. Mathias smiled. What a fool. With another hefting swing of his long-bladed claymore, the club fell from the guard's hands as he sagged to the ground.

One left. Then Bhaltair and the demon who stalked Kenzie. He sidestepped the blade of the ax again, then took off its bearer's head. Only Bhaltair and the last guard now. As he advanced, Bhaltair smiled and nodded toward the river. Mathias stole a quick glance. His heart sank to his gut.

The guard had captured Kenzie. With a burly arm around her waist and a blade at her throat, he shoved and wrestled her toward them. Blood covered his hands and arms. A trio of deep scratches ran from one of his eyes down to his jawline. His other eye was already swelling shut, and he sported a bloody nose.

Even though the situation was dire, Mathias's heart swelled with love and pride. His precious one had given a good fight.

"Sword on the ground, Mathias," Bhaltair ordered. He tossed a rope to the man holding Kenzie. "Bind her wrists and ankles. Gag her if ye wish."

"I'll be gagging her all right," the guard growled as he shoved her to the ground and twisted her arms behind her back. "Witch bit me!"

Bhaltair laughed, but the sound held no humor. "Bed play with this one will be enjoyable."

Mathias lunged, but halted as the guard jammed his blade

back to Kenzie's neck.

"Kill him, Mathias," she shouted as the guard yanked her head back, exposing her throat even more. "They willna hurt me."

"Draw the wench's blood," Bhaltair ordered. "Show her how wrong she is."

"No!" Mathias retreated a step, knowing Bhaltair valued no life other than his own. "Dinna harm her."

Bhaltair chuckled. "Ye know me well, old friend." His smug gaze slid back to the guard struggling with Kenzie. "The day grows old. Get her gagged, tied, and thrown over my saddle, so ye can take care of that one." He sheathed his sword but drew a dagger from his boot and showed the blade to Mathias. "Ye will allow yerself tied, or I will gut her like a deer in front of yer verra eyes."

"I will kill ye for this." Mathias itched to yank the bastard out of the saddle and snap his neck. Kenzie's muffled cursing stayed his hand. The fear in her eyes as the guard slammed her belly down in front of Bhaltair sent a raging jolt of fury coursing through his veins. He would kill them both if it was the last thing he did. "And I swear, I will kill ye slow."

Bhaltair rewarded the threat with a smug chortle and wedged the dagger's point in Kenzie's ribs. "I doubt ye get to keep that oath, old friend." He gave a curt nod to the guard. "I have changed my mind. Gather all the horses and tether them to yer own." With a glance at those who had died, he twitched a disinterested shrug. "Their kin can come here to recover them or leave them for the birds. I care not which." He pointed the dagger at Mathias. "Tie that one to the back of my saddle. He can walk behind me like the animal he is." With a tilt of his head, he smiled. "'Tis naught but a quick march to the keep. Aye, Mathias?"

Mathias clenched his teeth and remained silent as the man tied his hands, then secured the rope as ordered. He toyed with the idea of knocking Bhaltair from the saddle once they got going but cast it aside as he noticed the whoreson kept the point of his blade stuck into Kenzie's side. All it would take would be one hard thrust, and Bhaltair knew Mathias would know that.

He jogged behind the bastard's horse, trying to envision what lay ahead, but failed. As he watched his dear one bouncing head down across Bhaltair's saddle, he wished she had gone through that damn tunnel. Even though her loss would have killed him, at least she would have been safe and back in her family's arms by now.

Stronach Keep's towers loomed into view just beyond the River Loy's tree-lined banks. Bhaltair slowed his mount's cantering pace to a leisurely walk. It wasn't out of sympathy for his prisoner's winded state, but because the wily fox didn't wish to have too many lies to sort. The arseworm would be sore pressed to explain dragging the next chieftain of Clan Stronach behind his horse, as well as why their new seer traveled thrown across his horse, bound and gagged.

Before they reached the bridge, Bhaltair halted and frowned at his guard. "We best gag him as well." He twisted in the saddle and pointed his blade at Mathias. "Dinna fight him, or she bleeds, ye ken?" He jabbed the knifepoint hard enough into Kenzie's side to make her jerk.

Biting down on the knotted cloth between his teeth, Mathias promised himself again that Bhaltair would die by his hand. And in the slowest way possible. They crossed the bridge and passed through the gate, coming to a stop in front of the stable.

"Master Mathias," Rabbie called out as the men and women of the clan gathered to see what sort of prisoner Bhaltair had captured.

"Dinna speak to him," Bhaltair ordered. "Not before we have cast the demons out."

"Demons?" The word took on a life of its own, repeated again and again by those clustered in the courtyard.

"Aye, demons!" Bhaltair repeated louder. "The bloody Mac-Phersons set a curse upon them both, chaining their souls to the devil's own forces. Dinna get too close. We must exorcise them."

Mathias rolled his eyes, then fixed Rabbie with an imploring stare. The boy knew better. He knew what a liar Bhaltair could be.

"See?" Bhaltair pointed at him with the dagger. "He canna control his tongue nor his actions." He dismounted and waved for more guards. Several stepped forward, and another pair descended from the rooftop walkway of the gatehouse. "Take him to the dungeon to protect him from himself. Be sure and shackle him, ye ken? Wrists and ankles."

"And her?" one of them asked.

"Take care with that one!" Bhaltair's henchman warned. "Look what them demons gave her the power to do to me."

Another low murmuring rippled through the crowd as he turned and showed the onlookers his face.

"Lock her in the tower," Bhaltair ordered. "At least until Lady Lilias or the priest can pray the evil out of her." He pulled a heartbroken face that no one who knew him would believe. "I canna wed the lovely lady until we cleanse her of the MacPherson's evil curse."

Mathias watched them carry her away—she'd be taken to a room in the tower. One man grasped her shoulders while another held her feet. She twisted and fought to no avail. Her captors eyed her as if she had just risen from the deepest levels of Hell. At least Bhaltair's lie would make them fearful of her. Better than naming her a witch and putting her to death.

Another four guards treated him just as gingerly as they dragged him down to a cell dug into the tunnels that honeycombed the lowest level of the keep. Concern and confusion filled their eyes and hardened the lines of their face. One of them hung back a little longer than the others.

"I'll send Eumann to ye," the man whispered as he replaced the rope bindings with irons and removed the gag. "We know better than to trust Bhaltair."

Mathias lowered his chin enough for the man to see he understood. He wouldn't speak. Not yet. Not until he knew for certain how many and who could be trusted. As Kenzie had said earlier, Bhaltair could have filled the keep with lies before leaving to find them. He had noticed that none in the courtyard seemed surprised about the man's announcement that Kenzie was to be his wife.

Rubbing his rope-burned wrists, he shuffled back and forth across the slimy floor of the small enclosure. His chains clinked and rattled, making the chamber even more stifling. At least they had left several torches burning. The flickering glow lit the small square cut in the iron-banded wood of the cell door. They usually plunged prisoners into the darkness the bowels of the keep offered. He had to figure a way out, and fast. He wasn't certain of the entirety of Bhaltair's vile plans, but he knew the man wouldn't wait long to put them into play.

"Mathias?"

"Eumann!" Mathias rushed to the door's tiny window. "What lies has Bhaltair spread?" He could better devise his own plan by knowing all of Bhaltair's evil actions. Eumann's grim look tensed him even more. He clutched the edge of the window tighter. "Tell me. All of it."

"The bastard's turning the Stronach's mind. Making him question the choice of ye as *tanist*."

"I dinna give a damn about being chief." He kept his voice low in case someone listened from the shadows of the outer passage. "All I care about is Kenzie. We spoke our oaths before God. She is my wife, Eumann."

"And that's the only reason Bhaltair wants her." The man paused, glanced to the left, then to the right. "I dinna ken what the bastard means to do with sweet Lady Lilias if he convinces the chief to place him in yer stead. But it canna be good." His rounded jaw flexed. "I'll kill that bastard with my bare hands if he touches her."

"I have to get out of here and save them both." His original plan of escaping to the abandoned croft would still work, as long as he killed Bhaltair first. Then the Stronach could do whatever he wished with the chieftainship. Clan Stronach either would or wouldn't go on without him. He didn't give a damn which.

Eumann stole another look up and down the passage, then lowered his voice even more. "Ye understand that I'll be watched. Bhaltair knows where my loyalties lie." A wily grin plumped his round face. "But there is another who no one ever questions." He arched a scarred brow and nodded. "Can ye guess of whom I speak?"

"Annag." Everyone both feared and admired the strange old woman the Stronach had brought into the clan all those years ago. Not only was she an amazing healer and a fine maker of drink, but she knew things before they ever happened. Much like Kenzie had known about the Duke of Brittany's demise.

"Aye," Eumann agreed with another nod. "And she hates Bhaltair. Spits on his feet whenever he gets within range."

Mathias chuckled, remembering a time he'd seen her do just that. "Ask her to come. Tell the guards that Annag knows how to break curses and send demons back to Hell."

"It'll be done." The warrior blew out a heavy breath. "It willna be the same here without ye. Perhaps, I shall move on as well."

"I havena escaped yet," Mathias reminded. "But ye're welcome to come when we go. Lilias, Kenzie, and myself."

"Where Lady Lilias goes, I go as well." He stepped back from the door. "I best find Annag."

"Thank ye, my friend."

Eumann thumped his fist to his chest, then disappeared from view. His muffled steps faded off into the passage.

KENZIE STARED OUT the tall, slender arrow slit. Jaw clenched. Fingers drumming on the cold stone wall. Her captors had left little in the room that could be used as a weapon. Nothing more than a pile of straw in the corner covered with a ratty blanket and a chipped bit of crockery for a chamber pot. She turned from her narrow view of the outside world and eyed the squat earthenware vessel. It might be heavy enough to knock a man out, but she'd have to hit him just right. If her target happened to be tall, she'd be hard-pressed to send him to dreamland with just one whack. It also depended on whether more than one guard at a time brought food and water—assuming they provided her with food and water. She wouldn't put it past Bhaltair to leave her here to starve to death.

The heavy clank of the bolt unlatching the door spurred her into action. She snatched up the pot and backed up against the wall. Poised for the strike, she waited for the iron-banded portal of thick oak planks to swing open.

"Kenzie?"

She blew out the breath she hadn't realized she held and lowered the pot. "I'm surprised they allowed ye to see me, Lilias."

The lass clamped her lips shut in a tight line and cast an exaggerated side-eyed glance behind her. A silent warning.

Kenzie stepped back as the clan priest, a tall, bumbling man with a nose bigger than his body, marched through the door. He held a large wooden cross and worn prayer book as though they were shields. She noted the Father had allowed Lilias to enter first. What a coward. It shouldn't take much to run him off.

With a yodeling screech, she dove for the holy man, clawing and biting like a wild animal. "Only women may enter here!" She shrieked as she beat him back out the door, screaming unintelligible gibberish to make him flee even faster. "Enter again and die in here with us!" she warned with an ominous, theatrical wheezing. She'd done that in a Samhain play once while still in school. It had gone over quite well with the audience.

"Blessed Virgin protect us!" the frightened cleric shouted from the hall. "Shut it quick! Dinna let her escape!"

"But the Lady Lilias?" the guard said. "What about her?"

"Shut it! The Lady Lilias be in God's hands!"

The attendant yanked the door closed and slammed the bolt back into place.

"I wouldha thought they'd protect their chief's daughter better," Kenzie observed as she plopped the pot back on the floor and dusted off her hands. "Welcome to my chambers, Lilias. Forgive me if I dinna offer ye a chair."

Lilias pressed a finger to her lips and motioned for Kenzie to follow as she went to a spot farther from the door. After a glance back, she leaned close and whispered, "Have they hurt ye, dear friend?"

"Only my pride." Kenzie propped a shoulder against the wall. "Are ye all right? Has that idiot done anything to hurt ye?"

"Which idiot?" Lilias asked so innocently that Kenzie couldn't help but smile.

"Bhaltair."

The lass shook her head. "Nay. Not yet. But I worry about the time he spends with Father." She leaned closer. "I fear he means to take over the clan." After another glance at the door, she added, "I think he means to kill him."

"Mathias or yer father?" Kenzie wanted to be certain she understood.

"I fear Bhaltair means to kill them both." Lilias shuddered. Her thin frame swayed as she hugged herself. "And mayhap, the two of us as well. He is an evil man, Kenzie, evil to the core."

"We have to stop him."

"But how?" Hands clasped as though ready to drop to her knees and pray, Lilias's eyes filled with tears. "I have prayed and prayed, but no miracle has come."

"Sometimes, we have to make our own miracles, ye ken?" She wasn't certain how brave Lilias was. Even though the lass was a great deal more intelligent and mature than most knew, she still had led a sheltered life.

"What shall we do?" the girl whispered after another cautious glance at the door.

"I have no idea." Kenzie released a frustrated huff. "At least, not yet. Both Mathias and I need to be shed of this place and take ye with us."

Lilias bloomed with a relieved smile. "Ye willna leave me behind?"

"Of course not." Kenzie took hold of her hands and squeezed. "Ye're the sister I never had. I'd never leave ye to the likes of Bhaltair, and neither would Mathias. Ye know that."

"Be ye all right, Lady Lilias?" the guard called out without opening the door.

"I am well," Lilias answered without hesitation. "Still praying. Pray with me, aye? Pray for this evil to leave our keep."

"Aye, m'lady. I shall. Bang on the door and call out when ye've done all ye can and wish to retire to yer chambers."

"I'm impressed." Kenzie gave the lass a hug.

"Now, what do we do to escape?" Lilias whispered.

That was the quandary. Kenzie returned to the arrow slit, staring down at the treetops on the other side of the river. How could they all escape? A documentary she'd watched about medieval prisoners came to mind. "Castles have secret passages, aye? Tunnels inside the walls? Do ye know about any of those? We could sneak out that way."

"Stronach's only tunnels are beneath the keep, and they often flood with the river so close." Lilias's eyes flew open wide. "They put Mathias down there. The dungeon is dry now, but it willna stay that way long. Not with the spring rains and snowmelt coming off the mountains."

Kenzie held up a hand. "We have to stay calm," she insisted, more to herself than Lilias. Panic was just as deadly as any weapon. "We'll just have to get him out of there. And soon." She bounced the heels of her hands against the stones. "There aren't any corridors behind the walls of the upper levels? None?"

"Nay, dear friend. Not any."

The bolt rattled on the other side of the door, then clanked as it slid aside again.

"I said I wasna ready!" Lilias shouted. "Dinna enter! The demons could take hold of yer soul."

"Demons fear me," announced a gravelly voice that Kenzie had heard only once before. Old Annag gimped into the room, her twisted form bent double as she clung to her staff with both hands. Once she made it completely through the entrance, she stamped the knobby cane. "Dinna open that door again unless I command it, ye ken?"

"Aye, Mistress Annag. I willna open it. I swear."

"Then close yer maw along with that door," the scowling crone barked.

The door slammed shut, and the bar slid back in place.

With a wily grin, the old woman straightened, rubbing the small of her back as she did so. "The older I get, the harder it is to hold that position."

"Ye're not a cripple?" Kenzie stared at the matron moving around the room as spry as Lilias or herself. She also noted that Lilias didn't seem in the least surprised. "Ye knew?"

"I learned long ago to question nothing about Annag."

"I have a proposition for ye," Annag said in a hushed voice. She gave Kenzie a fierce up and down look. "Ye've proven yerself to be quite the fighter and cannier than most." Head tilted, she frowned. "Although, when ye ran the first time, why did ye not go back through the cave?"

"Why dinna ye tell me yer thoughts on the matter since ye seem to know so much?" Kenzie hadn't decided if Annag was friend or foe. It paid to be careful where you placed your trust—especially in the thirteenth century.

Annag grinned, pulled her clay pipe from the pocket tied to her belt, and placed the stem between her teeth. "Ye see? Cannier than most." She ran her hand deep into another pocket and frowned. "Bloody hell. I've mislaid me tinderbox again." Pointing her pipe at Kenzie, she gave a chilling smile. "I dinna suppose ye've a lighter or some matches on ye?"

Kenzie blinked. Twice. Unsure whether Annag had just made

a very twenty-first century reference or the stress of the past few days had caused her to hallucinate. "Beg pardon? I dinna think I heard ye quite right."

Annag's smile plumped her lined face, making her look years younger. "Oh, ye heard me right, lass." She gave a regal dip of her chin. "Allow me to introduce m'self properly. Professor Anna Flannagan, Dean of Medieval Studies. University of Edinburgh." With a reminiscent chuckle, she added, "At least, I was in 1979. I'm sure they have replaced me by now." She cocked her head to one side. "Ye wouldna have been a student there, would ye? What year are ye from?"

"2019," Kenzie repeated, struggling to process it all. "Why did ye not go back? Decide to stay and research yer specialty firsthand?"

Annag waved away the question with a snort. "Research firsthand? Are ye daft?" She shook her head and puffed on her cold pipe. "Nay, lass. I was sixty-five years old when I came through and found myself labeled a witch, tortured until I thought I'd never walk again, and sentenced to death by drowning. The Stronach saved me, but not without a price. I have been his prisoner nigh on fifteen years now. His *seer*. For a long while, I was too crippled to make it back to the cave. Now, I'm just too old." She shrugged. "Besides, after your arrival from the twenty-first century just fifteen years later, I now know that time doesna move in parallel linear layers. The stack of timelines must shift and slide as only a quantum theorist might understand." A deep sigh escaped her as she frowned at something only she could see. "And I'm certain the life I once knew no longer exists even if I could find my timeline and reenter it."

Kenzie bumped her butt against the wall and slid down to the floor. She needed to sit after hearing all that. "This is too feckin' amazing to be believed."

"I suppose so." Annag squinted and shifted the stem of her pipe between her teeth. "Unless ye're the one living it, aye?"

"Aye." Kenzie pinched the bridge of her nose and massaged

the corners of her eyes. The day's events had made her head pound. Then she remembered. Annag had spoken of a proposition. She looked up at her. "Your proposition?"

One eye squinted shut, the crone pointed her pipe toward the arrow slit. "I can help ye escape. But I'll nay tell ye how unless ye swear to take me with ye. With the Stronach dying and cruel Bhaltair taking the chieftainship by force, life here at the keep willna be pleasant. Especially not for the likes of me. I hate that bastard, and the feeling's mutual."

"I'll be going, too," Lilias announced with an excited grin.

"And we dinna go anywhere without Mathias," Kenzie warned, wondering if the old woman would still cooperate.

Annag smiled and waved her pipe. "Ahh, now I understand why ye stayed."

"So, what is this plan of yers?"

"The Stronach ordered me to examine ye. See how deep the evil rooted in yer soul." She meandered back and forth across the small room, her pipe cupped in one hand. With a wink, she continued, "He seeks to replace me. Knows I'm of an age that most never reach and could die and leave him without a seer. His hope is ye can be redeemed to take my place."

"Okay." Kenzie wasn't sure where Annag was going with this, but at least it was a start. "So, what is yer plan?"

"Many believe that a baptism by full immersion three times expunges evil from the soul." The old crone watched Kenzie with a sly grin. "In the river. Beside the bridge. At sunset."

If the woman was plotting what Kenzie thought she was plotting, it just might work. "Go under three times but only come up twice?"

Annag nodded, her sly grin becoming a proud smile.

"Ye mean to drown them?" Lilias asked a little too loud.

Both Annag and Kenzie shushed her.

"If we're next to the bridge, the third time Annag souses us, we'll swim underwater and hide. Since it'll be at sunset, the failing light will not only keep us from being seen but also delay them in searching for us until morning. By then, we can be far away." Kenzie liked the plan, but there was one slight problem. One man. Three women. They'd need at least two horses. "What about horses? How will we manage that?"

Annag's smile faded into a studious frown. "Well, damn. I didna think that far ahead."

"Rabbie can be trusted," Lilias offered.

"I agree, but Bhaltair and the guards would think it strange for a pair of horses to be saddled and waiting outside the keep." Kenzie rose from the floor and paced alongside Annag. "But we must have horses. Or maybe a wagon. We canna travel far enough nor fast enough on foot."

The guard banged on the door. "Lady Lilias! Mistress Annag! Himself has sent for the both of ye. Ye must come out at once, aye?"

"Crouch over there on the straw and act crazed," Annag whispered. "Lilias and I will figure a solution for our transportation. Dinna ye worry."

"Get word to Mathias," Kenzie whispered back. "Maybe he'll know of a way."

The heavy bolt clanged, and the door creaked as it eased open.

Kenzie dove for the straw and started flailing about as if possessed by demons.

"Stay back!" Annag hunched forward, resuming her charade of the crippled old hag. "'Tis worse than we feared. Come, Lady Lilias. More must be done for this poor soul, but it canna be done here."

Lilias crossed herself and bowed her head, clasping her hands to her chest.

Kenzie stole a peek at the guard to see if he believed what he saw. The hulking man had paled and looked ready to tuck his tail and run. Good. The more they feared her, the more rumors would spread, and they could use that to their advantage. As the door closed, she rose and brushed herself off, then returned to her narrow view of the world beyond. Annag's plan was good but incomplete. She didn't care if she had to stand at this arrow slit 'til a new day dawned. One way or another, she would figure a way to guarantee them some horses.

CHAPTER TWELVE

"How am I expected to examine the man's soul if I canna see him?"

Mathias smiled. He knew that voice. It was the old crone everyone feared. He rose from the corner nearest the door, the only dry spot left in the cell. The line he had scraped across the floor to mark the advance of the seepage had disappeared long ago. Dark water rippled across the room, determined to swallow the space. By the end of the day, the cell would be fully engulfed.

"Open this door at once!" Annag banged her staff against it. "Himself has ordered it. I must see if I can save this man."

"Bhaltair willna like this," the guard said. He added a stream of low grumbling Mathias couldn't make out, but rattling keys told him the man feared Annag more than he feared Bhaltair.

The door swung open, revealing the woman's hunched silhouette in the torchlight. Without a word, she hitched her way inside, then sidled around and twisted her neck to aim her scowl at the guard. "Water in the cell, and ye've nay moved him?"

"Canna be helped," the man muttered. "Always floods this time a year. It willna get deep enough to drown him."

"Come out here, boy." Annag backed out the door, waving for him to follow. "I canna see worth a shite in that watery pit they've thrown ye into."

"Nay!" The guard blocked the door. "He must stay in his cell." After a fearful glance at Mathias, he bowed forward to look her in the face. "The demons, ye ken?"

"No demon dares to defy me." The old woman dipped her staff toward the other end of the corridor. "Get thee to the entrance and stand guard from afar, if ye're so afeared." After puckering a scowl at Mathias's wrists and ankles, she shook a gnarled hand toward them. "God's beard, ye coward. Can ye nay see the man is shackled? He'll nay get far unless the demons decide to melt those irons, ye ken?"

"Melt the irons?" the guard whispered with a horrified look.

"Aye," Annag assured, her tone ominous and knowing. "If the demons decide to free him, ye'll nay be able to stop him no matter what ye try. Ye best hope something can be done afore they decide yer soul might be just as tasty as his."

"I'll wait at the outer door." The man loped away. The thud of the heavy main door clanked shut, echoing back to them.

"Yellow-backed eedjit." Annag snorted out a sound that resembled a chuckle. Resettling her staff, she turned and settled her squinty-eyed scowl back on Mathias. "Well? Do ye enjoy standing in a cesspool? Get out here."

"I was enjoying the entertainment." He had never feared the strange old woman. Always thought her odd but never feared her. After a glance down the passage, he gave a polite bow. "I thank ye for answering my call for help so quickly, wise one." He knew it couldn't have been easy for the crippled elder to manage her way down to the dungeon. "I had hoped Eumann would help ye down here."

Annag's sparse white brows leveled into a perplexed frown. "Eumann? I've nay seen that wee lump today." She stabbed her staff in the dirt floor again, working her shoulders as though the dampness of the dungeon made her aching stiffness worse. "I came here at yer lady love's behest."

Alarm charged through him. Demanded he flee the prison, no

matter the chains or guards. "My Kenzie? Is she all right?"

A hint of a rare smile tugged at the corner of the old one's thin lips. "More than all right. Ye have done well with that one, lad. Found yerself a canny wee fighter there." The smile faded just as quick as it had flickered into view. "Unfortunately, she's nay canny enough." With a pained grunt, the crone shuffled her feet and stretched her back from side to side. "I canna stand this way any longer. It's too feckin' wet down here to hold this farce." After inspecting the torchlit passage, she moved to stand just inside the doorway of the cell and stretched straight and tall. "Bless my soul that feels better." One hand clutching the cane, she rubbed her back with the other. "They shouldna be able to see me as long as I stand right here." She shook a finger. "And if ye say a word to anyone, I'll say it's the demons making ye repeat such foolishness. Understand me?"

Struck dumb by Annag's miraculous shedding of her hobbled form, Mathias dipped his chin in an obedient nod. He had known the woman ever since her arrival at the keep, and she had never walked with her back straight in all that time.

"Things are not always as they seem, ye ken?" She winked. "Especially not with yer lady love."

The old one knew Kenzie's secret. He could see it glittering in her eyes. "Why did ye say that my dear one is nay canny enough?"

"Because she thought of horses but canna figure how we can get them." With both hands propped atop her staff, she swayed back and forth as though the motion helped her think. "And, of course, Lilias is of no help at all. I know she's nay as addled as some believe, but she's still a might on the naïve side."

"Naïve?"

"Aye." She gave him a stern tilt of her head. "Young. Innocent. Too trusting?"

"Ah." Mathias nodded. "But ye nay said how or why we would come to need these horses, my Kenzie thought of." He felt like he'd walked in on a battle plan and missed the most important part.

"True." Annag peeped out the doorway, peering in the direction the guard had gone. In a hushed voice, while still watching the corridor, she explained, "I shall tell Himself that the only way to rid ye both of yer demons is by baptism in the river." Pulling her gaze from the passage, she locked eyes with him. "Immerse Kenzie and yerself three times—at the same time. Beside the bridge. At sunset. Soon as I can arrange it." She glanced back at the flooded cell. "Sooner the better from the look of things. I doubt ye can tread water in chains. I shall speak to Himself this verra day. See if they can do something about moving ye before we make our escape."

An inkling of what she hinted at came to mind, but he had to be certain. Too much was at stake to do otherwise. "Why would we need horses after ye've soused us in the river three times? And what about the priest? Would he nay be the one to do it?"

Annag's wily smirk returned. "Priest's a coward and happy to let me and Lilias handle the exorcism." She tipped her head to one side, looking more pleased than he had ever seen her. "We need the horses to make our escape. Ye're a braw warrior, but I dinna think ye can carry three women on yer back across the Highlands."

"Three women?"

"Aye." She held up three fingers. "Yer lady love, wee Lilias, and myself."

"Kenzie, Lilias, and *yerself?*"

"Aye, and if ye keep repeating everything I say, this conversation will take so long the guard will return before we finish. Are ye nay listening to me, lad? Or are ye struck with wonder that mere women have thought up such a foolproof escape?"

"My Kenzie is many things but being *mere* isna one of them." A noise from the shadows stopped him. The main entrance. The rusty creak of the door opening, then closing. "Someone comes," he whispered.

"How can we get horses?" Annag hissed as she returned to

her bent, twisted stance.

"Eumann and Rabbie can be trusted," he shared just as the guard, Bhaltair, and Ruari passed beneath the first torch in the passage beside the outer door. He prayed they hadn't overheard them.

"Get back in yer cell!" Bhaltair yelled. He backhanded the guard, bouncing the man off the wall. "There'll be lashes for yer stupidity. I ordered that man caged."

Ruari walked with a club in one hand and smacked it against the other. "Two for a beating then, my future chieftain?"

"Shut it." Bhaltair stopped and held up a hand, his glare settling on Annag.

Mathias edged to one side as the wily crone hitched her way out of his cell. As soon as she cleared the door, he stepped back inside, forcing himself to play the helpless prisoner a while longer when what he really wanted was to wrap his chains around Bhaltair's throat and strangle the bastard.

"What say ye about his demons, Annag?" Disrespect and abhorrence dripped from Bhaltair's every word.

"They are mighty," the elder said, stamping her staff harder with every gimping move. "The only hope is drowning."

"Drowning?" Bhaltair repeated, latching tight to the word. Mathias didn't miss how the man's expression brightened. The devil looked hopeful as a bairn wishing for a special treat. His smirk shifted to Mathias. "I shall be happy to see that done."

"Him and the lass both," Annag interjected as she shoved past him. "Tomorrow. At the river. Lilias and I will do what we can to save them."

Bhaltair's dark scowl returned. "Mistress Kenzie ye said? Must ye drown her, too?"

"I dinna mean to drown them 'til dead, ye mindless bastard." She blew out another snort as she wobbled down the hall. "I mean to drown the demons. Baptism by immersion. Three times should do it."

"And Himself knows of this?" Bhaltair spat.

Annag halted and glared back at him. "Aye. He does. So, dinna entertain any foolish ideas, ye ken?"

"What does she mean by that?" Ruari asked.

"Blind leading the feckin' blind," she intoned as she ambled out the door.

"I mean to kill that woman one day," Bhaltair observed as he stared after her.

"Kill the seer?" The guard grunted as Ruari's club came down hard across his shoulders.

"Back to the main door," Bhaltair ordered. "See that we're nay interrupted."

Mathias wound his hands in his chains. He might be shackled, but he was far from helpless. He backed deeper into the cell until he stood shin-deep in the murky water. "Come into my parlor, old friend. If ye dare."

Bhaltair grabbed Ruari and shoved him inside. "Humble that whoreson. Take him to his knees."

For the first time since his imprisonment, Mathias was thankful they had stripped him of his boots to lock the irons around his bare ankles. He dug his toes into the cold sliminess of the earthen floor. Advantages in this fight were few, but at least he had some.

He smelled Ruari's fear as the man edged closer with his iron-banded club ready to strike. As soon as he cleared the door, Bhaltair slammed it shut.

"Bhaltair!" Ruari spun and faced the door, a fatal mistake.

Mathias lunged forward, slung the chains over the man's head, then yanked them taut under his chin.

"Bhaltair!" The vile churl gasped and choked as he lost his footing. The club tumbled from his grasp, splashing into the water. "Help me!" he wheezed, clawing at the chains cutting off his air.

"Live or die," Bhaltair challenged from the safety of the door's small window. "Choice is yers, ye backstabbing fool. I'll nay be soiling my hands with either of ye. Filthy Stronachs. I'll be changing the name of this clan to MacSorley once I am chief."

"Ye never had any sense," Mathias told Ruari as he twisted harder. With one last bone-crunching yank, Ruari's struggling stopped. He went limp, hanging from the chain around his throat. Mathias freed himself from the man and marched to the door. "Come inside, coward. I dare ye."

Bhaltair laughed. "Ye can rot in there with yer cousin. Should go faster with the water helping ye."

"What evil goes on here?"

Mathias's spirits lifted even more. He recognized that growl. Hew MacVail. Eumann's uncle. A more sour, ill-humored man couldn't be found, but he was honest and loyal to the grave. Loyal to Mathias and Eumann alone. Hew had made it clear years ago that he thought the Stronach a simple-minded fool.

"Answer, ye bastard!" Hew also hated Bhaltair.

"I'll ignore that, old man," Bhaltair snarled. "If ye must know, there's been a murder. Mathias killed his own cousin."

"No loss there," Eumann observed.

Mathias craned his neck to see if anyone else accompanied Eumann and Hew, although he had no doubt those two could handle anything Bhaltair tried. He also wondered if the guard at the door still lived. "Eumann!"

"Aye, Mathias," Eumann called out. "The Stronach bids us bring ye to him. Me and Hew brought along a few of our own to ensure ye make it there alive."

"The Stronach can judge him for murdering Ruari," Bhaltair claimed, big and loud, as though the meeting had been his doing. "Our chief willna stomach a killing within our ranks."

"Ye said he had demons," Hew growled. "They knew Ruari for the pitiful arseworm he was and claimed him."

"One of them demons got yer guard too, Bhaltair," Eumann added with a chuckle as he yanked the cell door open. He waved Mathias forward. When he caught sight of the flooded room, he grabbed hold of Bhaltair and banged him back against the wall. "Ye filthy bastard. I ought to put ye in there to rot with Ruari."

Bhaltair pulled his blade and held it against Eumann's back, ready to plunge it into a kidney. "I am now the Stronach's favored one. I'd tread lightly if I were ye. The guards are divided in their loyalties, and ye know it. Those who follow me outnumber yers."

Eumann released him, shoving away with a frustrated growl. "Maybe. For now. Things can always change." He drew his own bollock dagger and held it ready. "Come, Mathias."

"Good to see ye, old friend." Mathias shuffled forward, chains clanking cold and wet between his feet.

"He doesna sound possessed to me," observed one of the replacement guards from farther down the corridor.

"Verra impressive." Mathias gave Eumann an approving nod. Not another man could be wedged into the passage. Each of them dipped their heads to Mathias and thumped their fists to their chests. Mathias returned the sign of loyalty as best he could with his wrists in shackles. Pride surged through him.

"To the front with ye," Hew snarled with a flick of his blade at Bhaltair. "No way in Hell will I put my back to the likes of yerself."

With his dagger leading the way, Bhaltair pushed through the throng and exited the dungeon.

Ravenous for battle, Mathias scanned the number gathered. Perhaps they had enough to take a stand rather than make their escape and run. "How many stand with us?" he asked as the men filed out the door ahead of him.

"For once, Bhaltair didna lie," Eumann replied in a hushed a tone. "Far less than half remain loyal to ye. It appears the man has been verra busy seeding promises and lies for ages." He nodded at the group they followed. "But the best are ours. That is something."

"That is everything," Mathias confirmed even though his heart was heavy that so many had pulled their allegiance from him. He had thought himself a good and fair commander. Apparently, he had been mistaken. He found the revelation painful and humbling.

They made their way to the large common room. The chieftain's ceremonial chair had been removed from the dais and replaced with a couch overflowing with pillows and furs. The Stronach, more weak and frail than the last time Mathias had seen him, reclined among the cushions. If not for the chieftain's sharp-eyed gaze flitting here and there, Mathias would think the man already dead.

Bhaltair stood closest to the chief's head. The scoundrel must have bolted to reach the hall first in order to seed more scurrilous tales.

Annag sat at the other end of the couch. Her expression was unreadable as she clutched her staff with both hands as though that was her only way of not toppling from her chair.

With Eumann to his left and Hew to his right, Mathias came to a halt a few feet in front of the dais. Shoulders back, chin set at a defiant angle, he didn't speak. Instead, he waited for the Stronach and Bhaltair to make the first move.

"Why did ye kill yer cousin?" the chieftain asked, plucking at the covers with his bony, blue-veined hands.

"Did Bhaltair not order me sent to the dungeons for my protection?"

The Stronach's gaze slid to Bhaltair, then returned to Mathias. "Aye, he reported such to me upon yer return to the keep."

"In all yer wisdom, do ye consider a room knee-deep in water and a beating with a club as protection for me or for Bhaltair?" He resettled his stance and pointed at the floor. "If ye need proof, see the muck in my chains."

The chief didn't answer, just shifted his gaze back to Bhaltair and waited.

"It was the demons, my chieftain," the smooth-talking scoundrel lied. "Took over Ruari and made him crazed with uncontrollable fury." He gave a sad shake of his head. "I couldna stop him from attacking Mathias."

"Then the killing was justified," the Stronach rasped. He pulled in a deep breath and twitched his shoulders as though deeply pained. "What of the flooding? Why did ye nay move him?

He is still *tanist* to this clan until Annag claims him irredeemable."

Mathias could tell by the way the redness crept up Bhaltair's neck that the man was furious. Good. Hopefully, the devil would show his arse in front of one and all.

"I had gone to inspect the cell myself. Eumann and the guards arrived before I could give the order to move him." Bhaltair stood with his chest thrown out, proud of his tales.

"A bald-faced lie if there ever was one!" Hew growled. "That whoreson—" He shook a fist at Bhaltair. "That whoreson right there was standing outside the door laughing."

A commotion from behind the chief's dais drew Mathias's attention. His heart jolted, then rage flared hot and fierce as Kenzie, gagged and bound, with a guard on each side of her, shuffled forward to stand beside Annag. He started to go to her, but Eumann and Hew yanked him back.

"Easy now," Eumann hissed.

"We be outmanned," Hew rumbled under his breath.

"'Tis the demons," Annag announced as she rose from her chair. "They always go toward their own. More power together."

"He had those demons before now," the Stronach said with a hint of his former strength. He pointed a shaking finger at Mathias. "My Lilias is to be yer wife." With a careless glance at Kenzie, he added. "Not that one. She needs Bhaltair's iron will to tame her."

Mathias clenched his teeth, burning to bash the filthy leer from Bhaltair's face.

"That is why I must take them to the water and drown the wickedness from them," Annag proclaimed. Her chilling announcement shot uneasiness through the room. "The demons sow discord among us. We must oust them afore they gain complete control of this clan."

"Take them now! Drown them away," the chieftain ordered, clutching his furs closer to his chin.

"Aye," Bhaltair echoed with a knowing smirk. "Drown them now."

"It canna happen today," Annag explained without twitching an eye. "Tomorrow. Soon as the sun sinks below the horizon. The dark of the moon will assist me in banishing the evil from them."

"'Tis true, Father," Lilias said as she appeared in the archway, moving with the grace and certainty of a mature woman rather than the poor addled lass everyone thought her. "I have prayed on it, and the angels said we must do it as Annag says."

"Angels?" her father whispered. "Ye have had visions, child?" He floundered among the pillows, weakly struggling to sit higher. "Come here, lass." He held out his hand. "Come, let me look into yer eyes."

She went to her father and knelt in front of him.

The man managed a trembling smile. His weary eyes took on a glistening sheen. A father's tears. Tears of relief and long-hoped-for joy. "'Tis a miracle, for certain." He touched her face, awe and thankfulness giving him strength. "Ye have been healed."

All these lies to prevent a battle that might be lost. Mathias flexed his fists, fighting to stand firm. This ploy could not be mishandled. Not with Kenzie's safety at risk. Eumann's hold on his arm tightened, as if fearing Mathias would lose control at any moment.

Kenzie shifted and caught his attention. Lowering her chin the barest notch, she blinked one eye shut with a quick twitch, but he caught it.

Aye, m'love. I shall play along. He wished she could hear his thoughts.

Bhaltair stormed forward, grabbed Lilias, and yanked her around to face him. "What witchery is this?"

"Unhand my daughter!" the Stronach shouted. He attempted to rise, then fell back limp among the pillows.

"Father!" Lilias cried out, twisting free of Bhaltair. Leaning over her sire, she touched a shaking hand to his face.

"Annag?" She looked at the crone, her face filled with fear. "I fear he has left us."

"Back wi' ye." Annag hitched closer. She fished a shiny black stone from her pocket and held it under the chieftain's nose. Frowning down at him, she finally nodded. "He breathes still," she announced, then returned the rock to her pocket. "But barely so."

"God bless ye, Annag. God bless ye, indeed," Lilias said. She caught Annag's hand to her chest and kissed her on the cheek. Turning to Bhaltair, she spat upon his boots. "A curse upon ye for shoving my father closer to death's door. A curse upon all who bear the MacSorley name."

An uneasy shifting rippled through the room as though the Angel of Death had just resettled its wings.

Annag stumbled to one side, clutching a hand at her throat. "'Tis a miracle. Lilias's touch has healed me. I feel it." She let her staff fall away and slowly straightened her back, standing tall with both shoulders smooth and level. Hands aloft, pure joy radiated from her as she flounced across the dais with the spryness of a young girl. "I am truly healed!"

Mathias clenched his teeth harder, this time to keep from laughing. To do his part, he fell to his knees and bowed his head. Kenzie dropped to the floor, trembling as though awestruck, but Mathias suspected she knew the truth as well and was having a hard time hiding her own amusement.

All in the room knelt—all except Bhaltair.

"Banish him, Lilias," Annag urged loud enough for all to hear. She pointed at Bhaltair. "Purge this clan of his evil. He is the demon among us!"

"Out with ye!" Lilias proclaimed. "And may all who follow ye go with ye and bear yer curse for all their days." Climbing to stand in Annag's chair, Lilias lifted her hands to the crowd. "Beg forgiveness and pledge fealty to Mathias to escape the MacSorley curse. I so command it."

"Lies!" Bhaltair roared. "My spies told me of Annag and her acting the cripple. Dinna allow these mere women to dupe ye. Dinna be such fools."

"Life and joy surround Annag and Lilias," Mathias shouted even louder as he pushed himself to his feet and faced the crowd. "Only death and suffering follow Bhaltair." He searched out the traitors in the room, easily found by their expressions. "How many have watched him abandon his own men? Leave them to suffer and die? Cared so little that he didn't bother to deliver their bodies to their families. Is that the fate ye want? As well as a curse to not only follow ye all yer days but follow yer children, too?"

"I shouldha killed ye long ago!" Bhaltair charged forward with his dagger raised but stumbled and fell headlong down the dais steps. The knife bounced out of his hand and spun across the floor.

"Ye see? The curse has already started," Annag proclaimed in a voice of doom. "Is this the man ye wish to follow into battle?"

A pair of guards closest to Bhaltair yanked him up and dragged him out the door. No one else followed.

Still standing in the chair, Lilias allowed her gaze to travel across the room. "I will brook no traitors. If ye mean to pledge yer fealty to Mathias and Clan Stronach, ye be welcome. Anything less, I will cast ye out as soon as the blackness of yer hearts are revealed."

"Nay, Lilias." Mathias strode forward and dropped to one knee in front of her. "Ye should lead this clan when yer father goes to his reward. Not I." And he meant every word. Nothing mattered other than a life with Kenzie. He knew that as surely as he knew day from night. Power. Leadership. Both were meaningless. He'd consider himself more than a little blessed to live his life as a guardian of Stronach and a happily married man. In his heart, he knew Lilias would make a fine chieftain. The lass had nary a treacherous fiber within her. He clutched his fist to his chest. "Ye have my fealty and protection. Always."

Kenzie crawled to his side and thrust her face close.

He removed the gag, replacing it with a gentle kiss. "I have missed ye, my love," he whispered.

"I missed ye, too." She turned and looked up at Lilias. "Ye

have my fealty as well, dear sister. Will ye grant us yer blessing?"

Lilias beamed down at them, hands clasped to her chest. "Aye, most heartily."

"Then let it be known," Mathias boomed, his shout echoing through the room. "Lady Lilias is rightful *tanist* to Clan Stronach. Pledge fealty to her."

Cheers and stomping threatened to shake the keep to its foundation.

"Lilias!" Annag shouted from the chieftain's side. She made a harried motion for her to come.

Lilias rushed to her father. Mathias and Kenzie followed.

"Father, I am here," Lilias said as she drew close so the fading man could see her. "Dinna be afraid, Father. I promise to do ye proud."

His eyelids fluttered, then drifted shut, but he gave her a peaceful smile as his chest slowly fell, then didn't rise again.

Lilias pressed a kiss to his cheek, then dropped to her knees and bowed her head.

All in the room followed suit in honor of their chief's passing.

CHAPTER THIRTEEN

"I WOULDHA THOUGHT Lilias would want to do this herself." Kenzie shaded her eyes, slowly turning as she scanned the meadow. "Are ye sure we're to go this way?"

"Aye." Mathias directed her toward a series of woodlands staggered in a haphazard line in the distance. "Up ahead. There among that second grove. She said we'd find the hive inside a hollow stump on its northern edge. They like all the clover here in the meadow."

Left hand holding a bundle of long black ribbons, Kenzie reached down with her right, grabbed a handful of skirt, and yanked it up to her knees. "It's going to take me a while to get used to tromping around in this garb. I miss my jeans."

"I prefer ye as ye were this morning." He scooped her up into his arms, intent on taking her again right here in the field. Even though they had enjoyed each other as soon as dawn awakened them, he wanted her as fiercely as if he'd been without her for an age.

She gave him a stern look that made her even lovelier and added a poke to his chest before snuggling closer. "Shame on ye! This is a solemn duty we're on. Not a search for a new place to tumble." Nibbling on his neck, she worked her way up to his ear, then gently caught his lobe between her teeth. "Shame, shame," she breathed into his ear, increasing the aching in his manparts by tenfold.

"Aye, a verra solemn duty." He dropped to his knees and lowered her into the soft carpet of sweet-smelling clover, perfect for what he planned. As he covered her body with his, he smiled down at her. "When an old one passes, 'tis time to celebrate a life well lived. What better way to celebrate than this?" After a long, slow kiss, he lifted his head and winked down at her. "Loving first, and then we'll go tell the bees he has gone, aye?"

"Ye are nay afraid the guards on the wall will enjoy the show?"

"I dinna give a damn who sees us." He teased a trail of nibbling kisses along her throat as his hand traveled lower and hiked her skirts out of his way. "But rest assured, m'love. We're far enough out. Even a man with the keenest eyes canna see us. And yon tall grasses hide us as well." He worked his hips, giving her a suggestive nudge so she might feel how much he needed her.

She returned his nudging then wrapped a leg around his. "Ye know I canna refuse ye."

Within minutes of undoing the flap of his trews, he had plunged back inside her exquisite heat. "I'll never get enough of ye, *mo nighean donn*. Never," he groaned as he ground deeper.

A fierce shuddering rippled between them as she met him thrust for thrust. "I love ye, my medieval warrior." She tangled her fingers in his hair and held tight. "Heaven help me, I love ye fierce."

Then all talking stopped. Instead, their bodies sang the perfect duet. Teased. Gave. Took. Enjoyed. The warmth of the sun on his back was nothing compared to the inferno she stoked inside him. Her nails dug into his shoulders, a silent bidding for him to drive harder. He gave his all to the request, pounding into her with delicious fury.

She cried out. His roars joined in, chasing her cries away.

Collapsing atop her, a movement to his right caught his eye.

Battle instincts flared. He jerked his head higher, ready to protect her. When he spotted the culprit, he huffed out a soft laugh and returned to nuzzling her salty-sweet throat. "Did I fail ye, my love?"

"Fail me?" she repeated in a dreamy tone. "Why would ye ask such a thing? Did ye nay hear me shouting?"

"Aye," he said. "But ye're still clutching the ribbons for the hive."

"I made a promise," she said, her attempt at sounding dutiful and solemn failing. "And no, my warrior. Ye have never failed me. I promise that, too. Every orgasm ye give me is real."

"Every what?" He stared down at her. She came out with the strangest words. Even with her being a Scot, the time she hailed from made her speak an unfamiliar language sometimes.

"Every…" she paused, then grinned. A playful wickedness gleamed in her eyes. "Ye know when ye growl out a roar, then spill yer seed because—"

"Aye, I know *because*." Women didn't speak of such things. At least, they didn't speak of them with men—not even their husbands.

She giggled, causing herself to shake quite nicely beneath him. "Well, when *I* reach that point and explode with pleasure, it's called an orgasm." She tickled a finger along his jawline. "Of course, they call yers an orgasm, too." Her grin took on a mischievous slant. "But I dinna think men can fake them as well as women can."

"Fake them?"

"Aye, some women fake their orgasms to get their men to hurry and finish so they'll leave them alone."

"Who are these women?" Had to be harlots who did such a heinous thing. That would give them time for more customers. "Whores, I reckon?"

She shrugged. "Probably. I dinna ken anything about prostitutes." She became thoughtful. "But not just them. Wives do it, too. Especially if they're tired and wish to be left in peace."

"That will never happen between us," he averred, finding the very idea insulting. "I never want ye to go along if ye dinna wish it." He stared down at her. "Promise ye will always tell me true, aye?"

"I promise." She pulled him down for a kiss. "And I also promise that ye've always satisfied me. As the clover is my witness, all my orgasms have been real."

"Well. 'Tis good to know I have never failed ye."

"Not a single time," she assured, then a heavy sigh shifted her against him again. "But I suppose we should be about our task now." She held the ribbons higher, watching them flutter in the breeze.

"I suppose so." With more than a little reluctance, he up-righted himself and fastened his trews.

Kenzie stood and shook out her skirts. Turning, she studied the wood in the distance. "Da said he and Mama always told the bees when one of us was born." Her thoughtful smile faded into sadness. "Births. Deaths. I remember hearing *go tell the bees lest they fly away* since I was a wean."

"'Tis good to know some of the old ways survived the decades." Mathias took her hand and steadied her as she hopped across a stream that was a mere trickle. "Did ye still open windows andcover the mirrors whenever anyone died?"

"Aye, Da did so when Mama passed." She spoke so softly he almost didn't hear. "Even though she was in a hospital. We did it there in her room and felt better for the doing of it."

"Ye sent yer mother to a place for the needy?"

"Nay. In my time, a hospital is a place for the sick and dying." She stopped walking as they reached the edge of the trees and tilted her head. "Listen," she whispered. "Someone's already here. Deeper in the woods."

Mathias rested a hand on a nearby trunk and tilted an ear northward. He knew that voice. "It's Eumann."

Kenzie pressed a finger across her lips and tiptoed through the forest, winding her way to the other side. Without a sound, she separated the spindly branches of a rowan sapling and peered through them. After a moment, she looked back at Mathias. "He's talking to the bees," she mouthed.

Mathias edged closer and peeped around a broad oak.

"Little bees, I wish ye could help me," Eumann said, his tone earnest. He sat on a rock at the base of a weathered stump that towered high above his head. Lightning must have blown away the top of the mighty tree, leaving behind a perfect place for the bees to build their hive. "I love her true, but I canna tell her." Then he paused as if waiting for the buzzing bringers of golden nectar to comment.

Kenzie made a move to push around the cluster of saplings, but Mathias held her back and shook his head. He had an inkling of who Eumann's *her* might be but needed to know for certain before he offered advice or help to his friend.

"I dinna think she means to take a husband," Eumann explained to the tiny, winged army. "She sees angels, ye ken? One so pure shouldna consider a bumbling fool such as me." He shook his shaggy head, then bowed it. "But I do love her," he swore quietly. "And I will protect her 'til I die, no matter if she never notices me."

Kenzie caught her bottom lip between her teeth and pressed a hand to her heart. She gave Mathias a pleading frown. He read her look as plain as if she had spoken.

"I will do what I can," he whispered. He motioned for her to follow, heading without a sound toward a downed tree large enough for them to hide behind. After they had knelt on the mossy embankment on the other side of the log, he added, "We have to leave the man his pride, ye ken? I dinna wish him to know we overheard him."

As they both peeped over the trunk and watched for Eumann to leave, she cut her eyes over at him. "He had to have heard us," she hissed. "The meadow is not that far, and we were verra loud."

Mathias shook his head, knowing his friend's focus and single-mindedness when something troubled him. "Nay, m'love. He's too deep in his worries. Praying that if he confesses to the bees, they'll somehow help him. He told me Lilias herself showed him the hive, and the wee buggers didna bother her a bit when she gathered a bit of honey for him to taste."

"She likes him, too." Kenzie ducked lower as Eumann rose to his feet with his head still bowed and tromped out of the woods.

"Has she said so?" Mathias whispered, hoping for his friend's sake that Lilias did care.

"Sort of. She wouldna give me his name."

Her eyes narrowed as they always did whenever she was plotting. *God help Eumann.* He'd find himself wed to Lilias before the month was out. Mathias rose as his friend disappeared from view. He shook a finger. "I dinna want him hurt or shamed, ye ken? The poor man's nay had an easy life."

Kenzie made an insulted huffing sound that informed him quite clearly how she felt about that. "Come on. Let's do our chore so we can get back to the keep and see about getting those two together."

They returned to the hive and stood beside the boulder Eumann had used as a seat. Mathias studied the massive trunk vibrating with the busy insects. A long, wide, teardrop-shaped opening in its middle had created the perfect sheltered doorway for the hive. A soft, contented humming filled the air. "Give me the ribbons. I'll tie them on what's left of those branches on either side of that split."

"Aye, that's a good place. Higher like that." She separated them out, smoothing the wrinkles where she'd clutched them. "I fear I've brought too many."

"Nay. They are for a chieftain." He stepped closer to the hive. "Little bees," he began. "I fear I bear sad news." Resettling his feet in the soft leaf mold, he displayed the black ribbons to the humming split in the trunk. "The Stronach has died, but never fear, his daughter, Lilias, is our new chieftain, and she will see ye well protected."

After a moment of silence, he tied the ribbons on every available spot on the dead tree, hoping the bees wouldn't decide him an enemy and swarm him. He'd always heard they could smell fear, and if a man remained calm and didn't threaten the wee buggers, the insects would stay kindly, too. With a step back, he inspected his work. The strips of black fluttered in the wind, making the stump look as though it had sprouted hair.

"Well done," Kenzie proclaimed with a respectful nod. "May the Stronach find peaceful rest, and may Lilias prosper as the new chieftain."

"Aye.' Mathias offered his arm. "Come, my lady love. We have much to discuss and decide."

"That sounds ominous."

"Not ominous at all," he said as he helped her free her skirt from a snag of nettles. He headed toward a peaceful bend in the river, westward of the keep. "'Tis a fine place up ahead where we can sit and enjoy the sunshine as we plan our future."

Once they reached the embankment overlooking the flat, rocky beach inside the curve of the waterway, Kenzie grew disturbingly quiet. As he helped her step down from the washed-out shelf of earth, he noticed her eyes had taken on the sheen of unshed tears.

"What is it, *mo nighean donn?*" He caught both her hands in his and turned her to face him, but she looked away. "Kenzie?"

"Brodie fought like a ferocious wolf right here," she said, her voice breaking. "He did his best to keep the MacPhersons from taking me until I ordered him to hide with Ramsay." Her quivering mouth turned down into a frown.

Mathias's heart swelled. He wished he could take away her pain. "Ye miss him still."

"Aye, I fear I will always miss him." She sniffed and blinked faster, pulling her hands free as she turned away and walked closer to the water's edge. "I know ye must think I'm stupid for feeling such love for my dog, but he wasna just a dog to me. I loved him like family."

It was hard for him to understand how she could still be so heartsick, but he accepted it for what it was. Her sorrow was heartfelt, and that was all that mattered.

"I would never think ye stupid, and it hurts me to see ye grieving." He gently curled her to his chest. "Cry if ye wish, my dear one. Mourn yer sweet pup. I know how ye loved him."

"Well, is that nay the most precious thing I have ever seen? Makes a man want to vomit."

Mathias spun and pushed Kenzie behind him. "They banished ye from here, ye bastard."

"Banished?" Bhaltair strutted back and forth across the embankment, his dark sneer more menacing than ever before. "That simple-minded bitch might have thought so, but the Stronach still breathed when those fools took away my sword and dragged me outside the walls. That addled spawn's order means nothing to me."

"She is chief now." Mathias spotted the pommel of Bhaltair's dagger peeping out from the top of his boot. Careless guards. They might have stripped the man of his sword, but they'd not left him defenseless. He pulled out his own blade and stepped forward, all the while praying Kenzie stayed out of the way. "If ye choose battle, only one of us will walk away from this, ye ken?"

With a haughty toss of his head, Bhaltair winked. "I count on it, friend. May ye rest in peace." He stepped down from the embankment. Slow. Cautious. Stealthy as a cat ready to pounce.

Mathias bided his time, knowing if he waited long enough, Bhaltair's uncontrollable temper would force the fool into carelessness. He'd bested the man before. This time would be the last. The black-hearted fiend tried to circle him away from Kenzie, but Mathias countered the move. Kenzie's protection would not be sacrificed.

The longer they stalked one another, the more Bhaltair's face reddened. Good. The unsettled bastard would make a faulty move at any moment.

"Enough dancing!" the miscreant roared and lunged.

Mathias was ready. He blocked the thrust of the man's dagger and punched him in the stomach, hitting so hard Bhaltair lifted to the tips of his toes.

The blackguard spun away, wheezing for air as he slashed his knife back and forth. He dove again, and they locked blades. This time Mathias twisted and pried Bhaltair's dagger free. It went flying into the river.

Teeth bared, face red as blood, the whoreson leapt backward with both hands raised. "Fight me bare-handed, lest ye're too afraid."

"Nay, my friend. I'd much rather snap yer neck with my bare hands than cut ye." After a stolen glance at Kenzie, Mathias tossed his dagger to land at her feet. She snatched it up and gave him a nod. Good. Now, she was armed, just in case.

The men collided, knocked themselves apart, then collided again, struggling to keep their footing on the rocky strand. Bhaltair hooked the toe of his boot around Mathias's ankle and yanked, bringing him to the ground. Ignoring the pain from the hard landing, Mathias rolled and brought Bhaltair down with him. He rolled again and crouched over the man, grabbing hold of his throat.

Bhaltair kicked upward and managed to worm out from under him. He grappled his way to his feet, coughing and rubbing his throat.

Mathias didn't give the snake time to recover. Instead, he sprang and delivered an uppercut that knocked Bhaltair stumbling backward. When he landed, the back of his head bounced hard against the rocks. Flailing with sluggish, jerky movements, the demon struggled to rise. As Mathias strode forward to finish him, a snarling flash of black and white sprang from the bushes. The enraged dog landed on the downed man's chest and clamped his jaws around his throat.

"Brodie!" Kenzie cried out.

"Leave him be, lass," Mathias ordered. "Give the lad his vengeance."

Locked on his prey, the dog gave a vicious twist that jerked both himself and Bhaltair. The man's legs kicked twice, then his arms went limp, and he fell still. The canine held fast, working his jaws to ensure the killing shake had done its job. He gave one last hard yank on the man's throat, then stepped back, blood staining the white fur of his chest. The animal turned to Kenzie, dropped its head, and whined.

"Good lad," she praised, dropping to her knees and holding out both arms. "Come to me, sweet boy."

The beast charged into her, rolling her onto her backside. Mathias couldn't tell if Kenzie was laughing or crying, but it didn't matter. Her precious Brodie had returned.

Arms wrapped around the dog, she beamed up at Mathias. "He came back to me. Can ye believe it? He found his way back through the cave."

"Of course, he came back to ye, lass." Mathias crouched down beside them and rubbed the animal's head. "I wouldha done the same. We both love ye so much we canna live without ye."

"I'm so verra happy." Tears streaming down her cheeks, she buried her face in the dog's fur.

"I am glad." Mathias stood and blew out a heavy sigh. Unfortunately, this place was no longer the peaceful sanctuary he had wished to use for their planning.

"Why the heavy sigh?" Kenzie rose and touched his arm. "Are ye all right?" She spared a glance at Bhaltair. "I guess it canna be easy, can it?"

"What canna be easy?" Puzzled, he frowned down at her while rubbing the tender spot where his hip had hit the rocks.

"The way Bhaltair died." She shrugged. "That he's dead at all, really. After all, I take it ye knew each other quite the while."

"If this fine lad had not done what he did, I wouldha killed the bastard myself." He hoped she wouldn't think less of him, but that was survival in this time. "That devil never wouldha changed his ways, m'love. Ye would not have been safe from him. Not ever." He brushed her cheek with the lightest touch. "I will do anything to keep ye safe." Cupping her face in his hand, he repeated the oath. "Anything."

She turned and kissed his palm, closing her eyes as she did so. "I never knew someone could mean so much to me. I love ye so."

"I love ye more, my lady love." After a gentle kiss, he huffed out another sigh. "But we must high to the keep and tell them of this." He spared a glance at the man's body, then tipped his head toward a mossy spot on the bank. "I had planned for us to take our leisure here and talk of where we should settle and start our life together. But that scum ruined the peace of the place."

Brodie barked and wiggled his way between them.

With a laugh, Mathias rubbed the jealous beastie's ears. "I reckon we've got the rest of our lives for planning, though."

She scooped up his hand and tugged him toward the embankment. "Come. We can plan as we walk back to the keep."

As soon as they cleared the thin line of trees and bushes cluttering the riverbank, a surprising sight halted them. Sheep. Everywhere. Meandering their way over the ridge and down into the meadow toward the river.

"Ramsay?" Walking at the head of his obedient harem, the ram meandered along with grass hanging out both sides of his mouth. A new bell around his neck clanged with every step. Kenzie shook her head. "Brodie brought them all with him." Her lips moved as she silently counted the flock. "Aye. A dozen looks like. Maybe more. That's almost all of mine." First, she nodded, then shook her head again. "I canna believe he herded them through those tunnels. My brothers and Da willna have a clue. They'll think them stolen."

"He didna wish to shun his duties, nor was he about to give up his search for his mistress." Mathias scrubbed his jaw, watching as the dog rounded up the stragglers and tidied up the herd.

"Sheep dinna graze the same as cows. I dinna think this size glen will do well with them both. Even with this size flock."

Her worry gave him the perfect opportunity to propose what he had in mind. After all, Bhaltair wasn't going anywhere.

"Remember the abandoned croft I told ye about?"

First, she frowned, then recognition smoothed her brow. "Aye."

"It'll take several long days and hard work, but the place is big enough for plenty of sheep." He hoped she'd warm to the idea. The more he thought about it, the more right it seemed. "Eumann and some of the other lads will help us get it livable and a stable built. I'm sure of it."

"I thought ye would want to live here at the keep? Ye're commander of the guard, not a farmer or a shepherd."

"Is that what ye wish?" he asked. "Live here at the keep so ye'll have the company of other women?" It made sense. Especially if they were eventually blessed with bairns. Women needed other women at such times. He had lived by the blade most of his life. A peaceful existence with family and farm called to him now, but the final decision was hers.

She pulled a face and stared up at him, as though about to confess a terrible sin. "Our own place would be wonderful. I love farming. It's in my blood. I helped Da and my brothers as soon as I could walk and tote a bucket." She glanced in the keep's direction and wrinkled her nose. "And there's nary a bit of privacy in that place. Ye canna take a shite without the entire clan knowing what color it is." With a shrug, she added, "I guess ye think I'm weird, right?"

"If weird means I think ye are an extraordinary woman, then aye, I do." He moved his thumb toward the animals grazing nearby. "And thanks to yer wee dog, we've got our own flock of sheep to start with."

She hugged his arm. "Aye, it will be lovely." With a flick of her wrist, she caught Brodie's attention, then pointed at the clear patch of land in front of the skirting wall. "In close, lad," she called out. "In close."

The dog set to maneuvering the animals in that direction.

"He'll keep them there 'til I call him in," she said. "The guards can help keep an eye on them whenever Brodie's not about. They'll do that, aye?"

"I'll tell Eumann. He'll see to it."

A companionable silence fell between them as they strolled arm in arm. The longer they walked without speaking, the more he wondered what thoughts furrowed her brow this time. "What is it, love?"

"While I dinna wish to live at the keep…" She paused. "Will Lilias be all right without us?"

He had wondered the same. While Lilias had shown herself much more adept than anyone thought, she had also lived a very sheltered life. He feared she might place her trust in the wrong people. "Eumann will protect her. And Annag, as well."

"Mrs. Kerr and Sorley seem to have her best interests at heart," Kenzie mused. "Do ye think they'll still be loyal now that she's shown herself to be more able-minded than they thought?"

"I believe so." He patted her hand where it rested in the crook of his arm. "It will take a bit of work to get the croft and new stable ready. Weeks, probably. We could stay here at the keep 'til it's done. Think ye the sheep and cows can share the glen that long without one herd starving out the other?"

"Aye." She smiled up at him. "Brodie and I will keep them on the move to make sure they dinna do too much damage."

His dear one's worried look disappeared, making him breathe easier.

"I reckon I'll have to give ye back yer staff for good now."

She spun around and blocked his way, squeezing both his arms. "Ye found it? I feared it lost forever."

"I fetched it from the bushes beside the river. It's hid beneath our bed. I thought to surprise ye with it once we moved into the croft, but if ye'll be herding yer wee balls of wool, ye'll be needing it now."

She pulled him down for a kiss, drawing whistles and hoots from the guards walking atop the wall.

Guards be damned. Mathias tightened his arms around her and deepened his tasting of this wondrous woman that fate had seen fit to bring him. When next he passed that cave, he'd pour out a healthy dram of *uisge beatha* in thanks.

With a seductive nudge that promised more to come, she pulled away. "I suppose we should behave with more propriety since the keep's still in mourning." With a delightfully wicked look, she added, "At least, publicly."

"If we must," he agreed as they entered the bailey. "We should speak with Lilias and let her know we completed our task."

"Should we tell her of our plans or wait?"

Mathias scanned the small community inside the skirting walls. While the door to each building still displayed a black ribbon in honor of the Stronach's passing, all appeared to have returned to normal everyday life. Women on the benches in front of their homes chatted as they weaved their baskets or tended to their mending. The smithy was busy at his forge. Children laughed and played. Life went on. "We should speak with her now before word gets back to her. After all, I'm sure the guards will tell her of the sheep."

"But first, I must have Bhaltair fetched so Daw can bury him." Mathias didn't relish the task and was sorely tempted to let the man rot where he lay. After all, Bhaltair had done that very thing to several of his own. Unfortunately, his conscience wouldn't allow him to lower himself to that black-hearted bastard's level. "Ye find Lilias. I'll join ye as soon as I'm finished."

"Warn them about Brodie and the sheep, aye?"

"Aye, m'love." A wonderful contentment filled him as he watched her hurry inside the keep. A contentment such as he had never known before.

CHAPTER FOURTEEN

"THEY SAID I'D find ye here in the garden with Henny."

Lilias, with her sleeves rolled up above her elbows, knelt in a plot of freshly turned soil. The dirt was rich and black, and rife with bugs and worms. Her pet chicken scratched nearby, with a contented clucking.

"Riverbed land makes the best gardens," the lass said as she poked a hole in the dirt, planted a tender green shoot, and tucked the ground in firm all around it. "And here inside the wall, the hares willna rob us." She gave Kenzie an embarrassed smile. "They said I shouldna do such things now that I'm chief."

Kenzie dropped beside her and started helping to plant what looked like onion slips. "I'd say that since ye're chieftain, ye can do anything ye wish." She gave Lilias's arm a playful nudge. "Ye're the boss now, ye ken?"

"Boss?"

"Aye, the one in charge. The leader. Ye make the rules and decisions. No one else."

"Ye truly think so?"

"I know so." Lilias's hesitancy worried her. The lass was so unsure of herself. How could they possibly leave her to rule alone? Unless…Kenzie selected another plant from the shallow wooden basket between them. Time to ensure Lilias's safety and Eumann's happiness. It was better she handle this than leave it to Mathias. "Mathias and I told the bees of yer father's passing."

"Good." Lilias rested her hands in her lap and lifted her face to the sun. "I pray he finds ease from all the pain he suffered in this life."

"I am sure he will." Kenzie spotted an earthworm, plucked it up, and tossed it to the hen. "When we first found the hive, we had to wait a little while, though. Someone else was already talking to them."

With a tilt of her head, Lilias frowned. "Who? I sent no one but yerself and Mathias."

"Eumann." Kenzie struggled not to smile at the sudden flare of rosiness that brightened Lilias's cheeks. A sense of victory filled her. She had guessed right. Lilias fancied Eumann as much as he loved her.

The hesitant new chief stole a glance back at the open door leading into the kitchens. She leaned close and whispered, "What was he telling the bees? Could ye hear him plain?"

"Aye, every word he said." Kenzie gave a solemn nod. "He asked them for their help." Kenzie left it at that. Matchmaking was a great deal like fishing. The bait had to be dangled for a while before setting the hook. The tactic had worked quite well with her eldest brother and the woman he now called his wife.

Lips parted and eyes filled with worry, Lilias clasped a hand to her chest. "Heaven help him. Is he unwell?"

Without answering, Kenzie busied herself with planting another shoot. She wouldn't let the lass worry overlong, but a wee bit of anxiousness would give the girl incentive to take action.

Lilias poked her shoulder. "Kenzie! Is he unwell?"

"Not exactly unwell." She sidled farther down the row before reaching back for the basket, but Lilias snatched it out of reach.

"No more planting until ye've told me everything."

Smiling on the inside, Kenzie prepared to set the hook. Lilias was ready. "He is heartsick because he loves a woman he fears he can never have."

"Never have?" The wide-eyed young woman caught her breath and pressed a hand to her throat.

"Aye," Kenzie said. "He told the bees the one he loves is far too good for him. Says she has visions of angels and is too pure for one such as himself." With a tilt of her head, she admired Lilias's rosiness as it went even brighter. "He doesna think she'll ever take a husband, but he swore an oath to the bees to always love and protect her no matter what."

"He said that?"

"I swear it." Kenzie fixed the girl with the same stern expression Mama always used when driving a point home. "The question is, what are ye going to do about it?"

"Do?" Lilias caught her bottom lip between her teeth. Her expression became more pained with every passing moment.

"Aye, do," Kenzie encouraged. "Ye told me once ye had a warmth for a certain man, but yer father forbade ye to even speak of it. Was that man Eumann?"

"Aye," she admitted so softly that Kenzie almost missed it.

"Then do something about it. Ye're chief now. Ye can be with anyone ye wish."

"But what will folk say?" She stole another glance back at the door.

"Who cares what they say?" Kenzie said. "Ye're chief now. Ye've a right to be happy and lead Clan Stronach with Eumann at yer side."

Lilias stared down at her lap, still chewing on her bottom lip.

The girl's reaction made her second guess her tactics. Perhaps she had pushed too hard. With the lass's continued silence, Kenzie decided to back up and regroup. "If ye dinna wish it, ye dinna have to do anything about what I just told ye," she gently reminded. "Neither Mathias nor I will speak of it to anyone. Yer life is yer own, lass. Live it in the way that gives ye peace, aye?" She caught the girl's hand and squeezed. "Ye've a good heart, dear sister. Lead with that heart of yers. Let the chips fall where they may."

Lilias lifted her head and frowned. "Chips?"

"Never mind." Disappointed at her failed matchmaking attempt, Kenzie held out a hand for the basket. "Let's get this row finished. Mathias will join us soon. We've quite a bit of news to share with ye."

"More news?"

Lilias's fretting tone gave her a swift kick in the conscience. Maybe she should've left the matchmaking to Mathias. She attempted to calm the girl with a reassuring smile.

"Dinna worry. It's good news." Her conscience twitched again, and she almost crossed herself. The death of another, even one as evil as Bhaltair, should not be called *good news*. "Most of it is good news," she amended.

"Most?" Lilias squeaked.

Heaven help her, she'd never mangled a conversation so badly in her life. "Brodie's back!" she announced. Lilias loved the dog. That should chase away her tension.

"For true?" The lass jumped up, looked all around the sprawling garden, then turned back. "Where is he? Did ye nay bring him to see me? He's most welcome in the garden, ye ken? Any time he wishes. He's welcome to come and play."

"He's outside the skirting wall. Minding the sheep." Kenzie flinched. How would she explain the sheep to Lilias?

"What sheep?" Wiping her hands on her apron, Lilias paused as she headed toward the door. "Come, Kenzie. Show me."

At least the lass sounded like a chieftain now. Kenzie rose and followed Lilias through the keep, into the bailey, then out the main gate. "See? Sheep." She pointed to an area shaded by trees. "And look over there. Ramsay and Brodie. See them?"

Lilias stared at the wooly beasts, then turned to Kenzie. "Is that where he's been all this time? Searching the Highlands for sheep to keep Ramsay company?"

"Aye," Kenzie hurried to agree, deciding that lie was good as any.

Her worried look finally gone, Lilias headed for the dog. "I'm so glad he has returned," she called back over her shoulder.

"Me, too." Kenzie smiled as the dog gave the girl a warm greeting.

"So, ye've told her then?"

She jumped, spun about, and thumped Mathias on the shoulder. "Dinna sneak up on me like that."

"Ye've a guilty conscience."

What was it about the man's deep voice that made her melt? "I do not have a guilty conscience." She cringed before she could stop it.

"Aye, ye do. Ye should see yerself." He folded his arms across his broad chest and gave her a look that always forced her to confess all. "What have ye done now?"

"I told her about Eumann." She eased back a step, unsure how he'd react. "And Brodie and the sheep, of course."

Nostrils flaring and jaw tight, his head tilted to the other side. "Of course."

"But I havena told her about the croft. Or Bhaltair." She felt like she'd just admitted to stealing cigarettes and smoking them behind the barn. "She took the news about Eumann well. And feels the same. She's just not sure what to do about it."

"Ye're babbling."

"Well, I tend to do that when someone makes me feel like I'm in the confessional."

"Come on." He scooped up her hand and tugged.

"Where to?"

He glared down his nose at her as if he couldn't believe she'd just asked that. "Ye told her the tidbits ye wished to tell. Dinna ye think it's time ye told her the rest?"

"I was kind of saving that news for ye to tell her." She gave her most charming smile. "After all, I dinna wish to steal yer thunder."

"Oh, no." He shook his head and tugged again. "Ye'll nay saddle me with telling her the news that might displease her.

Come, wife. Ye've much to sort out here."

"Fine." She snatched her hand away and marched over to the tree, mulling over what she would say.

"He's happy to see me." Lilias looked up while still hugging the dog.

"Of course he's happy to see ye." Kenzie looked back at Mathias trailing behind.

With an arched brow, he gave her a pointed look, then tipped his head toward Lilias.

"Remember, I said some of my news was good and some was bad?" Kenzie started, wringing her hands as if forced to recite her homework in front of class.

Lilias's smile faded, and she straightened. "I had forgotten." Smoothing her apron, she nodded. "Best get on with it, then. Tell me the rest."

"Bhaltair is dead."

"That isna bad news." The girl's tensed stance relaxed. "He was a terrible man, but I shall still pray for his soul."

"Well, that was the terrible news," Kenzie started, only to be interrupted by Mathias clearing his throat.

Lilias looked from one to the other of them, then frowned. "The two of ye are leaving the keep."

The girl's accurate guess shot a chill down Kenzie's spine. "Aye, Lilias. There's an abandoned croft southwest of here." She patted Mathias's arm. "We mean to make a farm of it. With Brodie and the sheep."

"I see." Lilias turned away, then wandered out of the shade, squinting as she looked out across the wildflowers bobbing in the breeze. "How far from here?"

"Not far at all, lass. On the edge of Stronach land close to Loch Shiel." Mathias went to her. "But know this, should ye ever have a need, all ye must do is send for us, aye? We will be here for ye."

"I had hoped ye would stay here." Lilias blew out a heavy sigh, hugging herself as if the sunshine failed at keeping her warm. "But I dinna blame ye. So many turned on ye. Listened to Bhaltair's lies. If they turned on ye once, they could verra well do so again, so I'm sure ye canna trust them."

"Spoken like a verra wise chieftain," Kenzie said. "We willna leave right away. The place needs some work before we can live in it." She had never felt so guilty about doing what she wanted in all her life. Lilias was like a helpless puppy they were abandoning. "It'll take weeks before we leave. By then, ye'll have the chieftain-ship well in hand."

"Will ye be taking Annag and Eumann?"

"No. Of course not. Why would ye ever think that?" Kenzie gave Lilias what she hoped was a reassuring hug. "They dinna even know what we've planned. We wanted to tell ye first." She hugged her again. "Eumann will keep ye safe, and Annag is settled and happy in her own place here. Could ye see Annag happy on a farm?"

"It's for the best, lass," Mathias quietly added.

"Aye, I know." She patted Kenzie's hand. "I need a walk. Time to think of all ye've told me, aye? Ye've given me much to consider."

"Of course." Kenzie felt lower than a worm. She watched the unhappy lass stroll off into the meadow.

Mathias turned toward the keep, lifted a hand, then brought it down and pointed at Lilias.

"What was that for?"

"She shouldna walk alone. Guards will follow at a distance great enough to grant her the privacy of her thoughts but still keep her safe." No sooner had he explained, then two of the burliest guards strode across the drawbridge and followed their chieftain. A heartbeat after that, Eumann charged out after them.

"Eumann!" Mathias waved him over, while giving Kenzie the same pointed stare he'd fixed upon her earlier. "Plant yer seeds, wife. She needs him now more than ever."

"Thanks a lot," Kenzie muttered. "I thought ye were going to talk to him?"

Mathias grinned. "Nay, ye handle such things so well. I decided to let ye tell him."

"Tell him what?" His focus still locked on Lilias meandering in the distance, Eumann spared them both a quick glance. "Make it fast, I pray ye. I dinna trust those two with watching after their own arses, much less the Lady Lilias."

Kenzie remembered the advice her father had always given: the shortest route between two points is a straight line. And then he would always say, *Dinna be mamby-pambying about, lass. Spit it out and be done with it. Ye'll feel better for it.* She sent up a silent prayer for guidance and charged forward.

"We overheard what ye told the bees," she said, then lifted her chin and braced herself.

Eumann's attention snapped away from Lilias and locked on her. His rounded jowls tensed, then shifted as if he couldn't decide whether to smile, scowl, or spit. "That was betwixt me and the bees," he finally said, glaring first at her, then Mathias.

Superstition. Perhaps that was the key to get these two together. After all, since her foretelling of the Duke of Brittany's murder, even Eumann had been a bit more cautious around her. "Did it ever occur to ye that the bees wanted us to hear so we could help ye like ye asked them?"

Even though his eyes narrowed, and he looked away, she spotted a flicker of belief.

"Lady Lilias once confided in me that she had a warmth for a man her father never approved of. In fact, he thought this man so low, he forbade her to even say his name." She pointed at Eumann. "I know ye're that man, Eumann."

His focus jerked back to her again. "How do ye know this?" he asked, his voice rasping and filled with a heart-tugging mix of caution, hope, and longing.

"Because I spoke to the bees, too," she lied. "Ye know how they love Lilias. Did they not share their honey without so much as a single sting?"

Scrubbing a hand across his mouth, he turned and stared at

the lass in question as she picked wildflowers. "They did share their honey," he admitted as his hand fell to his side. He gave Mathias an almost pleading expression. "I dinna wish to cause her grief or worry. Nor do I want to be more the fool than I already am. What do ye think, Mathias? Dare I even hope her to have a kindness for me?"

Mathias glanced at Kenzie before clapping a hand to Eumann's shoulder. "Love is always a risk, man. But I swear, it's well worth it."

The troubled warrior stood taller and rolled his shoulders. "Perhaps, I might go walk with her. Reckon she would want help in picking her wee flowers?"

"I know she would love yer help," Kenzie reassured.

Mathias encouraged him with a single nod.

"Prayers for me, please," Eumann called back to them as he hurried away to join her.

"God help him," Mathias said under his breath.

"God help them both," Kenzie corrected, watching the two interact like a couple of painfully shy children in the schoolyard. "Has Daw gone to fetch the body?" She didn't want that scene interrupting what she hoped was the beginning of something Eumann and Lilias both wanted but didn't know how to handle.

"Aye. Said he intends to dump it in a ravine farther downriver." Mathias's jaw tightened the way it always did whenever he spoke about Bhaltair. "Appears even his own brother hated him."

As she watched Lilias meander farther across the field with poor Eumann stumbling along beside her, she wondered what else they could do to help the hesitant lass succeed in her new role as chief. "Are we terrible for leaving?"

"We willna leave until she is ready, aye?"

She hugged him, nestling her head against his chest. "I want us happy, but not at her expense. She is so…innocent."

"I know, lass." He kissed the top of her head, then rested his cheek atop it as he held her.

"Can we go to the cave?" She didn't know why, but she

needed to see it one last time. Say a last goodbye to her family and all she had left behind.

With a sharp intake of breath, Mathias tensed in her arms. "Why do ye wish to go back to the cave?"

She hugged him tighter. "I never said my proper goodbyes, ye ken?" Looking up so he could see the truth of it in her eyes, she smiled. "I will never go back to my time." She patted his chest. "Ye are my home now. I belong with ye."

"Aye. Ye do." With a possessive growl, he bent his head and teased her mouth with his. "And never forget it," he warned in a rasping whisper.

"Never," she promised as she pulled him down to complete the delicious connection and give herself fully to the ancient Highland thief who had stolen her heart.

EPILOGUE

Three years later,
Summer
Due north of Loch Shiel
Stronach Farm

"I'M GLAD YE came for a visit," Kenzie said. "Gives me a chance to sit and rest since ye brought Jeanette to chase after the wee ones." She massaged her lower back with one hand and rubbed her uncomfortably swollen belly with the other. This babe was riding much lower than the first. Made her wonder if it was a boy. According to Mathias, it was. Of course, he had also sworn the same about their now two-year-old daughter, Lyla.

"Fergus loves playing with Lyla," Lilias said. She smiled proudly at her son, toddling alongside the little girl in front of the watchful maidservant. The red-headed lad exploded with an angry squall when the wee lassie plucked his wooden sword away.

"Make her give it back to him, Jeanette." Kenzie shifted on the bench, searching for a comfortable position. "She has to learn to share sooner or later."

"Ye should make her a sword," Eumann advised as the two

men appeared from around the side of the white-washed cottage. "Or I could make her one like Fergus's."

"My fierce daughter is dangerous enough without a weapon," Mathias said. "Throws rocks like a warrior so, dinna cross her." He winked at Kenzie. "She's much like her mother."

"I dinna think Brodie is pleased about our visit," Lilias commented as she held out a hand for Eumann to come and stand beside her. "He seems tired of the puppies already."

Kenzie laughed. "He sired that litter with the keep's dog. The least he can do is teach two of his sons how to work a herd."

The black and white collie lay in the shade, nose between his paws, and ears cocked to a disgruntled angle as two plump puppies clambered all over him. One was solid black. The other was white peppered with gray and brown patches, making Kenzie think of a wild piglet. She hoped that their father's border collie instincts ran strong in their blood. After all, precious Brodie wouldn't be able to tend the growing herds forever.

Mathias fetched a good-sized log, upended it behind the bench upon which the women sat, and started rubbing Kenzie's lower back. "The least I can do, aye?" he said after pecking a kiss to the back of her neck.

"How much longer?" Lilias asked, hugging Eumann's hand to her cheek.

"Any time, according to Annag." Kenzie breathed in deep, her knotted muscles finally relaxing under Mathias's expert touch. "When's the next full moon?"

"Tonight," Eumann said. "Reckon we should leave Jeanette here to help? Sorley and Mrs. Kerr can fight over who lends a hand with wee Fergus."

Lilias shook her head. "Those two will spoil him for certain." She rose from the bench, then brushed a kiss to Kenzie's cheek. "I fear we must head back now, dear sister. I tire more easily these days," she said with a mysterious smile.

Kenzie caught Lilias's hand. "Another?"

The lass beamed with a happy nod. "Aye. Another. Fergus is

to be a brother."

"Ye dinna need to leave Jeanette here," Annag growled from the window. "Lyla's arrival was easy as could be. Kenzie's got good wide hips for birthing her babies. I can catch this one just like I caught Lyla-girl."

"Thank ye for the lovely compliment, Annag," Kenzie snapped without a glance back at the cottage.

The old woman had been staying with them for nigh on a fortnight now, and her blunt observations had grown a tad tiresome. Especially today. For some reason, Kenzie felt uncomfortable in her own skin. Maybe the bairn would arrive soon. "And thank ye, that's quite enough." She pushed Mathias's hands away. The thoughtful back rub suddenly irritated her to no end, and she didn't know why. As ungainly as an overfed cow, she pushed herself up from the bench and waddled around the clearing, ready to lash out at everyone. It took biting her tongue to keep her unreasonable rattiness unspoken. What the devil was her problem? Hormones had raged worse with this one, and today was the most frustrating day of all.

"Ye've dropped more," Annag observed from the window where she perched with her elbows propped on the ledge. "Keep walking. I'd bet my last three teeth that bairn comes afore midnight."

"Then we must stay and help," Lilias announced with a nod at Eumann. "With the fair weather, we can sleep in the wagon, aye?"

"Aye," Eumann quickly agreed, backing toward the wagon as if to make a run for it. "'Tis a fine night for camp. I'll sort the bundles around, and it'll do just fine."

Kenzie bowed her head and held her back. Her stomach tightened hard as stone, and the girth held the tension for a few moments, then relaxed. As much as she hated to admit it, old Annag was right. Labor had started. She felt like she walked with her feet spread a meter apart.

"That was a pain right there," the wise woman crowed. "I

knew it!"

"What can I do, love?" Mathias asked, pacing alongside her, his face at least two shades paler than before.

"Nothing." She shook her head. "This isna my first dance, remember?"

"Dance?"

"Never mind." Waving him away, she started another lap around the clearing. "You and Eumann tend to the bairns. Take them to see the lambs, aye?"

"Aye." She spotted Mathias's relief before he had the chance to hide it. "Take Jeanette with ye. She can be the adult supervision for the lot of ye."

Jeanette obediently scooped up Fergus, held him astraddle one hip, and took hold of Lyla's hand. "This way, my bonnie wee babes."

Mathias and Eumann obediently followed.

Lilias fell in step beside her. "Men are good at planting our bairns, but they're more than a little useless when it comes to bringing them into the world, aye?"

"Aye." Kenzie paused and held her stomach as a deeper cramping made itself known. Forcing herself to relax as much as she could and breathe deeply, she watched a beetle crawl across the packed dirt as she waited for the pain to subside.

"Keep walking or go inside?" Lilias asked as she pulled a linen from her sleeve and mopped the peppering of sweat from Kenzie's brow.

"Keep walking," Kenzie huffed as she resumed her waddling gait. "Seems to move things along that much faster, ye ken?"

"Aye, it does," Lilias agreed. "We must do what our bodies need. That's always best. I squatted in front of a chair to get my stubborn son out." She strolled alongside, holding tight and supporting Kenzie whenever another pain hit. "Do ye wish for a boy or another girl?"

"I dinna care." And she didn't. It was Mathias who yearned for a son. "As long as the babe is healthy. That's all that matters."

"Too true."

Water gushed forth, splattering the ground between her feet. "Tell Annag," Kenzie groaned as another contraction took hold. This child appeared to be in a hurry.

"Annag! Water broke!" Lilias called out, gently steering Kenzie back across the clearing toward the door.

"Time to come inside then." The old woman appeared and waved them forward. "Dinna want to drop the wee one in the dirt now, do we?"

"Definitely not." And from the feel of it, that was a possibility. Kenzie quickened her gait. "Help me, Lilias. It willna be long."

"The bed's ready with the sheet, and I've set out the extra linens." Annag took her place on Kenzie's other side and helped her make her way into the small dwelling and across the main room. "Let's get ye down to yer shift. 'Twill give ye as much ease as we can for now."

A staggering cramp bent Kenzie as close to double as possible, considering the size of her middle. A gasping grunt escaped her as the pain increased. It shook hard through her, feeling as though it would never end.

"Breathe through it, lass," Annag crooned. "Breathe and see yerself holding that babe. It willna be long."

Once the contraction passed, the women hurried to untie the sides of her gown and pulled it off over her head. They got her settled in bed and stripped away her shoes and stockings.

"More pillows so ye can sit up higher?" Lilias asked as she mopped a cool cloth across Kenzie's brow.

"Nay," Kenzie groaned as another pain hit. "Just get this bairn out of me." She'd thought Lyla had been a rapid birthing. This one was racing into the world. Wadding her hands in the bedsheets, she strained out another long, low groan as Annag took hold of her knees.

"I see a head full of dark hair, lass," the crone encouraged. "Just as thick and black as Lyla's."

Another contraction took hold with the uncontrollable urge

to push again. She sucked in a deep breath and bore down, cutting loose with a fierce growl as the babe slid out into the world.

"A fine boy!" Annag announced. "Well done, lass."

The angry infant bellowed with an infuriated cry.

"And he's a braw, strong laddie, too," Lilias laughed, still supporting Kenzie's shoulders. "Listen to that cry."

Kenzie laughed, then cried, holding out both hands. "Come to Mama, my wee Ari. Come now."

"Ari?" Annag repeated.

"Aye, it means *brave.*" Cradling the wriggling bairn atop her chest, she kissed his wet forehead as he screamed his displeasure at leaving the warm darkness. "Ari, for my eldest brother. Mathias promised if I gave him a boy, I could name him Ari." As she held the babe, she became aware of another painful rippling sensation that should have been finished and gone. She handed the infant to Lilias. "Something is not the same as last time. Annag?"

Annag placed her hands on either side of Kenzie's still swollen stomach, squeezing and pushing from several angles. "Do multiple births run in yer family?"

"Twins," Kenzie admitted. "My youngest brothers were twins."

The elder gave Lilias a worried scowl. "Tend to the wee one. I believe there'll soon be another."

"Come, little Ari," Lilias crooned. "Let's get ye cleaned while yer Mama brings yer sister or brother into the world."

The idea of managing twins, and Lyla, and the farm suddenly seemed more than a little overwhelming. Mathias was a great help, but he was a man. A man could only do so much. Even one as helpful as Mathias.

"I canna handle twins," she sobbed. Another contraction, much stronger than before, ripped through her. An agonizing groan, ending with a shuddering sob, escaped her.

"Ye must not panic! All ye need do is think about right now,"

Annag barked. "This moment. This child. Nothing else. One moment at a time. That is all ye must bear, ye ken?" She pushed Kenzie's knees toward her chest. "Hold tight to yer knees and bring this babe to us. I command it."

Somewhere in her daze of pain and unreasonable worry, Kenzie heard and knew Annag's words as the truth. She grabbed hold of both knees and bore down until she couldn't bear down any longer.

"Nearly there, lass. One more push, and then ye can rest. I swear it."

Little Ari had ceased his crying, making her fret even more. "Ari? Is he all right? Where is he?"

"He's resting in his cradle. Tired from all his fussing." Lilias took hold of Kenzie's shoulders. "One more push now, my weary sister. One more for the gift of another precious bairn."

Digging down to her last reserves of strength, Kenzie dug her nails into her knees, curled forward, and pushed.

A wailing cry filled the air.

"Ye've another son, lass." Annag held him up and turned him to face her. "And who might this lad be?"

Covered in blood and mess, black hair matted all over his head, red as a beetroot, and yowling like a cat with its tail caught in a door. Kenzie knew this one's name immediately. "Barkev. It means *gift*. After my next eldest brother."

"A fine name," Lilias proclaimed as she helped Kenzie ease back into the pillows. "Rest now. Soon as we get Barkev seen to, we'll clean ye up, and then ye can feed them both." She arched a brow at Annag where she perched on the edge of the bed. "There's nay anymore, is there?"

Annag pressed hard on Kenzie's much flatter stomach. "Nay. Just the leavings, and they're expelling now." She patted Kenzie's shoulder. "Well done, lass. Birthing twins in just a little over an hour. Well done, indeed."

Kenzie sagged back in the bed, completely spent. She barely found the energy to turn her head and look down into the cradle at her one son, who would soon be joined by his brother. "Mathias will have to build another cradle," she mumbled, floating in a numb fog of exhaustion and dwindling adrenaline.

Even though she wished to sleep, Lilias and Annag wouldn't allow it. They rolled and prodded. Washed, dried, and rubbed her with rose-scented oils. Kenzie soon found herself dressed in a clean chemise and propped in a mound of fresh pillows.

"Best feed these lads their first meal," Annag advised as she propped the bairns in Kenzie's arms and untied the neckline of her shift. "Then we'll let Mathias in. He's beside himself, and Jeanette's ready to kill him."

"What about Lyla?" Kenzie smiled as each of her sons latched on and suckled with a ferocity that guaranteed them to have the bottomless appetite of their father. Thankfully, she'd had milk to spare with the first one. That wouldn't be the case with these two. "Does Lyla know she has two little brothers?"

"She was nay impressed," Annag chuckled. "All she would say was *more puppies*."

"I'm sure she will be even less impressed with her brothers as they grow. I know I was." Kenzie tipped her head toward the door. "Let him in. If Jeanette kills him, I'll be a widow with three mouths to feed."

Annag smiled and opened the door.

Mathias stormed inside, then froze at the foot of the bed, his wide-eyed gaze locked on her and the bairns. "Two," he whispered.

"Aye, m'love." She smiled down at the babe to her right. "Ari. Means *brave*, by the way. After my eldest brother." Her smile shifted to the infant on her left. "Barkev. Means *gift*. After my next brother in line." She basked in Mathias's joy, love, and pride. "I didna think ye would mind me naming them both."

He eased down beside her and touched a tiny hand. Little fingers wrapped around his. "Two," he repeated.

"Is that all ye can say?" she teased.

"Nay," he said as he cupped her cheek in his palm. "I love ye, *mo nighean donn*, and I'm forever thankful for whatever brought ye through that cave."

"Aye, m'love. Me, too."

About the Author

"No one has the power to shatter your dreams unless you give it to them." That's Maeve Greyson's mantra. She and her husband of almost forty years traveled around the world while in the U.S. Air Force. Now, they're settled in rural Kentucky where Maeve writes about her beloved Highlanders and the fearless women who tame them. When she's not plotting her next romantic Scottish tale, she can be found herding cats, grandchildren, and her husband—not necessarily in that order.

SOCIAL MEDIA LINKS:
Website: maevegreyson.com
Facebook Page: AuthorMaeveGreyson
Facebook Group: Maeve's Corner
facebook.com/groups/MaevesCorner
Twitter: @maevegreyson
Instagram: @maevegreyson
Amazon Author Page: amazon.com/Maeve-Greyson/e/B004PE9T9U
BookBub: bookbub.com/authors/maeve-greyson